THE LOCKET

By
SM. Stryker

Jeanette,
Thank you so
much for your friendship
& support &

THE LOCKET

Copyright © 2015 S. M. Stryker

EBOOK EDITION

TO JOIN MY MAILING LIST PLEASE SIGN UP HERE.
www.smstryker.com

Cover Design by Jo-Anna Walker with Just write Creations

Editing by Cheryl Keene, Keene-Eye Editing

TABLE OF CONTENTS

THE LOCKET

TITLES BY SM STRYKER

STOLEN INNOCENCE
NEVER FORGOTTEN LOVE
LOVING REDEMPTION
ANCHORED TO LOVE
NEVER EXPECTED LOVE
SACRIFICE OF LOVE
THE LOCKET

SECOND CHANCE SERIES

NEVER FORGOTTEN LOVE
LOVING REDEMPTION
ANCHORED TO LOVE
NEVER EXPECTED LOVE
SACRIFICE OF LOVE

NEVER EXPECTED SERIES

NEVER EXPECTED LOVE
SACRIFICE OF LOVE

THE LOCKET

SOME ARE BORN GREAT, SOME ACHIEVE GREATNESS, AND SOME HAVE
GREATNESS THRUST UPON THEM.

WILLIAM SHAKESPEARE

PREFACE
THE COLD HARD TRUTH

SAMANTHA

As I sit on the cold vinyl exam table listening to what the doctor is telling my mother and me, I think I'm in a dream or maybe an alternate universe as in one of my books. My stomach twists and turns. Bile creeps up the back of my throat at his declaration. The smell of antiseptic surrounds me, sinking in and imprinting into my brain. The thin paper sheet crinkles every time I move, and although the room is warm, the examination gown I am wearing is cold and stiff with its slit that exposes my entire back, and as the air blows, it hits my exposed skin sending shivers through my body.

How can I be pregnant? I just turned thirteen. I don't even know what to do to get pregnant. He has to be looking at the wrong file, although I am getting fatter, I thought it was because I am always hungry and eating more protein bars.

THE LOCKET

I've heard girls at school talk about boys, but my mom didn't want someone else teaching me about boys so I never took sex education. Mom always thought I was too young to talk about the birds and the bees, maybe because I have not ever been interested in boys, well other than Oliver, but he is my best friend. He's one of those friends that you don't always have to talk to everyday, but he always knows when I need him. Besides, I am more interested in school than the drama boys bring.

My mother glares at me, throwing questions at me. Her eyes red with tears, anger, shock, I don't know that look. She hasn't ever looked at me that way before. I'm asking those very same questions to myself, *who is the father? When did you sleep with someone?* Moreover, the worse yet, *how could you do this to me?* This is a very confusing situation for my young mind to process.

I've never slept with anyone, well, other than a few girlfriends when they spent the night at my house or me at theirs. Can a girl get a girl pregnant? I do remember hearing a man got pregnant. I don't know.

Mom steps out of the room to talk to the doctor as I get dressed. When she re-enters the room, she tells me she has made the necessary arrangements. It is cold and icy out, so I have to watch my step not to slip as I walk out to the car. I wish I would have remembered my gloves and scarf. I peer over to my mom, her face is tear stained, long streaks run down her face through her make-up. I don't wear make-up; she says I'm not old enough yet.

I slide into my seat as mom scraps the ice off the windshield. She puts the key into the ignition but she doesn't start it. When the windshield is cleared and she gets into the car, we just sit there in silence. The inside of the windows start to fog up and I see my breath every time I breathe. It seems as if we sit there for hours. She is just sitting there, holding the steering wheel, staring out the fogged up windshield. All I know is that I think I'm freezing to death. The cold and bitter December afternoon has my teeth chattering. I rub my hands up and down my arms trying to warm them up as my mom sits in an almost a catatonic state. I wipe my cold, running nose on the sleeve of my sweater and stick my hands between my legs trying to keep them warm.

She slowly turns to study me tilting her head. I'm still not sure what is happening to me. In a quite calm voice she finally asks "Sam honey, do you understand what's going on?"

I shake my head no, but deep inside I know what it all means. I know when you are pregnant you have a baby growing inside, but I don't know how it gets there.

"Do you know how you get pregnant Samantha?"

I peek up at my mom's face as tears start to run down her cheeks again. I bite my bottom lip and shake my head "No, not really, someone at school said you get it by kissing a boy."

She reaches over, takes my hands in hers, and gives me a reassuring squeeze. "Honey, has anyone touched you in your private area and hurt you?"

I think back to the night when Grady, my stepbrother was babysitting me, my mother and his father were not married yet and had gone out on a date. Gosh, it was four years ago;

I recall I had just celebrated my Golden Birthday; I had turned nine on the ninth. Grady told me that we were going to be family, that his father had asked my mother to marry him. Our parents had planned to get married, and as family, that entitled him privileges that other boy's did not get to have. He told me that his father did it to my mother and that made it okay. In fact, that night he came into my room and took me to their closed door so I could hear his father with my mother. He was three years older than I was and he was going to be my brother, so he had to know what he was talking about, didn't he?

That was the day after my birthday. I'll always remember it. He told me to get into my bed and I was supposed to be naked. My stomach feels funny, it aches, but also it feels like I have butterflies, as it did when I was in the school play. Maybe because I was nervous about being naked in front of a boy, even if it was just Grady, but I was excited because I wanted a family so badly. I was finally going to have a big brother, someone to protect me and watch over me. If this is what families did, I would do it. It had been a long time since my daddy left, and I do not want to do anything to make Dylan, Grady's dad, get upset and leave my mother.

I remember it as if it were yesterday when my daddy left. I recall him saying it was for our own safety, but I didn't understand, wasn't the man of the house supposed to protect us? Who was going to protect us now? I remember how sad my mother was. I would wake up to her crying in the middle of the night and see her red, swollen eyes every morning.

I flashback to Grady as he walked into my bedroom in just his underwear; it appeared as if he had something in them because there was something bulging out the front, I didn't know what it was until he pulled them off. That was the first time I had ever seen a boy's body. I smiled to myself as I thought of an elephant.

I couldn't stop staring at it, it appeared so weird.

"Do you want to touch it," he asked. "This is my penis, it's going to make friends with your vagina, okay?"

"My what?"

"Your vagina," he answers as he pulls the covers back and touches my bottom. My tummy felt as if it flipped, as if we were going fast over a dip in the road, like the one going to the pumpkin patch, there was also a little tingle I felt in my bottom too.

"Oh, okay." I nod my head as I reach my hand over and touch it. He made a funny sound in his throat when I did. It was soft, but hard at the same time. As I touched it, it twitched and scared me. I quickly pulled my hand away.

"It's okay; it is just excited to get to know you." I noticed a clear liquid came out of the hole at the tip. He said that it would help lubricate me, whatever that means. Wow, I am so lucky to have such a smart brother. I wonder how he knows all this.

He told me what he wanted to do and that it would be fun, just as his dad had done with my mom. *"Have you done this before,"* I ask.

"No, this will be both of our first times, so we can experiment and play."

"Are you sure this is okay?"

"Of course it is, we're family and this is what families do, they play together, but, this has to be our little secret because I don't want anyone to know how special you are to me. This is a secret all families have. Do you understand?"

Wide-eyed I nod my head. *"Okay Grady."*

"Because if anyone finds out, our parents won't be together anymore, and you don't want your mother to be sad again do you?"

"No," I cry out. *"I never want that to happen again."*

"Then this is just between you and me."

"Okay Grady."

He climbed up onto the bed and pushed my legs apart, crawling between my knees. He grabbed his penis with his hand and pressed against my private area. My stomach felt funny, like a hundred butterflies were fluttering around in there. The more he moved himself around my bottom, the more it tickled. It felt nice, and I can see why my mommy sounded so happy when she and Dylan were playing.

Suddenly, he pushed into me. Hard. I screamed out as pain shot from my private area to my tummy. I tried to move, to push Grady off of me, but he was holding me down by shoulders as he pushed into me over and over again. Harder and harder with each shove of his body.

I couldn't move no matter how much I shoved at him, and tears fell down my face. He finally stopped and looked into my eyes shushing me to be quiet. "You don't want your mom to be alone again do you?" he asked with a hard edge to his voice.

I shook my head and bit my lip to take my mind off the feeling in my bottom. I closed my eyes tight, found a place in my mind to hide, and laid there in silence as he again rammed inside me then he let out a growl like a wild animal and fell on top of me, the weight of his body now pressing against me. I was trapped under him. I was afraid he was going to stay like that. I couldn't breathe very well, and he was so heavy on me. I don't understand, Mommy sounded as if she liked it. Is there something wrong with me because I don't?

After that first night, he would come into my room making me play again, even though I did not want to anymore. It did not hurt anymore after that, but he would come into my room several times a week. He told me that this is what love was and that if I loved him, this was how I was to show it and that, 'We are bonded together now, we will always be together, forever. You are mine, Samantha. Nothing or no one will ever separate us.'

"Honey ... Sam?"

I'm pulled back to my mother's voice as tears start to fall down my cheeks. I don't want her to be sad again, but I can't see how I am going to fix this. I am pregnant, my stomach is getting bigger, and I have no other choice but to tell her.

"Grady told me that all families did it."

"Did what Sam?"

I stare down at my hands in my lap and in a whisper I say, "Put their bottoms together." I peer up through my damp lashes into her face. "He told me that since we were family, this is something I had to do, and that it is a way to show that I love him."

The expression on her face is one of shock, no, it is more than that, it's one of horror.

"Samantha honey," taking a deep breath, her voice almost a whisper. "How long has he been doing this to you?"

"Right after my ninth birthday." Her eyes go wide, as she turns and glares into my face. Then, oh God, her face, she is mad at me. I see it in her eyes, in the way her eyes squint and wrinkle and her lips are straight, flat then she bites one. I must have done something wrong. Maybe this is a test to see if I would say something. Oh God, what did I just do?

She gasps as she puts her hand to her mouth, "But that was four years ago."

"I know, it started the night that you and Dylan went out the day after my ninth birthday, I remember because it was my golden birthday."

Mom grabs her purse and starts to dig through it frantically, searching for something. She finally turns it over and dumps her purse out. All the contents scatter on the seat and floor until she finds her phone, flips it open and presses a button.

"Dylan, we need to talk. The whole family. Yes, including Grady! I don't care that he has Boy Scouts tonight. Yes, I know he's working to get his Eagle," she starts to raise her voice, "Because this is more important than a goddamn badge. I don't fucking care, I want him at the house tonight."

I've never heard my mother cuss before, now I know I'm in a lot of trouble. I jump as she yells into the phone and I know tonight is going to be very bad.

When we get home, the house is empty. Dylan isn't home from work yet and Grady is still at school.

CHAPTER ONE
GRADUATION DAY

SAMANTHA

I stand in the bathroom staring at myself, I can't believe I'm graduating from college today; I finally made it. I've worked so hard to make something of myself, and now all I want to do is get out of this city, away from all the ghosts. Without mom, there's nothing to keep me here anymore. Kassidy has Derek, and Oliver, well I don't know where he's at. He still knows somehow when I need him, he always calls me in those times, but I haven't seen him for a long time.

When mom's cancer returned, she wouldn't fight anymore, she just gave up, not that I blame her, chemo was hell on her, and she couldn't get over what had happened to me as a child. She always blamed herself for what had happened, but I know it was my fault not hers. I try not to think about it, I know she did what she thought was right, but I'm still haunted by the memories of that day.

I am still racked with guilt for destroying her marriage, her happiness. Even after years of therapy.

As I gaze in the mirror, I adjust the silver chain that supports a locket similar to a shadow box. A little girl angel and a tanzanite birthstone inside, enclosed by a glass egress. It was to remind me of that bitterly cold December day so many years ago.

I hear the bathroom door squeak open. I start to peer up as I hear a shrill cry as Kassidy barrels into me, grabbing me around the shoulders, almost knocking me off my feet. She continues to shriek with excitement. "I can't believe it, today's the day," she says as she bounces up and down bringing a smile to my lips. I haven't really smiled for a long time. "Have you decided what you're going to do yet?" She steps back regarding me. "Your boob is showing," she says and takes the clasp of my necklace, turning it so the clasp is in the back. I smile at the name she calls the clasp. Really…Boob.

I shake my head. "I have a couple of interviews this week, but I think I'm going to take the job in Seattle. They have already offered me the job. I just need to accept it."

"Seattle? That's hours away, you can't leave me here. What am I going to do without you?"

I run my hand down her arm. "This is a good opportunity for me, it's a new company, and I can work my way up. With my degree in marketing and business, I can be a step ahead of everyone else and move up faster." I stand in front of her and peer into her sad eyes, "I really need a change of scenery Kass." I exhale loudly as I tuck a tuft of hair behind her ear that had fallen out of her ponytail. "There are just too many ghosts here and I need to get away. Besides, as you said, it is only hours away. It's not as if it's across the country."

"Are any of those ghosts going to be here today?"

"I doubt it." I think Dylan only came back for mom's funeral out of respect for her, I know he loved her, but she just couldn't live with the past.

"You never told me what happened; it must have been really bad for him to send his own son away."

"Well, today's not the day either." I plaster a fake smile on my face, making sure my mask is securely in place and throw my arm around her shoulder. "Because today we graduate," I squeal. I grab her hand and pull her out of the bathroom.

I wander around the reception area after graduation trying to find Kassidy when my phone vibrates in my hand. Without checking at the screen, I answer the call knowing its Kassidy trying to find me. "Where are you bitch! I'm searching all over for you."

"You looked especially lovely today sis, I miss you, I miss being with you. You know we belong together; we tied our souls together. We were each other's firsts. That will never change," says the deep, husky voice on the other end of the phone. My heart starts to pound in my chest, my hand flies to my throat, the taste of bile hits the back of my tongue, my hands are clammy, and I can't catch my breath. I stop dead in my tracks, turning, searching, looking for the face I fear. Shit, I can't breathe. Perspiration coats my skin and my lips start to tingle as I start to see flashes of light in my vision. The room starts to spin. I hear voices, but can't understand what anyone is saying. Someone bumps me, I feel my phone slip from my fingers and I hear it crash to the floor. *Oh, fuck.* Everything goes black.

I feel something cold on my forehead. My head is throbbing. "Sam, Sam can you hear me, open your eyes for me."

I smell him before I can see him. God I love the way he smells. I slowly open my eyes, as I try to focus them, blinking a few times, I say, "Indigo blue."

"What? Sam?"

"Indigo blue." I close my eyes as everything goes black again. His scent lingers in my head.

CHAPTER TWO
MY CONSTANT

SAMANTHA

When I open my eyes again, I'm lying in a dark room. Frightened and not knowing where I am, I bolt upright and my head explodes with pain. I groan and touch my hands to my head, as if that will stop the throbbing. My heart races and I hear the blood pulsing in my ears to the throbbing in my head. The door opens, but the light behind the door is so bright all I see is a shadow. *Oh God! Did he get me?* A low, calm voice says, "You really need to lie back down, but before you do take these." I glance back up into the eyes that always makes me feel safe. Opening my hand, he lays pills in my palm and I take them without question. I scoot back down in the bed and close my eyes.

"*NO,*" I yell, shooting up from the bed, "*NO! You can't take my baby, NO!*" My heart is pounding against my ribs as I desperately place my hand over my belly, trying to feel my baby and realize there is nothing there. *"My baby, my baby, they killed my baby,"* I cry out, tears burning my eyes.

I feel someone smoothing my hair. "Shhh, it's okay Sam, Shhh, you're safe with me." He pulls me into his lap as I start to sob.

I wake the next morning with a start, trying to recognize anything around me, but nothing looks familiar. As I turn I see him in a chair, his hair is mussed up and he has a day's worth of stubble. He's in dress slacks and a white button-up shirt with the top two buttons undone. His biceps stretching the shirt tight as his arms are crossed over his chest. My heart flutters at the sight of him. My knight in shining armor. He has always been there to rescue me.

I glance down at what I have on and see that I'm wearing one of his t-shirts, my bra and panties are still on. I slip out of bed to find the bathroom. I start the shower and go in search of my clothes and purse. My head is still sore but more bruised than anything. I find my purse and clothes and take them into the bathroom.

I search my purse for my phone but can't find it. I vaguely remember it dropping out of my hands in the auditorium. I know Kassidy has to be worried about me. We were supposed to meet after the ceremony.

Glimpsing around I realize I'm in a hotel, a nice one by the looks of the sample toiletries. I don't know why I didn't realize it before. *Well maybe because you were having a nightmare and were unconscious when you got here stupid.* Why would he bring me here instead of to my place or his place?

Stepping into the hot shower, I try and wash the remnants of yesterday away as the hot water soothes my tight muscles.

I put my clothes on minus my cap and gown and throw my hair up into a messy bun. I find a little bottle of mouthwash and rinse out my mouth. In the desk in the living area, I find notepad and pen and write a note, quietly placing it on the pillow of the bed, and slip out of the room.

I step outside hoping I'm not too far away from the auditorium. I find I am only a few blocks away. The walk in the fresh air feels good. I get to my car and notice my phone on the seat with a note attached.

My God Sam! What happened? Who was the Adonis that swept you out of there? Call me!

I plug my phone into the charger so I can call Kassidy. I press the button next to her name on my phone, it doesn't even ring, before she's on the other end. "Sam! Are you okay? What happened? Where are you? When I finally found you, some hunk God was over you taking care of you then he picked you up and took you away. Someone handed me your phone and said you were talking on it when all of a sudden you fainted. I used your hide-a-key to get into your car; I knew you would be panicked without your phone. So spill bitch, is he the secret you're running from?"

I can't get a word in; Kassidy is talking a mile a minute. "Hi Kassidy, thank you for getting my phone, I have an interview today and it has all the information in it."

I was searching for you after the commencement when my phone rang, I thought it was you trying to find me, but when I answered it... shit Kassidy it was Grady, he was there. I panicked and couldn't breathe, everything went black, that was the last thing I remember until I woke up in a hotel with a nightmare."

"You woke up in a hotel? Who's? Sam, when are you going to tell me what happened to you? We've been best friends and roommates for the last four years. You're going to have to trust me some time, and who was the Adonis?"

"Oh Kassidy," I say with a sigh, "It's not about trust, I haven't told anyone other than my mother and Oliver. I was hoping that everything would go back to normal after she died."

"Well, how's that working for you?"

"Smartass! I'm on my way home. I need to get ready for my interview. Maybe if you can break away from Derek for an evening, we can talk and share a couple bottles of wine."

"Oliver? Is he the Adonis?"

"Yes, he was my best friend growing up. He was always there for me. He was my constant."

"Oh, I remember you speaking about him, but you didn't tell me he was a God."

I laugh. "Yeah, he's always been easy on the eyes, but I didn't see him that way, he was my best friend. So tonight?

"Yeah, okay. I'll see you later, and I want to know more about that mystery man too," she says. I chuckle as I hear Derek in the background trying to coax her to come back to bed. I end the call and drive to our apartment.

As I walk up to the door, I see there is a flower arrangement waiting. Nervously, I pull the card out and see it's from Dylan. I take a deep breath and relax as I smile, they are lovely, and it's nice to know he still cares. I unlock the door, pick up the arrangement, and with my back, I push my way through the door. My eyes close as I inhale the fragrance of the light pink roses, pink lilies, and gardenias. I turn as I get through the door opening my eyes. The smile slides from my face, as does the vase of flowers from my hands, shattering all over the floor. Shards of glass fly everywhere nicking my bare legs as the flowers bounce and land in a heap trapped in a floral oasis. I glance up, my eyes wide and my breath hitches. All I can see are vases upon vases of flowers; orchid, roses, lilies, and more, filling every flat surface. *Oh, Fuck*. I reach into my purse and pull out my phone dialing Kassidy again.

"What's up, bitch, you're kinda..."

I cut her off and in a whisper I ask, "Kassidy, how did the apartment appear when you last saw it?"

"What are you talking about?" Her voice is breathy from her activity with Derek.

My voice getting louder as I start to panic, my pulse spikes. "I'm saying that unless you have started a new floral business out of our apartment, someone has been in here. The place is covered in flowers. I can't do this Kassidy; I've got to go. I've got to leave."

"What about your interviews?"

"Fuck it! I'm going to accept the job the farthest away from here. Don't tell anyone where I'm going, okay? I'll call you when I get there to let you know that I've made it. Love you, Kass! Tell Derek bye."

"Love you too Sam, be careful."

I hang up the phone, slam the door closed, and lock it. I think I'm going to be sick from the mixture of fragrances from all the flowers. I quickly sweep up the shattered glass and flowers, dumping them into the trashcan as I mentally make a list of things I need to do and pack. I hurry to my room, grabbing my suitcases from the closet and start to throw my things into them. I don't even pay attention to what I'm packing. As I pack, I call and cancel my interviews and then call and accept the job in Seattle. I load my car down with as much stuff as possible, knowing that in my haste I've probably forgotten things, but I'll have Kass send them to me if they are important.

THE LOCKET

On the way out of town, I stop at Starbucks, picking up a vanilla latte and a breakfast sandwich since I haven't eaten since yesterday morning before graduation. I'm nervous as I start my new journey, but know this is for the best. After all, this is a new start a new adventure, a clean slate, but still, I'm constantly checking my rearview mirror in fear of being followed.

As my mind slowly starts to calm down, I reflect on the last twenty-four hours. Graduation, the call from Grady, the flowers, the fainting, and I woke up in a hotel room with Oliver. God, Oliver, the nightmare that had him rocking me back to sleep. I don't understand and probably never will now that I left, but how does he always rescue me. I haven't seen him in years, although I vaguely remember seeing him at Mom's funeral standing in the back of the church. I need to call him, tell him goodbye, and thank him for caring for me,

I think back to when I first met him

I remember it was the first day of first grade. It was just after my father left us. Mom didn't want to walk me in to meet my teacher, she had cried all night and her eyes were red and swollen. She gave me a sad smile and asked me if I would be alright by myself. I nodded to her that I would be okay, but deep down I was so scared.

I walked inside the school. I didn't know where to go. The halls were crowded with kids of all sizes, and I was being pushed around and bumped into. Then he came up to me and helped me. With his kind blue eyes and caring smile. I didn't know how old he was, but he took me to my classroom. How he knew what class I was in I don't know, and to be honest, I was so scared back then, I didn't even think about it. Then he kneeled down and introduced himself to me. "Hi, I'm Oliver," he said as he smiled at me and all I could remember was that he had the prettiest blue eyes and a single dimple in his cheek. But his eyes, I knew I needed to look in my crayon box to see which color most resembles them and what it was called. I didn't even know him and he made me feel safe. "If you ever need anything just ask the office to get me, okay?" I nodded my head as he stood back up and walked away. I walked into my class and the first thing I did was pull out my box of crayons. Indigo blue. They were indigo blue and I will never forget it or them, that was the day I met him, my Oliver.

Through the year, things got better at school, just as time helped my mother. By the end of the school year, she wasn't crying anymore. I would see Oliver occasionally around the schoolyard, and in the event other kids started to pick on me, he was there. He didn't have to say anything, he just stood there, his presence alone made the other kids cower and scamper away.

We never really had conversations during school, but I knew he would show up if I ever needed him. He would often walk me home and I found I could talk to him about almost anything. I never had to take him up on his offer, because he always knew if I needed him.

The day after I lost my virginity to Grady, he knew. I don't know how, but he did. The concern was written all over his face. "Samantha, what's wrong, what happened, who hurt you?" I thought about saying something, but I kept remembering Grady's warning about not letting anyone know, so I just kept it to myself. I just shook my head as a tear fell. He wiped it away then he lifted my chin to look him in those caring indigo eyes. It was as if he could see everything in me. "Is it someone here at school?" I shook my head again. "Just tell me, and I will make it stop," my eyes flash to his. "You just need to tell me who."

THE LOCKET

"I can't Oliver, I just can't." He pulled me into him, and I melted into his arms. I fit perfectly in them. It was then that I knew I would always love him.

That was the last year we went to the same school, but everyone knew not to bully me. Whenever they did, someone would whisper in their ear and they would apologize and quickly walk away.

When I found out I was pregnant, I received a visit from Oliver. Again, I don't know how he found out since both my mom and Dylan told Grady and I we were not allowed to speak of it or what led up to it. It was my first day back to school and I was walking home when Oliver drove up beside me and told me to get into his car. I slid into the front seat, the car smelled of him. I took in a deep breath wishing it was the only smell that would stay in my head. He always smelled good. It was clean and fresh; it was my Oliver.

He took me to a little park. We didn't talk the whole way there. He took my hand in his and led me over to an old weathered picnic table. "How are you feeling?" I peek up at him, not knowing how he knew. "I know what happened and you've been gone from school for a couple weeks. Are you feeling okay?"

I sat on the table staring down at my fingers, playing with them in my oversized sweatshirt to hide what was left of my pregnancy as I nodded.

"Samantha, I know you're not the type of girl to sleep around, and I know you haven't ever had a boyfriend either. Why didn't you tell me all those years ago, I could have stopped him?

I gazed up at him as tears burned and blurred my eyes. "He told me I couldn't say anything, that if I did his dad would leave my mom and it would be my fault that she was sad again," I whispered. "It was so hard on her when my dad left. I couldn't bear to see her like that again. I would do anything to keep that from happening."

He took my face in his hands as he glared at me sternly. "This is not your fucking fault, Samantha, and don't let anyone accuse you of that. This is the fault of some sick fuck. He'll learn he shouldn't have messed around with an innocent girl. He shouldn't have messed with you."

Tears rolled down my face, and he brushed them away. "He's gone, Mom kicked him out, but now she and Dylan are fighting all the time. I think they are going to get divorced." I placed my hands over my face as I start to weep.

"If they get divorced, it isn't because of you, Sam." He pulled my hands from my face. "It's because his son hurt you and your mother feels guilty because she didn't stop it. And the baby," he asked with a sympathetic voice.

"I can't talk about this, Oliver." I glimpse up into his eyes that are full of sadness, "Not because I'm not supposed to, but because... she's gone."

He pulled me into his chest and held me there. He never told me that everything would be alright, and I knew it never would be. He told me we would get through this together and he would always be here for me.

That night when I pulled my homework out of my backpack, I found a little gift box. Opening it I found a beautiful shadow box locket, it had a blue and pink heart-shaped birthstone inside. They represented mine and my baby's birthstone. The locket and chain were silver and were the most precious gift I had ever received. I rummaged further in my bag and found a little note card that simply read:

I will always be near and watching over you.

THE LOCKET

~Oliver

It was no less than a week later that I overheard Dylan and mom talking about Grady. Dylan said that Grady had been beaten up really badly, and had a broken nose, fractured jaw and a ruptured testicle. Part of me wanted to feel bad for him, but I was sure that was nothing like the pain I went through and would have to live with for the rest of my life. My mind flashed to Oliver because I know that he had to have been the one to inflict that type of treatment on him.

CHAPTER THREE
MOTH TO THE FLAME

OLIVER

I think the only thing that would feel better than beating the shit out of this perverted motherfucker is if I could just put a bullet through his brain. However, the boss doesn't want to bring attention to Sam. He knows that if Grady goes missing or shows up dead, it might come back on her.

It took me a little time to find him, but once I did, I wanted him to remember that there will be pain if he comes around Samantha again. I will do everything in my power to keep her safe from now on.

Thinking back, I should have known it was him, but Sam wouldn't tell me.

I remember the day I was assigned to protect her. Mr. Perrotti had placed me with my mother, Savina, after my family was murdered. I was asked into Mr. Perrotti's office. It wasn't that I was scared about meeting with him, he had always been nice to me, but this was different. This was a job, my first job, and this was going to define who I was and what I would do for the rest of my life. Savina told me that I needed to respect him and do what he asked of me. Hell, I wasn't much older than Samantha was when the Di Fonzo family murdered my family.

My job was to watch out for Samantha at school. She was a pretty little girl. Her blonde hair was braided into two pigtails, but it was her beautiful sapphire blue eyes that told me everything; they were so sad and alone. I walked up to her and helped her find her class. I wondered where her mother was; hell, it was her first day of school, and this was a milestone in her life. She needed someone to share it with, not a stranger. She was so scared. I kneeled down in front of her, letting her know that I would always be there for her; all she had to do was ask. It was then that she captured a piece of my heart, with that face, those eyes.

As the years went by, I watched my girl, my Samantha. When she turned nine, she changed. I could see it in her eyes, in her face, and in the way she carried herself. She had been violated. Someone had stolen her innocence. I knew it didn't happen outside of her home because I was always watching her. I would walk her home from school and she never hung around boys in school. That only left one person, but I couldn't get her to talk about it.

Even when I switched schools and my job was finished, I couldn't stay away. I was the moth to the flame. There was something about her. I needed to be close to her, with her. I was always there, even when she didn't know it. She was my Sam.

That all changed right after she turned thirteen. She was pale and sickly. I was concerned for my girl. I watched several times as she ran to the bathroom during school. Over the course of several months, I could see her body changing, and she started to wear big baggy clothes. I started to ask questions when the rumors were flying about her stepbrother having sex with her. He walked around the high school, the arrogant bastard, bragging about taking her virginity. I wanted to kill the motherfucker. I informed Mr. Perrotti of my suspicions, and even though my job had been finished for a couple years, I received permission to take care of the situation. I was to teach him a lesson, but he disappeared and I had to track him down.

Samantha was absent from school for a couple weeks, she never took sick days as long as I had known her. I watched for her every day. That's when I saw her walking home from school by herself, alone and dejected, her hoodie pulled up covering her head. I pulled my car over and she got inside. I drove her to a quiet little park. I knew no one would be there, and we could talk uninterrupted. We drove in silence. I would glance at her, My Sam, her head hung in shame. I took her hand as we walked to a nearby picnic table.

Samantha wasn't like typical girls; she was quiet, smart, caring, and modest. Now she was filled with pain, loss, and most of all guilt.

I watched her as she worried her fingers in her lap. She wouldn't look me in the face. "How are you feeling?" I studied her and her reaction. I have observed her for so long I could read her as well as I could myself. "I know what happened, and you've been absent from school for a couple weeks. Are you feeling okay?"

She nervously stuck her hands into the pocket of her oversized sweatshirt as she contemplated her answer. She nodded her head. "Samantha, why didn't you tell me all those years ago, I could have stopped him?"

She gazed up at me and tears brimmed her eyes. "He told me I couldn't," she whispered. Dammit! I wanted to kill the motherfucker. He not only hurt her but threatened her, too.

It took all that was within me not to hit something, but I knew I had to keep calm. I took a deep breath and tried to compose myself. I didn't want to scare her and she was like a scared little kitten ready to bolt and hide. I took her face in my hands and sternly looked into her eyes and said, "This is not your fucking fault, Samantha, and don't let anyone accuse you of that. He shouldn't have messed with you."

Tears rolled down her face, and I brushed them away.

I pulled her close to me and just held her, and rocked her, in my arms. I knew, this would alter her whole life. I knew she would get through it, but she would never be the same.

I drove her back to her house. As I opened the back door of the car to pull out her backpack, I slipped a little box inside. As she walked around my car, she took her backpack from my hand. I took her in my arms and kissed her forehead. "I will always be here for you, baby girl. You might not see me, but I am here." My heart was breaking for her and her loss. I have always loved her, but it was then that I decided that one day I would make her mine. I would make her whole again. I would protect her with my life. This wasn't a job; it hadn't been for years.

When I finally found out where they had sent the motherfucker a week later, I took pleasure in teaching him a lesson. The first hit broke his nose and blood splattered everywhere. As he crashed to the ground, I hit him again in the jaw. I felt and heard the bones crack under my punishing hit. Good, let him suck through a straw for a while, but the best blow of all was as he lay on the ground writhing and moaning, I kicked him in the balls with my steel toe boots. He let out a loud scream as he grabbed himself. "Don't you ever come around Samantha again, you sick motherfucker. The next time will be your last, and I'll take pleasure in ending your sorry excuse of a life."

CHAPTER FOUR
ALL GROWN UP

OLIVER

I watch my girl proudly accept her diploma. I know how hard she has worked for it. She received two majors, God she's intelligent. She hasn't had it easy. Her mother found out she had cancer not long after Samantha's thirteenth birthday and although she fought it, it came back a couple years later and this time, she succumbed to it, leaving Sam without family. Well, at least family that she knows of. She will always have a family with the Perrotti's.

I had always kept her father informed of her progress. I was surprised that he was at the funeral and he appeared genuinely distraught.

She has never had to worry about anything. I have always made sure she is cared for and protected. She just didn't realize it was I taking care of her.

My mom, Savina, taught me about the stock market and encouraged me to invest the money I had earned from Perrotti. Since I wasn't of age, she introduced me to a broker who helped me decide what stocks to invest in. My investments did well, and It didn't take long before I was able to start Drake Enterprises. My company specializes in personal security. I figure I had been doing it my whole life and I'm a natural protector. There is no better job I am qualified to do.

I watch her as she searches for her roommate, Kassidy, after the ceremony. She finally seems happy; she's finding herself again as she gets ready to start a new chapter of her life. Her face is aglow as she pulls out her phone and answers it. The smile on her face falls and the color drains from it, leaving her ghostly white. The smile is gone, replaced by fear in her eyes as she starts searching. I do the same. The hair on the back of my neck stands on end as I see the motherfucker standing in a corner, but I have to get to her. Her hand flies to her throat, grasping at it. I can see she's struggling to breathe as her lips start to turn blue. I run to her as she hits the floor. "Get me a cold cloth and some water," I yell. Everyone is standing around. I yell again and finally someone hands me a cloth and a bottle of water.

"Sam, Sam! Can you hear me, open your eyes for me?"

She slowly opens her eyes. "Indigo blue."

"What?"

"Indigo blue." She closes her eyes and she's out again.

Fuck! I have to get her out of here. I can't believe he has the balls to show up in her life again. I would have thought that my threat would have warded him off. However, at this moment, my mind is on my Sam and making sure she's safe. I pick her up and carry her to my car, taking her to my hotel. I place her in bed, removing her clothes except for her bra and panties, and put one of my T-shirt on her so she's comfortable.

I cover her up and close the curtain to keep it dark in the room. I know she will have a killer headache when she wakes up. She might even have a concussion with the way her head hit the linoleum floor.

I close the door to a crack and start making arrangements to finally get rid of the motherfucker. He's ruined her life for the last time. I notify Mr. Perrotti about what happened and ask for his approval. I'm just starting my search for the prick when I hear moaning from the bedroom. I slowly walk in, not wanting to spook her. "Sam, it's me, Oliver, you're safe. Here, take these, they will make you feel better." She opens her hand as I lay Ibuprofen in her palm and then hand her a glass of water. She places the pills in her mouth and drinks all the water. She lays back into the pillow and closes her eyes.

Once I get her back to sleep, I lay her down in the bed and covering her up. I move to the armchair near the bed, and my tired eyes grow heavy as I watch her sleep. I want so desperately to sleep next to her. To pull her into me and wrap my arms securely around her to show that she is safe, let her know just how much she means to me, but I realize I can't do that. I'm just her protector, nothing more. It doesn't matter what I want, but more importantly, I didn't want her to wake up scared with me next to her

When I wake, the bed is empty. My neck is stiff, not to mention the kink in my back. Not the most comfortable chair I have slept in before, but even worse is the racing of my heart, because she's gone, and I don't know where she is. The bed sheets are cold, and with the motherfucker close by, I start to panic. I search for her, but I already know she is gone. I find the note she left for me on her pillow.

Oliver, thank you for always being there when I need you. My knight in shining armor. I don't know how you always know, but you do and I love you for it. You will never know how much it means to me.

Love you, Samantha

I get ready for the day and check out of the hotel. I need to finish the search for the son of a bitch.

I receive a call from Dunthorpe letting me know that Sam has accepted the position with my company. I wonder if something else happened for her to accept the job so quickly, or if it had to do with the prick at her graduation. I put everything in motion, making sure things go as planned once she makes it to Seattle.

CHAPTER FIVE
A NEW LIFE

SAMANTHA

On the drive to Seattle, I call my mother's lawyer, Mr. Costa, to let him know that I'm moving to Seattle, and I'm not sure where I'll be staying until I find an apartment. He proceeds to tell me that he has some business associates in Seattle, and he might be able to find a place for me to live. He says that he will check with them and give me a call as soon as he has something lined up. "That would be amazing! Thank you. I look forward to hearing from you." That would be so great if he could find something, hell anything, for me.

My day was getting a little brighter after my conversation with Mr. Costa. I don't know when or where my mother found him, but he has been a godsend since her passing. He contacted me after her death and told me she had a life insurance policy. I was skeptical, you know, a stranger calling me out of the blue, offering his services. I had never heard my mother mention him or having a lawyer for that fact, but he started transferring a monthly allotment into my bank account shortly after her passing. He even talked to the bank that held the note on my mother's home and was able to sell it at a good price.

I'm just taking the exit for downtown Seattle when my phone rings, I'm so glad my car has Bluetooth capabilities. My car was my one big splurge after my mother died. It wasn't anything too pretentious, but my old car was old, very old and it didn't drive well in the snow. So I traded it in for a Chevy Captiva. It gets good gas mileage, has four-wheel drive and the interior is spacious.

"This is Sam."

"Hi Sam, this is Mr. Dunthorpe, I hope your drive is going well."

"Yes, in fact, I have made great time. I'm just pulling off I-5 and taking the Stewart Street exit, heading into the heart of the city to find a motel until I get a place to rent."

"Good, I'm glad I caught you in time then. We have a hotel for you to stay at while you find a place of your own. It's close to Pike Place Market. With it being the weekend, you can play the tourist on the waterfront. The weather this weekend is supposed to be splendid. It's called Hotel Max you can't miss it. Just give them your name; they already have your reservation waiting."

"Oh, that's wonderful. Can you email me the directions to the office? I'd like to familiarize myself with the new surroundings before my first day."

"Yes, of course, you will have all the details in your email inbox by the time you get to your room. And, Ms. Hunter, welcome to Seattle and E. O. Drake Enterprises, we're very glad you chose us."

"Thank you, Mr. Dunthorpe, I look forward to coming aboard."

THE LOCKET

I find the hotel, and as he said, it was easy to find, and just steps from Pike Place Market. I don't think I have ever been treated so well before. The hotel is amazing, and I feel guilty about staying here. It's not as if I'm an executive, I'm just a marketing and business graduate who worked hard to get good grades to get this entry-level job. My room is amazing. It has a sitting area, which separates the bedroom from the rest of the room.

After settling in, I send Kassidy a text letting her know I made it safely. I then decide to go exploring through the hotel. As I explore the hotel, I find a range of works, photographs, paintings, and collages, reflecting a myriad of voices and attitudes. Each floors' hallway is dedicated to the work of an individual artist, each of whom chose a theme, from architecture to romance, showcasing it in works large enough to cover the guest room doors. It's like having a sleepover at an art gallery.

According to the information that I found, the hotel design was inspired by art, and much of the artwork throughout Hotel Max is original works from local Seattle artists.

I spend the weekend getting to know this beautiful city. I would love to live downtown, but I know there is no way I would be able to afford anything down here on my salary.

I'm still nervous about Grady, and I hope he's not tracking me somehow. There have been several times this weekend that I felt as if I were being watched. Maybe it's just my paranoia with everything that just happened, I don't know. I'm just trying to get to know my new city and not get freaked out.

Saturday evening, I receive a call from Mr. Costa. He informs me that he has found an apartment for me to stay in. He says the owner is leaving the country for work and just wants to make sure it's cared for. He has a couple of cats that would have to be cared for, too. However, it's fully furnished and he is leaving in a week. "He would like to know if it's something you would be interested in doing and if so, he would like it if you could stop by tomorrow at one."

"Where is it located and how much is he asking for rent, oh and how long is he going to be gone for?"

"It's downtown close to where you said your new job is."

"Oh, Mr. Costa, I appreciate your assistance in this, but... well, this is an entry level job, I'm sure there's no way that I will be able to afford..." he cuts me off.

"Ms. Hunter, Samantha, he's not charging rent; you just have to pay the utilities."

"What do you mean he's not charging rent?"

"He knows it's last minute, and he's just concerned about his cats and making sure the place is well taken care of."

"But..."

"No buts, Samantha, I have checked him out and he's a good man, so one o'clock tomorrow afternoon? I will email you his address."

"Okay, tomorrow at one. Thank you, Mr. Costa, for all your help."

"My pleasure, Samantha."

I put the address into the GPS on my phone and it is literally just four blocks from where the hotel is, so I decide to walk.

It's a beautiful, late spring day, and all the flowers are blooming. The smell reminds me of my mother's home; she had amazing, sweet smelling shrubs. The scent of a daphnia stops me dead in my tracks, my all-time favorite shrub. I search until I see them walk over to it, and kneel down to inhale the citrusy floral scent, that reminds me of my mother's house. I close my eyes and let it fill my senses. As I walk down the street, I gaze at the little gardens and flower beds that line the sidewalk. Pink dogwoods are all in bloom as they line the street.

My phone notifies me that I am at my location. I gaze up at the massive building in front of me. I walk inside where I am met by a concierge. I approach him and give him my name. "Oh yes, Ms. Hunter, Mr. Randolph is waiting for you." He points me to the bank of elevators and gives me a pin number to put in the code box. "There are only two doors once you exit the elevator," he states. "Mr. Randolph's is on the right."

"Thank you very much," I say. I anxiously walk to the elevators and push the call button to my possibly new home. I take in my surroundings and can't believe my fortune.

I step inside the mirror and glass elevator realizing I didn't even ask what floor it is on. As the doors close, I push the pin number into the code box and the elevator ascends. Coming to a slow stop, I step out and turn to my right to find the door. I nervously ring the doorbell. Several moments pass before I hear the rattling of the door handle and a middle-aged man answers. He holds out his hand and introduces himself to me. "Hi, you must be Ms.

SM. STRYKER

Hunter, I'm James Randolph. Come in, and excuse the mess as I have been packing to leave this week."

I shake his hand. "Hi, I'm Samantha, it's nice to meet you, Mr. Randolph."

"Please, call me James."

"Well, it's nice to meet you, James."

"Please." He motions to the sofa. We sit and he tells me about where he will be and that he could be out of the country for two years. As he talks, I glance around at all the furnishings. Everything in the apartment appears brand new. No wear marks on the sofa or the chairs; the carpet doesn't even have pathway marks.

Then out of nowhere, two kittens come running and rolling across the floor, they are darling. It's a shiny nickel moment and I forget everything I was thinking before. They come bounding right to me. They both have Siamese coloring, one darker than the other. "Well hello babies," I say as I pick them up. They couldn't be more than a couple months old.

He points to each kitten. "This one is Levi and that one is Maxx, I just got them a couple weeks ago, before I knew I would be leaving the country."

"They're so cute," I say as I lay Maxx on his back and tickle his nose with his tail. Levi swats at Maxx's tail, then they are off the sofa and wrestling on the floor again.

James shows me around the place and explains that there is a housekeeper that comes every week and that I would just need to make sure the kittens are cared for and the plants watered. Other than that... all I'll have to do is pay the utilities.

"You appear a little confused, Samantha." You can say that again. The thought of only having to pay utilities for playing with kittens that I have always wanted and living in downtown Seattle in the magnificent apartment for the next year or two has me speechless. My life has never been like this. First, the job, then the apartment, what's next, I trip into an office and fall madly in love? I shake my head at the obscurity.

"Well, to be honest, I just don't get it. I mean, you could rent this place out and find a new home for Maxx and Levi."

"That's true, but I didn't want to do that to them, and because this was a last minute decision, I didn't have time to advertise and go through the interview process. Let alone the time to pack and store my belongings. I value Costa's recommendation. I just need to make sure the place is taken care of. When I heard that you had just come into town and were inquiring about a place to stay, I jumped at the chance. You're only a few blocks away from your work from what Costa said."

"Yes, the Drake building is within walking distance so I doubt that I will ever have to use my car. Oh! Where would I park?"

"There's a parking garage underneath the building. The concierge will have all of that information for you." I walk around in a fog, I hear him talking, but there is so much going through my head it's hard for me to pay attention.

He continues to tell me about the apartment and shows me where everything is that I will need for the kittens.

"Okay, I'll do it. Do I need to fill out a rental agreement?

"No, I have all the information I will need from you."

I want to jump with joy, I'm so excited, and I can't wait to tell Kassidy. "Wow, this is amazing. When can I move in?"

"I'll be leaving on Friday, so maybe we can meet before I leave to the airport. I'll let the Stephen know that you will be moving in and that you have full access." He motions for me to follow him into the home office. "Maxx and Levi will need you to take them to their veterinarian appointments. The dates are already scheduled on the calendar here, but the office will give you a courtesy call to remind you. You'll have access to the bank account to pay for their care, food, and supplies." He pulls the top drawer open revealing the leather bound check book and credit card. He shows me where he keeps an address book with names and numbers of people and places I might need, from the local Chinese takeout to dry cleaners, and lawyers, to the local grocery stores that deliver. He hands me a key right before I step out the door. I'm in awe as I take the elevator back down to the ground level. My phone vibrates as I step out; it's a text from James.

Samantha, it was nice to meet you. I forgot to give you my number just in case you need something in the next week. Thank you for agreeing to care for my place and the kittens in my absence.

~James

I have to chuckle because he is thanking me for taking care of his place, when I should be the one thanking him for allowing me to stay there. As I walk by the concierge, he calls out to me, "Ms. Hunter."

I turn and walk back over to his desk, "Yes?"

He hands me a card key. "Mr. Randolph asked me to give you this. This card will get you into anything that is needed."

"Oh, thank you..." I look for his name badge.

"It's Stephen, Ms. Hunter."

I hold out my hand to him. "Thank you, Stephen." I place the card in my wallet as I turn to exit the building.

CHAPTER SIX
LIFE IS LOOKING UP

SAMANTHA

The sun filters through the sheers that are draped across the windows. I purposely didn't close the drapes because I wanted to wake with the sun. I wanted to feel its warmth on my face.

I feel as if I'm in a bubble and I don't want it to burst. Today is my first day at my new job, and by the end of the week, I will be in my new amazing apartment with two little furry roommates. I love kittens, I never could have one growing up because Grady was allergic to them, so I vowed to myself that I would get one when I had a place of my own. Well, they might not be mine, but I'll be the one they get to know and love for the next couple years.

I rummage through my clothes to see what isn't too badly wrinkled as I haven't unpacked. I was in such a hurry to leave town I just threw my clothes in haphazardly. I find a little orange power skirt with a floral blouse. I panic as I search for my orange stiletto heels. In my rush, I didn't even think about checking in Kassidy's room for my clothes that she had borrowed. I start tossing clothes in a frantic search. I finally find one and then the other. Taking a deep breath, I calm myself. I'm glad I woke up early. With the crisis of the day averted, I can leisurely walk to work after grabbing a breakfast sandwich and vanilla latte at Starbucks.

I walk into the lobby of the Drake Towers and to the security desk. "Hi, I'm..."

"Yes, Ms. Hunter, welcome to E.O. Drake Enterprises, Mr. Dunthorpe is on his way down to show you around."

I furrow my brows as I cock my head to the side in confusion. "How..."

"It's my job to know everyone's comings and goings. I'm David."

David is an attractive, mixed race man. He has the prettiest green eyes. He is maybe in his late twenties, and I can't tell with his suit jacket but he appears pretty firm under his shirt. He extends his hand out to me. "Samantha Hunter, it's nice to meet you David."

"I'll have you sign in and I will get you a temporary key card. Later today you will have your picture taken and I will have your permanent key card for you. On your way out tonight, you can just bring this one back."

"Okay, thank you."

I didn't even think about photo ID, I'm glad I spent a little more time on my makeup today. I'm just finishing signing in when I hear my name being called. "Ms. Hunter, welcome aboard." I look up at the man that is striding toward me. He extends his hand and says, "I'm Duane Dunthorpe; it's nice to put a face to the name. Did David get you all checked in?"

"Yes, sir," I hold up my temporary card, "All set." Mr. Dunthorpe appears to be in his mid-thirties, with dark hair and the early onset of gray fringing around the edges, a sharply trimmed goatee, and friendly green eyes with smile lines starting to show.

"Let me give you the grand tour." As we walk, he tells me that the company is only a few years old and that it started, as a personal security company, but now security development is what they are heading into as well. The owner is a computer whiz. He fills me in on the team I will be working with and what projects they are currently working on. We take the elevator to the floor I'll be working on, and he shows me to my office... an office, not a cubical... wow. I try to play calm, but wow. My inner child is doing a happy dance.

I step into my new office and I'm hit by two fragrances. I know where one is coming from, the large bouquet of daphnia displayed in a crystal vase on my desk. The other has to be my imagination. It's the smell of Oliver. I know it's silly, I'm sure other men probably wear the same cologne. But this scent I've always associated with just Oliver. It makes me smile, but I feel as if my heart is crying. I miss him, and although we don't see each other very much anymore, we still have a very special bond. I make a mental note to call him this week. Maybe once I'm in my apartment I can sit outside and talk to him for a while and catch up.

A computer tech is just finishing setting up my computer system, and as he leaves, he hands me a sheet of paper with several links to programs with all my temporary passwords. "Hi, Ms. Hunter, my name is Chris. I'm one of the computer techs here, if you have any problems just give me a call. My number is at the top of the page."

"Thank you, Chris," I say to him and turn, "What do you guys do, put wanted posters in the break room so everyone knows who the new kid on the block is," I chuckle as I glance over at Mr. Dunthorpe.

"Something like that," Mr. Dunthorpe says, "Why don't you get yourself settled in and we'll get together after lunch and you can meet the team."

"That would be wonderful, thank you."

Mr. Dunthorpe leaves my office. I study everything, trying to take it all in. A wall of built-in bookshelves lines the left wall as you walk into my office, and to the right is the massive 'U' shaped desk and hutch. Two leather chairs are positioned adjacent to the desk for visitors, and an ergonomic chair is behind the desk. I'm so mesmerized by the furnishings that I hadn't even paid attention to the view until a flicker of sunlight catches my eye. I walk over to the window and gasp, it's an unhindered view of the bay full of sailboats and yachts. Maybe one day I can go out on one. I've never been on a boat before.

"It's an amazing view isn't it?" I jump at the sound of a man's voice. "I'm sorry; I didn't mean to startle you. I'm Lucas, but everyone calls me Luke. You must have done something right to land this office."

I reach my hand out to Luke. "Hi, I'm..." he forgoes my hand and walks past me to stare out the window.

"Yeah. I know who you are. You're Samantha, the wiz kid from back east."

"Why do you say it like that and how does everyone know who I am?"

"You don't know?" I shake my head. "The owner has been talking about you for a while now and how you were going to revolutionize the marketing department." He flings his hands in a mock celebration move.

"How could he have known that when I only accepted the job last week? And who pissed in your cheerios to be so malicious to me," I ask, my brow furrows and prop my fisted hands on my hips.

"This was supposed to be my office and my job. You stole it out from under me. What did you do, sleep your way in?" He glares me, his eyes roaming up and down staring at my breasts longer than he should have, contempt dripping in his voice.

"Listen, Lucas, I don't even know who the owner is other than his name is Ethan Drake. I report directly to Mr. Dunthorpe, so if you have a problem with me, then I suggest you take it up with him. This conversation won't happen again, understood?" My tone is stern as I get in his face, and I tap my finger on his chest as I finish. "Now if you don't mind I have an office to get organized." I walk to the door and he slowly follows to stand in front of me. He snarls at me as he ogles up and down my body again. I swiftly shove the door to close it, making him jump back so he isn't hit with it as it slams shut.

I take a deep breath and try to calm myself. "What an ass," I say to myself. I start to wonder about what he said, though. As an entry-level employee, I wouldn't expect the treatment that I've been receiving, and what's with everyone already knowing whom I am?

I study the projects I'll be working on for a few hours before deciding to take my lunch break. I walk outside; it feels so good to enjoy the sunshine on my face. The smell of the bay wafts through the air, and it's refreshing as I take in the scenery of Seattle. There are several little vendors around the area, so I decide to grab a bento. I find a bench to sit down and eat and reflect on the day.

I walk back to the office and when I enter the atrium, I'm met with odd stares and whispers. Feeling a little self-conscious, I step in the restroom and check myself to make sure I don't have food on my face or that I hadn't tucked my skirt into my panties. Thank God, it was neither of those. I walk back to my office and close my door to finish organizing my desk.

Opening the draws and cabinets, I find that they're stocked with everything that I need, from sticky notes and pens to legal pads and gridded paper. I'm just finishing putting the rest of my things away when there is a knock on the door. "Come in," I call out.

Mr. Dunthorpe peeks his head through the door. "Are you getting settled in?"

"Yes, thank you, please come in." I come close to asking him about Lucas and his accusation but then decide against it. The last thing I want at a new job is drama, but unfortunately, it seems I have already attracted it.

"What can you tell me about the company?"

He stares at me with almost a shocked expression on his face. "It's kind of late for that don't you think?"

I chuckle, "I don't mean the company itself, I know all of that. I researched the company before I even applied or for that matter accepted the interview. I mean the owner and what made him who he is."

"He's pretty quiet about himself and his life, but he's a highly motivated man. From what I've heard, he walked in on a burglary gone wrong and his family had been killed. He felt guilty for not being there to stop them and he swore that he would do what it took to give everyone a little bit of security in their life, so as he got older, he started to develop new programs and products that were affordable so anyone could be secure in their own home."

My hand covers my mouth in shock and tears burn the back of my eyes. "Oh my God, how old was he?"

"I'm not sure, grade school age, I think."

"Oh God! How horrible that a child should have to go through anything like that.

"It's said that he started protecting a young girl in school and he has turned that into what you see here today."

"Wow, where is she now?"

"I think you need to ask him that," he says as he smiles down at me.

There's no mistaking the confusion on my face. "I'm sure he wouldn't have time for the curiosity of an entry-level employee. Nor would I waste his time on something that is none of my business."

"You would be very surprised at what he would do for you, Ms. Hunter." He slips his hands into his front pockets of his slacks.

"For me?"

"For his employees," he quickly corrects himself, as he pulls a hand out of his pocket. In a nervous gesture, he runs his thumb and index finger over his upper lip to his bottom lip.

"Oh." Still confused, I figure I will find out more over time.

"He's a very generous man, I'm sure it won't be too long before you get to meet him."

"I'd like that. Can you tell me what project I need to work on, I would love to see some of the campaigns you have done in the past and what you're working on currently?"

"Well, as a matter of fact I've set up a meeting for you to meet your team members." He glances down at his watch. "We might be a little early, but we can walk over to the conference room now."

"Being early is good. I think it will be easier to remember them as they come through the door." I grab a legal pad and pen before following Mr. Dunthorpe out of my office.

"Great, I'll show you to the conference room then. Do you want any coffee, tea, or water before we go in?"

"No, thank you."

We walk into the empty room. The smell of lemon polish infuses the room as the lights ping to life and gleam off the top of the highly polished, rectangular cherry conference table. I take a chair toward the front of the table. I don't know why, but I've always liked to be in the front, maybe because I like the unobstructed view of the dry erase board or maybe because I feel I have more control. I really don't know.

As my co-workers start to filter through, I stand to meet them. Lucas hasn't arrived yet. I wonder if this is just part of his personality or if it is his way of having a temper tantrum for not getting whatever he wanted.

After a few minutes, Mr. Dunthorpe closes the conference room door. I think he is wondering the same thing I am. *Ass Hole*.

Mr. Dunthorpe introduces me to my co-workers and foes over a list of my accomplishments. I feel my face flush; I'm not used to having the spotlight shone on me. He's well into my list of actuations when the door burst open and Lucas slowly meanders in. He finds an empty chair to sit in and tosses his notepad onto the table and it makes a loud plopping noise as it hits.

"Mr. Masters, it's nice you could join us," Mr. Dunthorpe says, sarcasm dripping from his voice.

"I figured I would set a precedent for the new girl. After all, she is the *Golden Child*."

I peek up at Dunthorpe; you could almost see steam billowing from his ears. The room is alive with escalating chatter.

I stand, glaring Lucas in the eye, and making sure I have his and everyone else's attention, "I don't know what is going on here, but I accepted this job because I fully believe in the company's mission statement and the vision Mr. Drake has for E.O. Drake Enterprises." I take a couple steps toward Lucas so I am close enough to smell his cologne. And although he smells goddamn good, I don't like him. He's a first class ass. "I didn't come here to put up with your junior high school drama and antics. So as I told you earlier, I've never met Mr. Drake, I answer to Mr. Dunthorpe. If you have a problem, I suggest you take it up with him." I square my shoulders and turn back to my chair as I take in a deep breath and exhale slowly to calm myself before sitting back down. The rumble of chatter starts up again until Dunthorpe calls the room to order and changes the subject.

The rest of the meeting continues uneventfully; I struggle to keep focused on what is being said. Thank God, I am used to taking notes and can focus on the important issues.

I walk back to my office after the meeting, leaving my door open. As I sit down, I hear a light tap on my door. I don't have a chance to tell her to come in before she has the door closed and the windows fog.

"Hi, Samantha, I know you probably don't remember me with everyone you have met today."

"Of course, I remember you, Addison." Standing in front of me is a petite little redhead with a flawless little bob hairstyle that swings perfectly as she walks. She appears to have just walked out of a Vidal Sassoon hair salon. "You had some great ideas back there." I'm not sure why she is in my office, but she seems friendly enough, and it would be nice to make a new friend, especially after the day I've been having.

"Thank you, Samantha, I just wanted to say thank you for saying what you did to Lucas, he can be a real ass. In fact, I don't know that anyone has ever stood up to him since I've been here, and that's been three years. He and I are some of the originals."

"Really, and no one has complained about him?"

"Oh, I think there have been complaints, but I don't think they have made it very far up the management ladder because he's good at what he does. Anyway, one of the other reasons I came in here is to invite you out this Friday. Several of us girls are going out dancing, and I know you just moved here and probably don't have any friends, so I thought you would like to come with."

Addison is pretty and I know she would be a blast on the dance floor, she has that kind of spitfire personality. "Thank you, I would love to come. Just tell me when and where."

Addison does a little happy dance and claps as she says, "We're going to have so much fun. I'll get you all the specs later this week. Bye." And in a blink of an eye she is gone. However, the aftermath of her lingers and I can't stop smiling at my new friend.

CHAPTER SEVEN
DRAMA

SAMANTHA

"I disagree!"

"Then tell me why you think I'm wrong. You have the statistics and demographics right there in front of you. You can see why this marketing idea will work better. You just haven't ever tried it before, and you're afraid that I'm right."

"That's bullshit! Just because you just graduated from college doesn't mean you know everything," Lucas says as he throws his notepad down and it slides across the conference table hitting Taylor in the chest, catching him off-guard.

"I never claimed to know everything, I think your way of marketing is good. I just think that there are better ways, new ways. Something people haven't seen before, something new and fresh," I say with a calm voice. The whole room glances from Lucas to me and back again, as if watching a tennis or ping pong match. We've been going over our ideas for the last two hours, and at this rate, we will be here all night. "Mr. Dunthorpe, ultimately this is your decision. You have both of our ideas, there's no reason to keep hashing this out."

"True, I will run both of your ideas by Mr. Drake. It's been a long week; why don't you take the rest of the day off."

The prattle from everyone sitting around the table starts to escalate as they get up and leave the conference room. I take my time, gathering up my papers from my presentation, going over it in my head and making sure I hadn't left anything pertinent out. No, I made sure my outline was followed. I did the best I could.

"Hey, Sam," Addison calls out. I glimpse up at her as I shake the after thoughts of the meeting from my head. "Do you want to come with us or just meet us there?"

"Can I just meet you there; I have a couple things I want to finish before I leave."

"Of course, but if you're not there in an hour I'm coming back to get you."

"Okay," I say with a smile as I pick up my stack of papers. Addison told me about a new club that just opened up in downtown Seattle. It's only a few blocks from my apartment. Stephen, the concierge, sent a courier over to the hotel to pick up my things, so I can walk to and from there and don't have to worry about drinking and driving. Not that I do a lot of drinking, but I might make an exception tonight. It's been an interesting first week.

I think back on the week and my curiosity gets the best of me. I pick up my phone and dial the extension for Mr. Drake's office; I want to know why he's had so much interest in me even before I decided to join the company.

"Mr. Drake's office, how can I help you?"

"Hi, this is Samantha Hunter. I would like to make an appointment with Mr. Drake, please.

"Good afternoon Ms. Hunter, and welcome to E.O. Drake Enterprises, I hope your first week has been a good one."

"Thank you...?"

"I'm sorry, my name is Tiffany, and I'm Mr. Drakes assistant. We're very happy you decided to join our team."

"Well, that's what I wanted to talk to Mr. Drake about. Is it possible to get an appointment with him?"

"Oh, I'm sorry Ms. Hunter; Mr. Drake is out of the office on business. Is there something I can help you with?"

"No, thank you, I would prefer to speak to him directly. Do you know when he will be back in the office?"

"I'm sorry, no. I can leave him a message that you would like a meeting with him, though."

"That would be wonderful, thank you, Tiffany."

"You are very welcome, Ms. Hunter."

I hang up the phone and wonder more about the elusive Mr. Drake. Maybe the girls can fill me in on him tonight. I clear off my desk then check my watch; I know that if I don't leave soon, Addison will be back here dragging me out. I still need to meet up with James to get his final instructions, too. I pull my door closed make sure it is locked.

As I walk out of the building, I decide to stop at the security desk. My curiosity is getting the best of me. David stands to greet me, "Ms. Hunter, how are you this evening? Any big plans for the weekend?"

"Hi, David. No, although I am going out with some co-worker this evening for a little while."

"Good! I'm glad you're making some new friends."

"David, can I ask you something?"

"Of course. I'll even answer if I know it." His eyes sparkle when he smiles at me.

"Can you tell me how often Mr. Drake is out of town?"

"Not very often, he's a very hands-on boss. He was out of town for a couple days last week for personal business, but he was back on Monday, why do you ask?"

"Oh, Tiffany said he was out of town for a while and didn't know when he was going to be back."

"Ah... Oh... Ah... Maybe he had to leave today for an emergency while I was at lunch, yeah, that's it, he probably left during my lunch hour." All of a sudden, the smile on David's face is gone and it's replaced with a look of fear, as his eyes shift from side to side.

"David, why do I get the feeling you and everyone here is hiding something from me?"

"Gee, I…I don't know, Ms. Hunter. Why do you feel that way?"

"Because your smile disappeared and was replaced with fear as soon as I told you that he was supposed to be out of town. And you now have sweat beading on your forehead. So spill it!"

"I'm sorry, Ms. Hunter, I will lose my job if I say anything."

"Why David? Why all the secrecy?"

"I'm sorry Ms. Hunter," David leans forward as if to whisper in my ear, "You know you might want to get to work early on Monday, say six. Maybe sit and have a cup of coffee in the lobby, it's a nice relaxing time to people watch." David winks at me to make sure I understand what he is trying to tell me.

"Thank you, David, have a good weekend."

"Thank you, Ms. Hunter, you do the same."

I walk out the door with determination. What the hell is going on, and why all the secrecy? I'm definitely going to have to see if I can get some information out of the girls tonight.

My meeting with James only took five minutes, which is a good thing since I was playing detective and I'm now running late to get to the club. As I walk up to the club, I hear and feel the bass pounding. If it weren't for the conversation with David nagging at me, I would be all for a little club action. Maybe I just need to lighten up and deal with it on Monday.

Addison is at the door as I'm showing the brawny bouncer my ID. He's dressed in black slacks and a black t-shirt that stretches taut across his hard chest. You can even see the ripples from his muscles through his shirt. Wow, just wow. He gives me a hard time about being a long way from home. Then he peers up at me, his eyes finding mine, and he smiles. "Welcome to Washington, Ms. Hunter, I hope to see you around here more." He winks at me, and I smile back at him feeling my face flush at his flirting.

Addison grabs my arm pulling me inside. She yells over the music, "I thought you would never get here, I was just about to go and get you."

"Sorry, I was trying to get settled."

"We're over here; follow me,"

Like I have a choice. She has me by my wrist and pulls me along until we get to a booth. No one is there, just everyone's belongings.

I set my phone on the table then she pulls me to the bar. "What's your poison," she asks, "My treat!"

I figure I need to loosen up. It's been an interesting week to say the least. "Don Julio 1942, chilled if you have it." The bartender pours it into a small snifter. I inhale its fragrance:

rich, sweet aromas of caramel and chocolate. Then I sip just a little, it's been a long time, but I have always loved the taste. It's silky and smooth, with a flavor of roasted agave, vanilla, and spiced with undertones of cinnamon and pepper. It slides down my throat long and smooth with no bitterness. I've missed this, the liquid warms my body as it sinks into my belly. As I set my glass down, the bartender refills my glass, and I repeat the process. He tries to refill it for the third time, but I place my hand over the glass and shake my head no. It's been such a long time since I have drunk. I can tell my body isn't used to it, and I'm already feeling the slight buzz.

Addison takes me by the hand again and pulls me to the dance floor. The floor is shaking with the loud beat of the music and I feel the vibrations trembling through my chest. Lights are flashing all around us as I try to take in the monstrosity of this place. It appears as if there are three floors and I am sure the upper floors are for VIP. I start to relax as the alcohol takes its effect on my senses. I close my eyes as the music washes through me, and I start to move to the music, letting it fill me until I don't even think about what I am doing, my body moving on its own.

I don't know how long I'm dancing for when I feel hands sliding up my hips. My eyes flash open as I turn my head to see who is touching me in such an intimate way, and I'm shocked to see Lucas. I stop, placing my hands on his and I shove them off me as I turn and scowl at him, "What the hell do you think you are doing?"

He leans forward and speaks into my ear, "I just thought I would see if you were willing to share what you've been passing around to get your job."

Before I can even think about what I'm doing, I slap him across his face, hard. *Son of a bitch!* I shake my hand as it stings then starts to throb.

I turn to walk away when he grabs me by the shoulder. I swing around getting ready to slap him again but this time he blocks it and grabs my wrist pulling me to him. I start to panic, but then remember what my instructor said, *'It's when you panic that you are going to get hurt.'* I take a deep cleansing breath as I place my hand on his shoulder lifting my knee into his groin. Hard. "You BITCH!" he yells as he doubles over grabbing his balls.

I lean into his ear and say, "Don't you ever fucking touch me again." I turn and walk to the table and pick up my phone when Addison comes up beside me.

"What the hell just happened back there?"

"Other than I probably just lost my job for hitting a co-worker... nothing."

"You won't lose your job, but maybe it's time to talk to HR."

"I've been here for a week and what? Go to HR to complain about an employee who has worked here for several years. I don't think so. I need to leave. Thank you, Addison, for including me." It's too loud here to think. I just need to leave and get some air. I think about what I'm going to do if I lose this job. I know I have enough money to last me for a while. I'll have to see what happens on Monday. It's not as if this happened at work.

I push the club door open and the cool air coming off the bay hits me like a slap in the face, sobering me. The loud chatter coming from the line of people waiting to get inside is hardly noticed as I walk toward my place. I'm almost to the door of my building when my phone buzzes. It pulls me out of my deep thoughts and I answer it. "Hello?"

CHAPTER EIGHT
IS IT A DREAM

SAMANTHA

"Hey sis, how's the Pacific Northwest?"

I stop dead in my tracks. How in the hell did he find out where I am? I turn, searching for any movement, anyone in the shadows. "Why are you calling me, Grady?"

"Is that any way to treat your brother?"

"You're not my brother; you're the monster who took advantage of a naïve, innocent child."

"Oh come now, sis, you wanted it just as much as I did."

I blink back the tears that are threatening to fall. "I didn't even know what *it* was. I just didn't want to see my mother unhappy again. I believed what you told me. I never would have..." I take in a deep breath and try to calm myself. "What do you want, Grady?"

"I think you already know the answer to that, Sam. I want you. You're my first love, and I'm yours. We belong together, and nothing will change that. So you can either come home or I'll come and bring you back myself. Your choice."

"I will never come back. I never would have done the things that I did if it hadn't been for the lies you told me. Just leave me alone, Grady, because I will never be with you." I press end on my phone. I lean against the side of the cool, smooth marble building, sliding down to the ground I bury my head in my knees and wrap my arms around them. I do everything to keep from letting my fears escape.

My phone vibrates again and I let out an exasperated breath as I answer it. "I told you to fucking leave me alone, Grady!" I yell.

"Sam? What's going on? Where are you?"

"Oliver?"

"Sam, where are you and what's going on?"

Just the sound of his voice makes my heart hurt. I thought I was stronger than I'm feeling at that moment. I've always felt safe with Oliver. He is always there when I need him, and right now, I need a friend; I need my Oliver. With everything going on at work and the call from Grady, I'm feeling overwhelmed. The last time I saw Oliver was only a little over a week ago when he rescued me at my graduation. I don't even think I told him thank you, well except for the note I left, but how impersonal. I just left. Shit, I didn't even tell him I was leaving the state. How could I do that? He's the only one who knows me… really knows me and what my childhood was like. I wish things had been different. Somewhere in the back of my mind, I had always dreamed about Oliver, but I know that would never be. I'm damaged goods, and no one ever wants damaged goods.

"Oh God, Oliver," I set my feet under me, push myself up the wall, and start to walk, "I'm so sorry."

"Sorry for what, Sam?"

"God Oliver, so much has happened in the last week. I didn't even say thank you for rescuing me, but I didn't know what to do."

"Do about what, Sam, where are you?"

"I'm in Seattle."

"What are you doing there?"

"I moved here the day after graduation. Grady got into my apartment. I just had to leave. I couldn't stay when he knew where I lived and how to get into my apartment.

"What the fuck, he got into your apartment?"

I tell him what I found when I got back to my apartment the day after graduation. "I hadn't heard from him since he called the day of my graduation. I hoped that by moving here, I'd be safe. But he just called, Oliver, and he knows I'm here." I let out a sob.

"Send me your address. I'll be there by morning."

"I can't let you do that, Oliver. You have your own life. I need to start standing on my own."

"Sam, you have been standing on your own all of your life, but every now and then you need to lean on someone. Haven't you learned that that's what I'm here for?"

"Oliver, I'm sure you have better things to do than to be a shoulder for me to cry on or be my rescuer."

"Sam, go back to your apartment and by morning I will be there."

"How do you know I'm outside?"

There is a pause. "I hear the cars driving by and the wind as it hits the phone."

"Oh."

"Go and rest. I will see you in a couple hours."

"Okay, thank you, Oliver."

"For what Sam?"

"For always being here for me."

"I told you a long time ago that I will always be there for you. Bed."

"Okay."

I end the call, walk into the atrium of the building and proceed to my apartment. As I walk into the apartment, both Maxx and Levi are at my feet, rubbing and weaving in between my legs as I try to walk. I reach down and pet them then try to make my way to the bedroom without tripping over them. This isn't the way I had envisioned my first night in my apartment.

I step into a hot shower trying to erase the events of the day. I don't know how long I soak under the torrid raindrops of the shower, but it's long enough to drain what little energy I have left in my body. I walk out into the bedroom and to my surprise both Maxx and Levi are both waiting for me on the bed. I slip a T-shirt on and climb into my covers.

"No, Grady, stop, I don't like this. Stop! Oh God! It hurts, no! My baby, don't take my baby."

"Shhh, Sam, shhh, you're safe, Sam. You're safe. I'm right here. I have you now. It's just a dream. He can't hurt you anymore."

I wake terrified, my eyes flash open as I search to recognize my surroundings. I recognize the fragrance before I realize I'm in Oliver's arms and he's rocking me as he whispers in my ear. I turn my head to stare into his beautiful blue eyes just before I wrap my arms around his neck and hold onto him for dear life. Maxx and Levi are there as well, rubbing against me as if to tell me that everything is all right.

"It was a dream, shhh," he holds me tight as he continues to rock me. "He can't hurt you anymore."

"He's always going to be there; he always knows where I'm at. He's going to find me again. He knows I'm here. How did he find me?"

"I will do everything in my power to keep him from hurting you anymore," he reassures me.

"You promise?" I peer up at him with hopeful eyes, as he nods his head.

"Yes." I rest my head on his chest.

I've wanted Oliver for so long. I've never told him how I feel, but tonight I want to show him. I know showing him how I feel might change things, but that's the chance I'm willing to take.

I let my body take over as I curl into him. I look into those amazing indigo eyes, searching for any sign that he wants the same thing as I want. Butterflies fill my stomach as my core starts to ache. He runs his finger down my cheek. His touch sends goosebumps over my entire body and my clit starts to clench. I feel his erection against my panties as I feel the wetness soak through them. Bravely, I straddle his lap, and take his face in my hands, searching it, studying and finding the longing that I feel. I have loved him for so long. I slide my tongue across my bottom lip in anticipation as his eyes flash to my mouth. A groan leaves his open lips and his tongue mimics mine. I want to feel his tongue and lips on me, all over me. I've never wanted this before. His eyes flash to mine, and mine never leave his.

"Samantha, you are so beautiful. I've dreamt of this day." That is all the confirmation I needed. I pull his face to mine as I brush my lips across his. I run my tongue across the seam of his lips and he opens for me to enter. I can feel he is trying to restrain himself, but that's not what I'm wanting. I've waited too damn long for niceties. I touch my tongue to his as I slide my fingers through his thick curls. Closing my eyes, I try to memorize what I'm feeling.

He twines his fingers through my hair, pulling me closer as our tongues start to move. The energy between us turns primal and I wrap my arms around his head, pulling him closer; I need more of him.

I can't catch my breath, but that's okay, because he's all the air I need right now. I pull my T-shirt off then grip for his. I want to feel him, run my hands up his body, and touch every inch of him. This is the dream I have had of him for years. He pulls off his shirt, tossing it on the ground. Then he glances down at my breasts. My nipples are hard and long for his touch. He leans down, taking one in his mouth and the other with his hand, gently massaging. "Oh God," I moan as I arch my back, pressing my breast further into his mouth, needing to feel more as he rolls my other nipple between his index finger and thumb. I mewl loudly and I pull his hair as he lets out a loud growl.

I scramble for his belt then the buttons of his jeans, but he stops. He pulls away, his eyes searching mine. I don't know if I did something wrong. Maybe I moved too fast. Maybe he remembers what was done to me. Maybe he just doesn't want me this way.

He takes my face in my hands as he continues looking deep into my eyes, searching. "Before anything happens between us, we need to talk. I need to make sure you really want this."

"I do, I have..."

He interrupts, "I know you were scared tonight. You need to really think about this because there will be no going back. Once you give yourself to me, you will be mine. Do you understand?"

I gaze up at him and nod. "Yes." Oh God, he does want me. My heart overflows with the love I have felt for him for so long. That's what he said right, I ask myself.

"You also need to know who I am."

"I know..."

"No, you don't. You need to really know who I am."

"Okay."

"Right now we sleep, and tomorrow we'll talk."

"Okay, Oliver, but it won't change my mind or how I feel about you."

He kisses me on the forehead. "I hope not, baby." I slide down into the covers as he pulls me into him so I lay on top of him.

I don't know how long I cling to him before I finally drift back to sleep.

I wake in the morning to the feeling of soft touches skating over my shoulder and arm as I remember the nightmare and... Oh my God, Oliver is here. "How did you get in last night?"

"You left the door unlocked."

The sun is shining through the curtains that I left open last night.

I turn out of his hold and the moment I do, I wish I hadn't, I love the way he holds me. Oliver is the only man who can make me feel this way, and I think that deep down inside I have always loved him. I've never told him how I feel, never wanting to do anything to ruin our friendship, but I want more.

Turning onto my side so I can stare into his eyes, he reaches over, taking a strand of hair and tucks it behind my ear. He runs his finger down my jaw line to my chin. "I did? I was so upset last night. I guess I didn't even think about it."

"Tell me, Sam, what's going on? What brought you here? What are you running from? I think it's time for you to tell me the whole story."

I sit up in bed as I feel the burning of unwanted tears threatening to fall. I can't look at him. I don't want to see the pity in his face. He sits back against the headboard then takes my crossed legs and turns me toward him. Taking my chin, he lifts it so I have no other choice but to look him in the eyes. "Sam, it's been thirteen years, don't you think it's time?"

The first of my tears start to fall. "It's a long story Oliver, and it's not a happily ever after story."

"I have all the time in the world Sam, I'm not going anywhere, and your story isn't over yet so don't label it as a tragedy until the fat lady sings. Why don't you take a shower and I'll make coffee, then we can either stay in or we can walk along the bay and talk."

"Okay, but I think it would be best to stay in."

"Well then take your shower and I'll meet you in the living room."

I slide off the bed and walk into the bathroom. I sink into the shower, soaking my sore muscles. I never realized how much I thrash around when I'm having a nightmare. As I reflect on the events of last night, I wonder how Oliver found me. I don't remember giving him my address. Maybe I did and I was so upset that I just forgot.

I get dressed as the aroma of fresh coffee drifts back into the room making my mouth water. I walk out into the kitchen, and Oliver has a cup of coffee ready for me. He also has pastries and fresh cut fruit. How the hell did he do that so fast? We carry the food into the living area and place it on the coffee table, then sit and get comfortable.

"How did you fix this so fast?"

"I just called a store and had it delivered."

"How did you even know who to call? I've been here a week and I don't even know who to call."

"I just Googled it." He walks back into the kitchen and brings back our coffee and some plates. He's so comfortable wherever he's at that he walks with authority.

He hands me my coffee and looks at me expectedly. I try to get comfortable, but I don't know where to start.

We're sitting on the couch cross-legged, my heart is pounding hard against my ribs and my breathing is rapid. I stare down and run my finger around the rim of my mug. Oliver reaches over and touches my hand. I glance up at his face, so full of understanding and care. I shake my head as the first tear slides down my cheek. He reaches behind himself and grabs a box of tissues. I didn't even know they were there.

"Sam, how long have we known each other?"

"About seventeen years," I say quietly as I gaze up at him.

"And in those seventeen years have I ever once made you feel scared or ashamed?"

I shake my head no. "Oliver, I don't even know where to start. I have buried this so deep, I don't know what will happen if I let it all out."

"Baby girl, look at what it's doing to you know. You can't keep hiding this. It will break you."

"I know, I just don't want it to change us. I did something horrible, and I don't know how to live with myself."

"Start at the beginning, and we will work through everything else."

I begin at the day my father left and what my mother's reaction was. "That first day, the day we met, my mother was so upset. She had been crying for so long, she didn't want anyone to see her so I told her that I would go to my class by myself. You came up to me, and I immediately felt so safe and comfortable with you." I glance up at him.

"I'm glad. You looked so scared, and all I wanted to do was to protect you and keep you safe."

I tell him about mom and Dylan, and that he had a son, Grady. Then I start to tell him about the night that Grady babysat me. I watch the expression on his face go from sympathy to shock then murderous. I tell him how Grady said that all families have sex together and how he would come into my room whenever our parents' were gone and even sometimes in the middle of the night.

"Why didn't you tell someone? Why didn't you tell me?"

"He told me I couldn't tell anyone, that if our parents' found out his father would leave and my mother would be sad again." I peek up at him through tear-filled eyes. "I couldn't bear to see her so upset again."

"But they got divorced anyway, didn't they?"

"Yes, it wasn't that my mother wanted it, but she felt as if she didn't have a choice. My sins tore the family apart."

"What the fuck are you talking about," Oliver raises his voice, almost yelling. I don't think I have ever heard him raise his voice unless it was to help me. I jump at his harsh statement. "I'm sorry; I just can't understand why you're blaming yourself for this. What do you think you did? What sin do you think you committed?"

"When I was thirteen, I found out that I was pregnant."

"Oh fuck, it was his."

I'm staring down at my hands, and I unconsciously rip the tissue apart. "I think you knew, didn't you? You beat him up because of it." I glance back up at him.

"Yes, I did, and he deserved it; for not only what he did to you, but also what he was saying about it."

I can feel the heat of his penetrating gaze, but I can't force my eyes to meet his.

He sighs and rubs his thumbs across my knuckle. "I had heard rumors about him. He had told his friends that he was fucking you. He was dragging your name through the mud, and I couldn't have that, you were too important to me. I don't regret it, Sam."

A sob catches in my throat, and I brush the tears from my cheek.

"So what happened after you found out you were pregnant?"

"I was in shock. I wasn't even sure at that time how to get pregnant. I couldn't imagine being a mother at thirteen, and my mother didn't know what to do. She didn't want me to have the stigma of being promiscuous and a teen mother, so she did the only thing she believed to be right. I didn't know until later what was happening. I was very naïve when it came to things like that. All I knew was that I scared. I was too far along to go to a clinic so she took me to the hospital. I thought I was having tests done because that's what the doctor had talked about. They put me in a little room; it seemed just a little bigger than a closet. I laid there by myself for a long time. Then I started having cramps. No one was telling me what was going on. I just remember the pain, being alone, and being very scared. Then she was born. She was so tiny, and when the nurse finally came in and saw her, she was surprised. She called another nurse in and took her away in the bloody sheet that was under me. I realized then that I had just killed my baby. So yes, as far as I'm concerned, I sinned. I know others don't see it that way, but that's what I believe. I sinned by having sex, and I paid the ultimate price."

I bury my face in my hands and sob uncontrollably. The gut-wrenching reality of losing a child rips me inside out and my body jerks and shudders through my cries. I'm so distraught that I don't even realize that Oliver has placed me in his lap, rocking me gently until his voice breaks through my tears moments later.

"Shhh, it wasn't your fault, Sam. You didn't do this, and I'm sure your mother felt she was doing the right thing for you."

Oliver runs his hand down my hair, soothing me. I tuck my head in the crook of his neck and continue to weep. When my crying subsides, he leans back, and taking a tissue, he wipes the tears and smeared makeup off my face. His face is full of concern as he kisses my forehead.

"So what made you come to Seattle?"

I try to crawl off his lap, but he doesn't allow it; he holds me tight. "When I left the hotel, I couldn't find my phone and I knew Kassidy, my roommate, was going to be worried sick. I had an interview that day, and my phone had all the contact information in it. When I got to my car, Kassidy had left me a note that said she had found my phone, and had left it in my car. I was going to call you when I got back to my apartment. There was a flower arrangement on the doorstep from Dylan, and when I went into the apartment, it was filled with flowers from Grady. It was then that I made the decision to get as far away as possible. I had interviewed with Drake Enterprises before graduation and was offered a position. I hadn't made up my mind, but when I saw the flowers and knew Grady could get into my apartment, I felt I only had one choice. So I called the manager and accepted the job right then. I packed everything I could into my car and drove to Seattle. I didn't mean to leave without saying goodbye, but the only thing I could think about was getting away as quickly as possible."

"What is Grady doing that scares you so badly? Is he threatening you?"

"He told me that we belonged together and that I belonged to him and only him. He said that if I didn't come back, he was going to come and bring me back because I was his, and if he couldn't have me no one could."

"So that's the only reason you moved here? You didn't want to come to Drake?"

"It wasn't that I didn't want the job; it was so far away, and I guess I was a little scared. Even though I don't have any family, I was moving from the only two friends I had; you, and Kass.

"Drake is a wonderful place to work. They've bent over backward to make me comfortable, but they glare at me funny."

"Funny?"

"Well, there's a guy there that thinks I slept with the owner to get the job. I tried to tell him I hadn't even met the owner. Then last night I had been invited to go to a club with a couple of the girls I work with. While there, this same guy came up to me and started harassing me on the dance floor, so I slapped him. As I was trying to get away from him, he grabbed me and I knee him in the groin. I don't know if I will even have a job come Monday. But the weird part is that I was trying to meet the owner to tell him what a great job I thought he was doing, but when I tried to make the appointment, they wouldn't let me."

"Oh?"

"I was told the owner was out of town, but when I questioned a few other people they said he was in town. It's weird because he had talked me up to all the employees and everyone knew who I was, even though I had just made up my mind to accept the job. I'm going to get some more coffee; do you want some?"

"No, thank you I'm fine."

I scoot off his lap to go to the kitchen. As I'm walking back out, I hear the ring of his cell phone.

"Drake speaking."

CHAPTER NINE
DREAMS COME TRUE

OLIVER

I hadn't been asleep long before I woke to the sounds of whimpers and cries. I reach for her as she thrashes in the throes of her nightmare, hollering out in agony, pain, and guilt. I do the only thing I know to do, the only thing I've ever done, I take her in my arms, whispering her name and let her know that I am there to protect her.

She wakes, terror set in her sapphire eyes as they flash open, searching to recognize her surroundings. Tears start to fall as she clings tight to me and sobs.

I reassure her, holding her, rocking her.

"He's always going to be there; he always knows where I'm at. He's going to find me again. He knows I'm here. How did he find me?"

"I promise I will do everything in my power to keep you safe from him."

"You promise," she reaffirms, peering up at me with hopeful eyes.

"Yes." She watches me closely as if trying to read my reaction. She nods and rests her head on my chest.

Then as if in a dream, she curls into me. Her beautiful blue eyes search mine, my gut rolls with anticipation with that simple glance, and my dick starts to strain against my jeans. She continues to turn. She's now straddling me as she takes my face in her hands, holding me there, searching my face, looking deep into the depths of my soul as if she can read my inner thoughts, wants, and needs. She runs the tip of her tiny pink tongue across her bottom lip as my eyes flash to it. A groan slips from my lips. I've waited for so long to do just that, to run my tongue over her soft, plump lips. I'm so hard now and I know she can feel my erection pressing against her. I feel the heat of her arousal as her scent wafts up and infuses me. My eyes flash back up to hers, and hers never leaving mine. God, I want this. For so long I've dreamt about it, fanaticized about it, but never thought it would happen. *Fuck.*

"Samantha, you are so beautiful. I've dreamt of this day..." She pulls my face to hers, just brushing her lips softly across mine. Both of us are still gazing at each other, watching, waiting. She pulls me to her again and runs her warm tongue across the seam of my lips as if asking for permission, which I gladly accept, and hers slowly enters. I'm doing everything in my power not to devour her right now, but I'm losing all self-control. She touches her tongue to mine. I can still taste the mint of her toothpaste. She slides her fingers through my hair, her eyes close and I'm lost.

I twine my fingers through her long golden waves, pulling her close as our tongues start to dance, then more. All control is lost as her tongue starts to fuck my mouth. She wraps her arms around my head, pulling us together closer, not knowing where I start and she ends.

My heart is pounding in my chest, my breath ragged. I feel goose bumps forming on her arms. She pulls her T-shirt off and she frantically grasps for mine. I want that skin-to-skin contact. I want to feel her tits pressed against my bare chest. I pull off my shirt, only breaking our lip contact to pull it over my head as I toss it on the ground. Then I glance down at her soft supple tits, and they stand hard. I lean down, taking one in my mouth and the other with my hand, gently massaging it as a low moan seeps from her open lips. She arches her back, pressing her breast into me as I roll her nipple between my finger and thumb. Another moan escapes. She threads her fingers through my hair, pulling it. Fuck, it feels good and I growl.

She claws at my belt then the buttons of my jeans, I long to free my dick, to be inside her fucking her, making her mine. Then realization hits me, I can't do this. I am her protector. I have to stop this.

I pull away, as her eyes search mine. Uncertainty, sadness, and doubt fill her eyes. I cup her face in my hands, staring deep into her blue pools, I need to tell her how I feel, how I have loved her for all these years, but I also need to get Perrotti's approval.

"Before anything happens between us we need to talk. I need to make sure you really want this."

I lean forward, brushing my lips over her forehead. I know this might be the last time I hold her like this. This isn't the life I would want for her. I slide down into the covers as Sam lies on top of me.

I wake to the sun peeking through the curtains as I gaze down at the woman I have been in love with for over ten years. I daydream of her, of us as I run my fingers over her shoulders and arms, needing to touch her, feel her, hold her forever. For the first time I'm scared. I'm scared that I will lose her. That she will not want me after she knows, that she will slip through my fingertips. It's taken so long to get to this point. I have to tell her everything today.

CHAPTER TEN
CAT AND MOUSE

SAMANTHA

Oh my God! Now I get it. Now I know why everyone knew who I was. My mug slips out of my hand and shatters on the hardwood floor. Hot coffee splatters my legs. Dressed in shorts, a tank top, and bare feet. I jump from the burning of my legs, but land on shards from the mug. I let out a squeal. Within seconds, Oliver is there. I drop to my hands and knees picking up the shards from the ground in pieces embed in my knees, tears burn my eyes and blur my vision. I'm so upset about what I just heard that I don't even realize that I am gripping the broken pieces of the mug so tight that they're slicing into my hand and fingers.

"Shit! Sam, give me that."

I slowly glance up at him, in a daze. I'm numb, I feel the blood trickling down my arm. I'm vaguely aware that it's dripping from my elbow. Oliver runs into the kitchen grabbing a towel. He comes toward me and I scoot back from him. "STOP," I yell holding up my uninjured hand. He instantly stops in his tracks but only for a moment before he starts to come toward me again. "NO," I yell again, "Get away from me!"

"Sam, I need to stop the bleeding."

"Get away from me," I say in a whispered voice. However, he comes toward me again. "Get the fuck away from me," I yell this time. He stops. Tears stream down my face as I collapse on the floor, my world spinning out of control.

Oliver grabs a towel and a broom to sweep up the ceramic shards into a corner, and then wipes up the floor with the towel, making sure there are no more pieces to step on. I still haven't dropped the broken pieces of the mug; they are still slicing into my hand as I squeeze tighter and tighter. The pain feels good. It's the only part of me that isn't numb, that lets me know that this isn't a dream; it's real.

Oliver comes over to me again. I've backed myself into the corner and I have no place to go. "I said leave me the fuck alone," I growl at him

Oliver roars at me. "I will not! I haven't stopped trying to protect you since you were a child."

My eyes shoot to his, as I gasp for air, "What? What are you saying to me?"

He leans down picking me up. He takes me to the kitchen sink, removing the broken pieces from my hand, and drops the shards into the sink. He then turns the faucet on and places my hands under the cold water to try to stop the bleeding. He tries to pat it dry, but the bleeding won't stop. "We need to take you to the hospital, you need stitches."

"No," I say sternly as I glare at him defiantly.

"What do you mean no?" He stares at me with confusion.

"No, I'm not going to the hospital."

"Yes, you are." His brow is furrowed and his eyes are narrowed and burning.

"No, I'm not." I know I'm acting like a child, but at this moment, I don't care.

"You can either come with me or I will physically take you. Your choice, but you are going to the hospital," he says with a rumble in his voice. He grabs another towel and wraps it around my hand then he grabs a Ziploc bag filling it with ice. "Hold this," he says. "Stay here I'll be right back." When he comes back, he slips a pair of my flip-flops on my feet. He makes a call as he picks me off the counter top and walks out of the apartment to the elevator.

"Can you put me down please? I can walk on my own."

"Only if you promise to come with me to have your hand examined." He sets me down. I wince as I think there is still a ceramic shard in my foot. "Are you okay, do I need to carry you?"

"No, I'll be fine. I'm not a typical girl you know," I say gruffly.

I disdainfully glare up at him. His face is full of concern, and it takes all the strength I can muster to not fall back into his arms, but fuck.

"Believe me, I have known that for years." A shy smile breaks across his face revealing his dimple, and his beautiful indigo blue eyes start to sparkle.

"Why are you doing this? Why all the secrecy? I'm nobody to you," I say in a soft tone.

"I can't tell you why, at least not all of it, not yet. You're far from being a nobody, I knew that the first day we met."

"I don't understand, you knew that I would come and work here before I even did. This is your company isn't it?"

"Yes it's my company, and I knew you would come here because of your past. I knew you would need to get away, and now that your mother has passed, and you have graduated from college there was nothing holding you there. Well except for Kassidy, and I know she'll come out to visit you a lot." I gawp at him with confusion. I never realized he knew that much about me.

"But your last name isn't Drake."

"Drake was my real last name before I was adopted. When my adoptive mother died, I changed it back."

"Mr. Dunthorpe said the owner of the company walked in on a robbery and that his parents were murdered. Was that you?"

Oliver closes his eyes and just nods his head, not saying a word.

"Oh God, Oliver. I am so sorry."

"It was a long time ago, and Savina was a wonderful mother to me," he says in a quiet voice.

As we get off the elevator, I limp into the lobby, still feeling the shard digging into my foot the more I walk on it. Oliver notices and bends to pick me back up.

I regard him and shake my head. "I'll be fine." As we walk outside a car pulls up to the curb and an ex-military type exits the car and opens the back door for us.

"Reynolds, I need you to take us to the closest hospital."

"Yes sir, Mr. Drake."

I peer down at the towel, it's crimson from the blood. "I'll have to buy Mr. Randolph a new kitchen towel."

"I don't think Mr. Randolph will mind too much."

I glance up at him still wanting to know more of what is going on. Why me, and for how long has he been watching over me. "The apartment… it's yours isn't it? That's how you knew where everything was."

"Yes."

"Oliver, I need to know more, I need you to tell me. My mind won't rest until I know."

"I…I can't." He glances up at Reynolds then back to me. "I shouldn't have even revealed myself to you yet. That was never the plan."

"What plan? Do you realize that co-workers think I slept with you to get my job?"

"They're just jealous."

I slip my free hand into his. With that simple touch, just the feeling of his hand in mine sends goosebumps down my body and a strange throbbing in my belly. Oliver stares down at our hands and quickly pulls his hand away, leaving an unwanted empty feeling in my gut. I study his face, his eyes are closed, his jaw tense as if he's trying hard to concentrate.

"What did I do? I know you felt it too. I saw it on your face. Last night in bed. Tell me you don't feel the same way."

"What I want and what I can have are two different things, Sam."

"Tell me. Tell me what the hell is going on then."

Oliver glances at Reynolds in the rear view mirror then closes his eyes again. "I can't. Not yet."

We're just about out of downtown as we come to a red light. I grab the handle of the door and just as the light turns green I yank it open, slamming it shut behind me before he can react. I weave in and out of cars until I get to the sidewalk. Horns from impatient drivers come from the cars that are stopped behind them as they try to maneuver to the curb.

I try to run but the shard in the bottom of my foot slows me down. Oliver yells for me to stop, but I keep going, trying not to look back at him. I need to find a place to try to pull the shard out. I see a drug store and duck inside, hoping

Oliver didn't see me. I quickly go to the first aid section and grab a pair of tweezers, first aid kit, and hydrogen peroxide. On the way to the register, I pick up super glue and a sewing kit. I take it to the cashier in the back of the store. Thank God, I always keep my debit card in my pocket, I've never been much of a purse girl. "Do you have a restroom I can use?"

"Yes, down the hall and to the right."

"Thank you." I grab the bag and slip into the bathroom and into one of the stalls. I take my flip-flop off and try to find the shard, but my feet are too dirty and covered in blood. I move out to the sink, sliding up onto the countertop. I stick my foot into the sink and turn on the water to wash the blood and dirt off. I need to examine my hand too, I know it's bad, I just don't know how bad. Taking the needle out of the package, I pour the hydrogen peroxide on it, at least to clean it a little bit. I start to dig in the wound to find the shard. Clenching my teeth, I bring it close enough to the surface. Using the tweezers, I pull it out the rest of the way. I pour hydrogen peroxide over it then dry it off with the towel. I open the super glue and holding the cut closed, I spread a little on and blow it dry. I cover it with a bandage and hop off the countertop. What a difference in how my foot feels now without that shard in there.

The ice has melted and I dread looking at my hand. I throw the bag of melted ice away and remove the towel. I don't want my hand to start bleeding again, but I know it needs to be cleaned. I run it under warm water and blot it dry. I feel around the cut for any foreign objects. The smaller, shallower cuts I super glue closed but the deeper ones I stitch up with the needle and thread. I then pour the hydrogen peroxide over my hand and it bubbles up. I use the

Neosporin that is in the first aid kit, putting it on the worst of the cuts, and wrap my hand with the roll of gauze.

I just finish when there is a knock at the door. I jump with a start as I toss everything into the bag. I glimpse down on the floor and see footprints of blood leading to the first stall I had been in. I tiptoe to the last stall and climb onto the toilet, trying not to fall in. I don't lock the stall door. I want him to think it is empty. There's another knock, "Sam I know you're in there, your footprints lead inside. You can either come out or I'm coming in after you." My heart is racing, and for some reason I have a defiant smile on my face. Not that I want to be caught, but maybe the thrill of it all. Hell, who am I fooling, a part of me would love to be caught by him. The thought of hiding and seeing if I can out think him to get away is exhilarating. I hear the door creak open.

"Sir."

"Yes Reynolds"

"The cashier said she bought a first aid kit, a sewing kit, and hydrogen peroxide. It sounds as if she's going to stitch herself."

"My God, what is she thinking? Even the toughest men have a problem stitching themselves up."

"What are you going to do sir?"

"I don't know, Reynolds. I can't lose her."

"Maybe you should tell her how you feel."

"I can't, just knowing what she knows has pushed her away, if she knew the rest..."

"Does she know how long you have been watching after her for?"

"No. But we need to find her before that SOB does. Come on, we're just wasting time here."

I hear the door squeak closed. I slowly step down from the toilet and peek through the crack of the stall door. So far so good. My pulse is racing, but I'm feeling enlivened. I slowly open the bathroom door, making sure the coast is clear. I stay to the outside wall as I walk to the door. I have to figure out what I'm going to do. Maybe I can get back to the apartment, grab my keys and a few things, and get out undetected. Maybe if I go now while they are still out searching for me, I can get away. I walk out the door and peer around for either of them. I start for the apartment. At least if I get my car I can sleep in it.

My phone vibrates and I jump. I see that it's Oliver. I take a deep breath. "Hello," I say in a quiet tone.

"Where are you, Sam?" I can hear the concern in his voice, and I fight hard to keep the tears from falling. My heart feels broken.

"I'm fine, Oliver, go back to your life and I will find mine again. You don't have to babysit me anymore, and like I've told you before, I'm not like most women... or men, I can and have withstood more than most."

"You were in there, all that time, you were there and... FUCK!"

"She was in there? That whole time," I hear Reynolds ask.

"Yes, she was."

"Oliver, when you are ready to talk to me and tell me what the hell is going on, then and only then will we talk. I don't know what you are afraid of, but we've known each other for a long time. These secrets will just tear us apart. If that's what you want and are willing to do, then so be it, but I'm finished with secrets. I told you all my secrets and obviously, you don't trust me enough with yours, and that's what's really sad. I thought we were closer than that."

I search the streets as I make my way to the apartment. I enter through the garage so I don't have to walk into the lobby. I don't want the concierge to see me just in case Oliver told him to notify him if I came back. I get to my floor and glance around the elevator before exiting. I knock on the door to see if anyone answers, but there is silence. I slowly open the door and I'm greeted by the kittens. I had placed my phone on mute so Oliver couldn't hear the elevator beep or ding for the floors. I rush into my room, throw some clothes into my suitcase, and then grab my things out of the bathroom. I hear the elevator ding through his phone and make a mad dash for the door. I get to the stairwell just as the elevator door dings its arrival. I wait in the stairwell until I hear the apartment door close. I slowly open the door and push the call button for the elevator. The doors open immediately. I slip inside and hit the garage button.

"We are, but there are things I can't tell you. Not yet anyway."

I un-mute my phone to answer him. "Then I guess there isn't anything else to discuss." The elevator dings its arrival to the basement, and I know he had to have heard it. I hear him running through the apartment as I stride quickly to my car. I toss my bag in the front seat as I see Reynolds in my mirror. He's walking over to the doors. He hasn't seen me. "You want to know the sad part of this whole story, Oliver?" I hear him panting in the background. I put my car into drive as soon as the elevator doors close with Reynolds inside. "You used to be the one I would run to. The one I always felt safe with, but look at me now. I'm running from you, because I don't know what to believe anymore, and you don't trust me enough to tell me what's going on."

"Sam, I can't."

"I've heard that before, Oliver, and until you can, I guess this is the end. Tell Lucas to enjoy my office." I press end on my phone.

CHAPTER ELEVEN
ON THE RUN

SAMANTHA

I have no idea where I'm going, but I have to get out of Seattle and away from Oliver. I can't be in an environment where I don't know what's going on. Let alone a friendship that's based on lies.

I feel sick. My heart hurts so badly, and my eyes burn with unshed tears as my stomach twists at the thought of losing him. I have to be strong, but God, I just want to crumble. I have to start standing up for myself. It's time to put my mask back on. The mask that hides my true feelings and emotions. Taking a deep breath, I find my resolve.

Oliver tries to call several times, but I let it go to voicemail, hoping that he gets the point.

I know he felt the same thing that I felt, that's why he pulled his hand away. Whatever this is, he's fighting it with all he has.

I finally turn off on a little road and end up in a small lake town. I stop at the gas station that is also the general store. Any other time I would love it, it's so romantic, rustic and charming. I feel as if I can breathe for once.

As I walk inside, I see a little diner and my stomach reminds me with a growl that I haven't eaten today. With all the revelations and then my hand, I never had the chance.

I'm greeted with a friendly 'hello' as I walk through the door. I walk over to the counter to where a girl maybe my age is standing. She's pretty. She is the extreme opposite of me. She has long black, shiny hair, amber eyes, with an olive complexion. She's tall and thin, almost model thin. She has a natural beauty about her. I, on the other hand, am golden blonde with blue eyes, and although I am thin, my body changed a lot when I was thirteen and I have more curves than most.

"Hi, my name is Samantha, and I am new to the area. Can you tell me what's around here to do? I also need to find a job and a place to stay."

"Hi, Samantha, I'm Amber." I smile as she says her name, it's perfect for her because of her amber eyes. She reaches out her hand, and I take it in mine. "Oh my gosh, what did you do?" she asks referring to my bandaged hand.

"It's nothing, I dropped a mug, and cut my hand when I was cleaning up the pieces."

"Oh, Samantha, who or what are you running from?" she glares at me with an all-knowing smile.

"Why would you think that? I..."

"It's fine, you'll tell me sooner or later."

I shake my head, staring at the floor, and then I straighten myself as I collect my resolve. "I'm just considering for a new place, that's all."

"Okay, whatever you say, Sam. The diner is hiring, they have good food, and it's not the typical diner food. The Guest House always has rooms to rent. The last girl that 'wasn't running' stayed there until she was found."

My eyes flash to hers, she's not stupid, she must see this all the time. "Thank you, Amber." I turn to get my affairs in order. First on the list is to get a job and it sounds as if the diner is the only place in town. As I start for the door, I turn, "Who are you not running from?"

"I'll tell you when you tell me."

I smile at her. "It's a deal." I give her a quick wave as I walk out the door. I like her, I think she'll be a good friend.

I take the 'Help Wanted' sign out of the window as I walk into the diner. There are several customers sitting around waiting as a middle-aged woman is at the window in the kitchen cooking. Several of the couples glance around impatiently, and it appears as if they need more coffee and well, more. Not seeing anyone else to help I walk behind the counter put the sign down, wash my good hand, put a glove on the other hand, and grab an apron that is folded on the countertop. I grab the pot of coffee, feeling it to see if it is still hot. As I pass the cash register, I pick up a notepad and pen then walk over to the first couple and fill their mugs. "Hi, my name is Samantha. I'm new, I apologize for your wait time. What can I get you?" They tell me their order and I place the order slip on the window in front of the woman. I then go to the next table then the next until all the orders are placed. The woman calls out 'Order Up.' I walk up to the window and smile at her as I glance at her nametag, "Thank you, Val, I'm Samantha, just call me Sam."

Val doesn't smile or acknowledge me until she says, "Why are you standing here gabbing when food is getting cold." I take the plates of food and deliver them to the tables as the orders start to come up. I had the mind to just walk out and let her sink or swim, but I figure we all have bad days; all I had to do is look at my day, and I cut her some slack.

I'm surprised at how busy it is, and Amber was right, although you can get the regular diner food, it's a step above. When all the customers have left and the tables are cleared and wiped down, I head to the back room to start washing the dishes. I was just finishing putting the last of the dishes away when Val walks back into the room.

"What makes you think that you can just come tromping into *my* restaurant and take over the front of the house?"

It's been a long and stressful day, and I still haven't eaten. The last thing I want is to be bashed for helping someone out that obviously doesn't appreciate the help. Well, screw that. I wipe my hands on my apron then untie it. Holding it in one hand, I walk over to her and stand directly in front of her. She isn't much taller than I am, but when I square my shoulders and get into her space the expression on her face changes. I purposely glance at her nametag again. "Val, I have tried to be nice, Lord knows I've had a shitty day today myself." I gesture to my hand. "So I was going to give you the benefit of the doubt and chalk it up to a bad day. I came in here to eat and ask for the job until I saw that you had no one to help you, and your customers were getting ready to walk out. I thought that you would appreciate making a little money since you were ready to lose business. You want to be a one-woman show, fine. Work your ass off, and lose your customers. You might be the only place in this town to eat, but once you get a bad reputation for bad customer service, it doesn't matter how good the food is, people will go elsewhere." I take her hand and put my apron in it as I turn to walk out of the kitchen.

"And who are you to tell me how to run my business?"

"I'm a customer that has a degree in business and marketing, which could've built this place bigger than you would ever imagine, but hey, you have your own ideas on how to market this place, good for you." I turn and glare her in the eye. "How's that working for you... Val?" I say in a sarcastic tone as I walk out the door. Frustrated and still hungry I walk to the boarding house and take the last room they have. It's nice, and for the price, I can't beat it; it's better than sleeping in my car.

I had just finished unpacking when a knock comes at the door. I open the door to find Val. In her hands, she is holding several takeout containers. "I figured the least I can do is feed you since you never had the chance." I glance up at her as my brows furrow, trying to figure out why the change of heart. "Do you mind if I come in?"

I move out of the way as she steps around me into the room. Taking the containers from her hands, I set them on the table. "Thank you for this."

"Well, as I said, it's the least I could do for saving my bacon today.

I laugh at her metaphor. "Well, as I said earlier, I didn't want you to lose your customers."

"I didn't know what I was going to do without a server. Please sit and eat before it gets cold. I have a proposition for you."

Intrigued, I narrow my eyes at her comment, "What kind of a proposition?" I pull the chair out to sit. I gesture for her to sit, too. My stomach growls at the aroma of the food. I laugh and place my hand on my stomach. I open the first box "Oh my God." I close my eyes and just inhale, my mouth is watering. I gawk at the container full of Garbage Fries; crosscut fries slathered in homemade beef chili, cheddar cheese, scallions, sour cream, homemade salsa, and guacamole.

She pulls out a stack of napkins from her apron. "I figured you would need these."

I dive into the fries and moans escape my lips. "I'm sorry, I know it's not polite to moan and eat, but my God!" I peer up at her and she has a big smile on her face. "That's nice."

"What is?"

"I don't know if it's just the stress of the restaurant, but you need to smile more. I didn't once see you smile while I was there."

"Thank you, yes, it has been stressful. It's hard for me to ask for help, and it's finally getting to me I guess."

"What good is it to have your own business if you can't enjoy it? I mean it's one thing to work hard, but if you can't enjoy going to work, then there's something wrong."

"So help me."

"Excuse me?"

"Help me get things on track, show me what I need to do to bring in more customers, even the ones that don't live around here."

"Why would you ask me that, you didn't even like me serving your customers today?"

"Like you said, let's just chalk it up to having a bad day. I know I was an ass, I'm sorry." She lays her hand on my arm. I peer up at her. "Samantha, as I said, it's hard for me to ask for help, but I know you're the one to help me. I don't know why I feel this way, but there's something about you, and this time, I'm going to trust my gut feelings. Please say yes."

"I have to be honest, I don't know how long I'm going to be here."

"Then work with me until you leave, we can work something out. I don't want to beg."

I gaze into her desperate eyes. "Fine," I say as I huff out a breath. I grab my legal pad and start taking notes and writing ideas down on how to grow her business. "First, you need to get someone in there that will do a good job serving and take an interest in you customers. Then we need to get a press release out to introduce you to the rest of the world. However, you need to get someone to help you. I don't know what all you do in the middle of the night, but maybe you can get someone in there to do that shift so you can do your magic during the day. After all, it's your food that will brand this place." After eating most of the fries, I opened another container that had Mac 'N' Cheese. I remember reading the ingredients in the menu and my mouth watered. Mac 'N' Cheese is one of my weaknesses. Three kinds of cheese, bacon, mushrooms, tomatoes over bow tie noodles and then baked with homemade seasoned bread crumbs sprinkled on top. I know that if I keep eating her food, I'm not going to be fitting in any of my clothes. I open the last food container, not that I'm still hungry, but just curious what else she brought. Oh God, it's my all-time favorite, a six-layer carrot cake. Well, it doesn't have to be six layers but just carrot cake in general. I think I've died and gone to Heaven. I peek up at her. "Raisins?"

"No, I don't like cooked raisins except in bagels."

"Walnuts?"

"Pecans, they have a better flavor than walnuts and they don't burn your mouth."

"Wow. We must be sisters." We talk about what she is considering and I throw out more of my ideas. I agree to help her serve and hire someone to take my place so she can concentrate on the food. I've just put the leftover food in the fridge when there's a knock at the door. First night in town and I have a second visitor.

Val gets up and starts to leave as I open the door. It's Amber. She looks me up and down. "Go change your clothes. You need to go dancing to work off that food Val brought over. Hey, Val."

"Hi, Amber, it's good seeing you, too. I'll see you in the morning."

"Okay, and thanks, Val, for the food."

"Again, the least," she says as she walks out the door.

"Come on, times a wastin'."

"Really?"

"Yes, it's your first night in town and your fresh bait. This means I might get lucky, so chop, chop."

I have to laugh. "I don't have very much, I just grabbed a few things before I left."

"See, I told you, you were on the run." I peer at her and roll my eyes.

I change into some ripped skinny jeans and a tank top with lace at the neckline. I throw a little blush on my face and put some lip gloss on and I'm ready. I grab my phone and key, and we are out the door.

I hadn't even realized that there was a club in town. I guess it's more of a bar, but they have a great sound system and a big dance floor. There aren't many people here, but it's still early. What's nice is that it's within walking distance.

I order a glass of Riesling and Amber orders a gin and tonic. We find a table and sit for a few minutes. The music is loud, but not so loud that we can't hear each other talking.

"So what are you running from?"

"I'm not really running. I'm more trying to find my own way."

"And that brought you to our little town?"

"What can I say, I just started to drive and I ended up here."

"I have a feeling you're not a waitress."

"No, I'm not. I just graduated from college."

"Wow, that's pretty ambitious."

"I needed to be able to take care of myself, an education was the only way I felt I could do that."

"Your parents'?"

"My mother died a few years ago, my father took off when I was a kid."

"I'm sorry."

"My turn now, have you always lived here?"

"No, I'm a runner. I've been here for the last three years."

"What are you running from?"

Amber's face falls, but she puts on a fake smile that doesn't even come close to her eyes, and if I didn't know better, it appears as if there are tears swelling the brim of her eyelid. "It's time to dance." She pulls me up out of the chair and drags me to the dance floor.

As the night progresses, the club gets busier. Two glasses of wine down, and I'm feeling a little buzzed. We're in the middle of a crowd of people, and I close my eyes and feel the music pulse through me. Hands slowly pull my hips so my back is to his front. Nothing like déjà-vu. The sound of a soft, low voice breathes in my ear. The warmth of his breath sends shivers down my body. "Do you mind sharing the dance floor with me?" I don't say anything. I just shake my head no and keep my eyes closed. I long to be touched. I hadn't been with anyone since that day almost ten years ago. Just before I found I was pregnant. A tear runs down my cheek at the memory, and I quickly wipe it away.

He skims his hands up and down my sides and follows my arms that are up in the air. He takes my arms and places them around the back of his neck as I hold him tight to me. He has his arm around my stomach and I feel his hard body against mine, and then I feel his erection at my back. I rub it with my ass, grinding on him, feeling his reaction to me. I imagine it's Oliver. I want it to be him, but I know it's not. I don't want to be a tease, but this feels good. I love to feel a man's desire for me, I crave to be desired. I've never had the opportunity to just take what I want. I need something to dull the feelings I have inside me. I just want to forget.

Maybe that's a sick notion that I picked up from all those years with Grady. I knew how to make him hard. He always told me what he liked. Maybe I was just as big of a freak as he was, or maybe it was all those years that he made me do the unthinkable. Maybe it was my fault, maybe I did something that I didn't know would turn him on, and that's what started this whole mess. Grady was right, I had only been with him, and even though I didn't like him that way, I like the idea that I knew what he liked. I wonder if it's the same for all men. Maybe if I hadn't gotten pregnant, Grady would still make me have sex with him. I wonder if I would like it now. All I know is that I'm lonely and I longed to be touched.

I miss Oliver. I want him to touch me, but whenever we get that close, he pulls away. Was I wrong in leaving? Should I have stayed and talked it out? No, because he already said he wouldn't tell me anything. I can't be in any situation where there isn't honesty and trust.

The song ends and a new one starts, my arms are still wrapped around Mr. Hard Body's neck. This song has a faster beat and he pulls me into him as he grinds into me harder and harder. I know I should stop and walk away. This will only lead to trouble, but I'm tired of being alone, I'm tired of being afraid, but that doesn't change things; As much as I want to be touched, I only want Oliver to touch me, no one else. I gave him my heart years ago, and I don't want anyone else to have it. I turn to him, gazing up into his dark eyes. I can tell he's not going to take my rejection well. He tries to pull me close to him, but I press my hands on his chest and try to push away. But he won't have it. He grabs my wrists, twisting them behind my back and pulls our bodies together. I let out a shrill cry, "Stop! You're hurting me." I try fighting to free my wrists, but his grip on me is too tight. I stare into his face and there's a wicked grin leering back at me. I peer around for Amber, but she is in her own little world with her own tall dark and handsome.

I continue to struggle to get free, and he leans into my ear, "We both know you want it, but I like the fight you're putting up; it just makes me harder." I gasp at his admission. It is my fault. I brought this on myself. I'm going to have to get out of it. I come up with an idea, but I'm not sure it will work.

I paste a fake smile on my face and gaze up at him through my lashes. "You're right, I was just playing hard to get. I don't know your name."

"Paul. Let's get out of here."

"Let me go to the bathroom and we can leave. I just need to tell my friend, though."

His grip on my wrists loosens then he lets go. He has a cocky arrogant smile across his face. I rub my wrists trying to get the circulation back into my hands as I walk over to Amber. I touch her arm and she leans so I can whisper into her ear. "I need to sneak out the back, please tell me there's an exit by the bathrooms?"

She nods her head. "Yes, at the end of the hall that the bathrooms are on."

"Thanks, Amber, I'll talk to you later." I head to the hall and I glance behind me to make sure Mr. Tall, Dark, and Dangerous (TDD) is still there waiting for me. He's standing at the bar with a drink in his hand. I slowly slip through the door, and stay to the shadows of the night as I walk back to the boarding house.

Once back in my room, I start getting ready for bed. I've just snuggled down into my pillow when my phone vibrates. I glance at the name on the screen and know I need to at least let him know that I am okay. "Hello," I say in almost a whisper.

"Samantha, are you alright, where are you?" The concern in his voice brings tears to my eyes.

"I'm fine, Oliver." I wipe away a stray tear. "Go back to your empire, and just leave me alone."

"You don't mean that, Sam."

"I do, I don't know what is real and what isn't. I can't go on not knowing what secrets you are keeping from me, and since you can't tell me, then I'll have to start to live my life without you."

"I can't say any more than I have, Sam."

My heart is breaking, I want to feel his comforting touch, he's always been my constant; now I'll have to learn to find my own safety. "Then I guess this is goodbye, Oliver." I hit end on my phone and lay it on the nightstand as another tear runs down my cheek.

CHAPTER TWELVE
SCAVENGER HUNT

OLIVER

Fuck! I throw my phone across the room, and it smashes into a vase, shattering them both. Maxx and Levi quickly slither away hiding under something. I can't believe I lost her. I knew she would be good, but I underestimated her.

I call Tiffany to make arrangements for a private jet to fly back home. I need to talk to Mr. Perrotti and Nicolas. While I'm back there, I need to take care of unfinished business with Grady Price. Reynolds found him and we'll be making a personal call on him.

We board the jet. Reynolds sits across from me and gives me a knowing look. Reynolds was in the Special Forces and has been with me for since I started the company four years ago. Although there is respect, he also knows that I'll listen to what he has to say.

"What are you going to tell them," he asks.

"Fuck if I know. Things were so much simpler when she was younger, but now she's too smart for her good." I rake my fingers through my hair, trying to figure out how I'm going to find her. Shit, she could be anywhere. In all the years I've watched her, this is the first that I have ever lost her.

The smell of coffee fills the cabin of the jet as Piper, the flight attendant, brings us a tray with a carafe of coffee on it.

"I can't believe she was in that bathroom the whole time." I have to chuckle at her cat and mouse game, not locking the stall door, then placing her phone on mute so I wouldn't hear the elevator; she definitely went into the wrong business.

"What's so funny, boss?"

"Just thinking how she gave us the slip today. Not only once but twice. She's damn good. She's going to need those instincts." I glance up at Reynolds just as a thought pops up in my mind. My eyes go wide.

"What is it? What are you thinking?"

"Did Costa help get her car?"

"Yes, I believe he negotiated the price, why?"

I pull out my phone and hit Costas number. "Costa, it's Drake, have heard from our lady today?"

"No, Mr. Drake, not since last week. What do you need?"

"Does her car have OnStar?"

"Yes, I made sure the model she bought had that feature. I also knew it could help us keep an eye on her."

"Thank God! I need you to find out where her car is. Make up something, but I want it found within the hour."

"I'm on it."

I peer at Reynolds. "I can't believe I didn't think of this before. I hope I'm not slipping."

"You're just emotionally involved and it takes some of your shrewdness away."

I stare up at him. "You're right, and if I'm going to keep her safe, I have to get my head back on right."

"What are you going to say to Nicolas? Are you going to ask his permission to see her?"

My eyes flash to his. "That would be ludicrous."

"Why? Because you've been in love with her for the last ten years, or because you'd rather be lonely all your life. How I see it is, she's the closest thing to a soul-mate that I have ever seen."

"Fuck!" I run my hands over my face and through my hair again. "What am I supposed to do? I'm supposed to be protecting her, not falling in love with her. I've tried so hard to keep her at arm's length, but now..."

"And how's that working for you today, boss?"

I throw him a pointed look. "I'd like to live to see my thirtieth birthday. Hell, my next birthday at this rate."

"Besides, you were only supposed to be watching her for three years. You've been watching after her and caring for her for the last seventeen. He has to see that. Perrotti is a good guy. He likes you. He knows you're a straight shooter. I think you should tell him and see where the chips fall. The worst he could do is say no."

"The worst he could do is put a bullet in my brain for even thinking I could have a relationship with her."

Once we land, we head straight to Perrotti's club where we're taken to the back room to meet with him and Nicolas. Costa leaves me a message letting me know where Samantha is and I send a couple guys over to watch her. I breathe a big sigh of relief that she's safe.

Reynolds stands outside the door as I enter the office.

I reach out my hand to both Mr. Perrotti and Nicolas. "Oliver, what brings you back home?"

"Thank you for meeting me on such short notice, but there are two important matters that I wanted to meet with both of you about."

"I'm intrigued. Please sit."

"Thank you, sir. First, I want to talk to you about Samantha."

Nicolas's eyes light up, "Is she alright?"

"Yes, sir, she is," I address Nicolas, "But I want to ask your permission to take care of an old problem."

"What type of old problem?"

"The step brother, sir."

"I thought that was dealt with years ago."

"No, sir. The orders were to rough him up and tell him never to contact her again. That lasted up until a couple weeks ago. He's now harassing her and to be frank, scaring her. She's been having nightmares again. I would like to rectify the problem so that she'll never have to fear him again."

"I see," Perrotti says as he runs his index finger and thumb around his mouth, then places his index finger over his lips and places his thumb under his chin as if contemplating another solution.

"Oliver, I would like to know how you know that she's having nightmares. Have you been taking advantage of her?"

Nicolas questions me sternly. Perrotti raises his brows for my answer.

"No, sir! Although I would like to talk to you about her."

"Oh?"

"Yes, sir, I have been watching after and protecting Samantha for the better of seventeen years, and I have grown very fond of her. In fact, sir, I'm in love with her and have been for quite some time now."

"Oh? And have you expressed your feeling to her?"

"No, sir. I wanted to express my feeling to you first and ask your permission."

"And if I say no?"

"I won't like it, but I will abide by your answer, sir."

"I see," Nicolas says.

"And what of your business? Does she know what you do?"

"Only that I own my security business," I glance from Perrotti to Nicolas nervously. "But if you allow me the chance for a relationship with her, I would tell her about my other activities. I believe she has the right to know what she is getting herself into if she agrees to have a relationship with me."

"You do realize that I left her and her mother because of this life, correct?"

"Yes, sir, I do, but Samantha is smart, and I wouldn't want to start a relationship if I can't be honest with her."

"So you love her," Nicolas asks.

"More than life itself, Sir."

"And how does she feel about you?"

"I believe she feels the same. However, I let her go because I couldn't tell her who I am. I wanted to talk to you first."

"I'm not happy about her being involved with the family business. There are too many threats against us. I want her safe."

"With all due respect, sir, she has never left the family. She just doesn't know about it, which might make it that much more dangerous for her. She doesn't know that she could be in danger. At least if we are together, I can keep her safe. This brings me back to the original issue. Obviously, he didn't heed my warning about staying away. I am asking your permission to end her fear."

"Permission granted," Perrotti states, "But it needs to be clean, no trace of this back to you, to the family, or to Samantha."

"Thank you, sir. I will let you know when the problem is resolved."

I peer over to Nicolas for his answer but it never comes. "Give me some time to think about this, Oliver. I'll be in touch."

"Thank you, sir." I stand and shake their hands before turning to leave. I hope I have expressed my feeling for Samantha enough that he will see what's in my heart and how much I want to be with her.

As I exit the door, I stare at Reynolds. "It's time to pay someone a visit," I say.

CHAPTER THIRTEEN
LET'S TALK

SAMANTHA

A month has gone by. Every day I get a text from Oliver asking me to come back. He tries to pull me in, either using Maxx and Levi, or Addison or even better, rubbing my face in the fact that Lucas now has my office. As much as it all affects me, the point is still the same. I can't be somewhere where I'm not trusted, and ultimately that's what this is all about. I don't know what secrets he's hiding from me or why, but that's what's keeping me from going back.

I always answer back the same way.

'I can't come back to something or someone that can't trust me with the truth... the truth of my life.'

During the day, I help Val at the restaurant then when things slow down I work on a marketing plan for her. I've sent out a couple press releases that have drawn in some business to not only her restaurant but to the town itself. Val has hired someone to help her in the kitchen so she doesn't have to get up in the middle of the night to make her specialty bread and desserts, as well as a server. You can see the love Val has for this place; it's on her face.

Amber and I have been spending time together getting to know each other more. I know she wants me to tell her what I'm running from, but it's not that simple. It's not that I'm running from Oliver, because that's really not what I'm doing. Yeah, I'm upset with him because there's a whole other side of him that I don't know, but shit, he needs to recognize his feelings for me, too. We have never had a physical relationship with each other, and with what happened that last night together everything changed.

I haven't been to the club since that first night. The last person I want to run into is (TDD), especially after I snuck out on him.

Amber and I are going to go to the lake for the day.

I make some sandwiches, cut up some fresh fruit, and place it in a basket with a couple of bottles of water. By the time I've finished, Amber is walking into the diner. I say my goodbyes to Val as I pick up my bag that holds my towel and some extra clothes and the basket of food, "You ready?"

"Yep," she says.

I don't even know the last time I actually spent the day just relaxing. Amber takes us to the spot that she usually goes. It's a secluded area, out of the way of the tourists. No one knows where it's at; much less how to get here. We lay our towels down on the sandy shore then I open the basket of food and set it down between us. The smell of the pine trees has me thinking clearer as the sound of the water lapping at the shoreline serenades with the birds singing in the trees.

As we nibble on the fruit, we talk. "This is so nice out here." We both have stripped down to our bathing suits. The sun is hot, but not unbearable yet. "Tell me what brought you here." I glance up at her. She had already told me that it had to do with a relationship, but she didn't indulge anything other than that.

Her eyes flash to mine. There's sadness in her eyes. "Tyler and I were high school sweethearts and voted *most likely to be married within a year of graduation.*" She picks up a grape and bite it in half before putting it in into her mouth. She peers up at me as if to get my approval. "We were heading that way. We had talked about getting married our senior year of high school, but I wanted to go to college. I didn't want to be like my parents', struggling to make ends meet, living paycheck to paycheck. I wanted more for myself than that." She glances back up at me, shrugs her shoulders and continues. "I'd been accepted to my first choice university. I was so excited. Everything was opening up for me, but Tyler didn't have it as easy. When he wasn't accepted to the same university I got into, he tried to get me to change my mind about going. I didn't want to stay. I wanted to see other parts of the United States, hell the world." She stopped and was just gazing at the ground as if in a trance or just remembering something.

"Amber?"

"I'm sorry. It's still hard to talk about."

"If you don't want to tell me, I'll understand."

"No, it's okay." She never looked up but shook her head. "He agreed to move with me, but he wanted to get married first. I didn't see anything wrong with that, after all, it's not as if we hadn't been together for several years. We knew we were going to get married, we were just doing it sooner."

"Where are you from?"

"Idaho. I got accepted to University of Washington."

"Wow, that's great."

"We had a little wedding with a few friends and family before we left." She shrugs her shoulders as if it wasn't a big deal. "When we moved out here it was as if we were on an adventure. We were actually. We didn't have any friends or family out here. We found a cute little apartment close to campus and fixed it up.

"I started school that fall and Tyler tried to get a job, but had problems because he didn't have any experience working. He played football, basketball, and baseball in school, which left him no time for a job. The more rejections he got, the more depressed he got.

"He started spending his days in the gym at the apartment, and all of a sudden he was bulking up." She squints up at me, and I know she's telling me that he was using something to help him bulk up. "He started to get angry. When I would have an evening class, he would accuse me of cheating on him." She shakes her head as if denying it. "That went on for a couple years. Then he began getting in my face and pushing me around. He still never got a job. I had received some good scholarships, and I was working at the university so we were able to pay our bills... barely, but we were doing it.

"Then all hell broke loose. I had been working as a tutor and one of my students was a football player. He was nice and we were able to really open up and talk. I felt comfortable with him. Tyler came home one night, and he accused me of cheating again. This time, he took it to the next level. He pushed me around, and when I wouldn't back down, he hit me. He told me it was my fault, and that I had brought it on myself. I told him he needed to get help and to get off the drugs that he was on for 'bulking up', but he refused. I told him that if he ever laid another hand on me I would leave. It wasn't but a week later that he showed up at the university and caused a scene. It was then that I knew I didn't have a choice but to leave before he got more violent. I left with just what I had with me. Luckily, I had my car that day so I didn't have to worry about him finding it and taking it."

"Oh my gosh, did you talk to your parents' or even his about what was going on?"

"I tried to, but we are from a small farming area and they don't know a lot about steroids and things of that nature. They just thought I had changed my mind about being married. You know, big city and all." She glimpsed up at me, guilt on her face. "I couldn't tell them about what he had done to me."

"Don't you think they deserve to know what he did? This wasn't your fault."

"I know," she says with a catch in her voice, "I just didn't want them to think less of him."

"Well, I still think they need to know what he got himself into so they don't think this is your fault, so he doesn't take it out on someone else and hurt them."

She changes the subject quickly. "Okay, enough of my story, it's your turn. What brought you to our fine town?"

"Well, mine goes a lot deeper than that."

"Hold that thought then." Amber gets up and grabs her bag, then pulling out a bottle of wine and a couple of plastic cups. She opens the bottle and pours some into the cups.

"Aren't you the prepared one?"

"I knew this story was going to be hard for you to talk about, so I figured wine would help."

I tilt my head to the side and smile at her, knowing the smile didn't reach my eyes. "Okay, go," she says.

I take a big draw of my wine, and the fruity oak taste invades my mouth, I can already feel the tears burning the backs of my eyes, but I blink them away. "It was just after my ninth birthday; my mother was dating Dylan. Dylan had a son a few years older than me, and his name is Grady." I explain to her about Grady babysitting me and what families are expected to do. Amber gasped, raising her hand to her mouth in disbelief. I tell her how he would come into my room and make me have sex with him. I felt something wet fall on my hand and peered up thinking it was starting to rain, but then realize it's tears falling from my cheeks. I didn't even realize I was crying.

"How long did this go on for," she asks in almost a whisper.

"Until I was thirteen," I whisper back.

"Oh, Fuck."

She takes my hand in hers, I think for moral support. "I was thirteen and was getting sick, my mother was concerned and took me to the doctor. He asked a bunch of questions then did and exam. He put something cold on my stomach, I didn't know back then what it was, but I knew what it did after a couple seconds and I could hear the heartbeat of the baby that I was carrying."

"Oh, fucking hell." Amber squeezed my hand tighter as tears started to run down her cheeks. "Oh God, Sam."

"That night when Dylan got home from work and Grady got home from school, there was a big fight. I stayed locked in my room, not wanting to come out."

"Oh honey, I don't blame you. Did your mom kill your step-brother?"

"No, but they sent him away."

"Good, they should have sent him to jail. So' what happened after that?"

"I was so naive. My mother made an appointment at the hospital. I thought it was for testing. I had people touching me everywhere. I was placed in a tiny little room not much bigger than a closet when I felt the first of the cramps." I proceeded to tell her what happened to my baby girl as I started to sob.

"Mom and Dylan eventually got divorced, and mom died of cancer a couple years ago. I don't think she ever got over the guilt of not only what happened to me, but what she did about the baby."

"So what are you running from?"

"Before I graduated I was offered an amazing job with a security company here in Washington. I interviewed for it and knew I could have the job if I wanted it. The day after my college graduation is when I decided to accept the position." I tell her about Grady's call and that he was there watching me and that he snuck into my apartment and all the flowers he put in there. Then about Oliver.

"Oliver? Who is Oliver?" The look on her face was one of confusion.

"Oliver has always been my knight in shining armor. He was always there for me, from first grade until now, just like at graduation. Someone beat Grady up, and I knew it was Oliver after finding out what he had done to me."

"So, what's the problem then?"

"He owns the company that hired me."

"Yeah, So?"

"He's hiding things from me. We have this deep connection with each other, but I don't think it's wise to start a relationship with someone when the foundation is built on deceit. He won't tell me anything, so I left, my job, my new apartment and I found this place."

"Tell me about him."

A smile spreads across my face just thinking of him. My heart beats faster and butterflies fill my stomach. "He has dark brown hair, the most amazing indigo blue eyes, and a dimple to die for."

"You know the color of his eyes?"

I fill her in on how we met my first day of school and how I found the color of his eyes in my box of crayons. That he was always there to protect me. Well, except when Grady started to abuse me. "He knew something was going on, but I couldn't tell him."

"And you're hiding out here why again? Because if I didn't know better, you're in love with this Oliver guy, and it sounds like he's in love with you."

"God, Amber. I think I've been in love with him since that first day of school. I've never felt safer than when I'm with him. I know he feels something, but every time he starts to let his guard down, something happens and the wall goes back up. Not to mention, there are things he knows about me and my life that he's not willing to share with me. I can't be with someone that can't trust me enough to confide in me."

"What if he has a good reason? What if he's afraid there is something that could hurt you?"

"I don't know, Amber, I just... Maybe I should just talk to him. He texts me every day trying to get me to come back."

"Are you crazy, woman? I would give anything to get Tyler back to how he used to be, and you have someone who wants to work things out?" Amber shakes her head.

"When's the last time you talked to Tyler?"

"It's been a while. He was supposed to have gone home. He didn't have money to pay for anything."

"Did you ever get divorced?"

"No, I tried, but he wouldn't ever sign the papers, so I just stopped trying."

"What about your parents'? Do you ever talk to them?"

"Not a lot, not after they treated me as if it were my fault for what he did."

We continue to talk as we lay out in the sun. It feels good to just lay there and not have to do anything for the day.

I must have fallen asleep, because I wake with a start when my phone vibrates. I already know who it is, Oliver texts me every day about the same time. Shit, I can't believe how late it is.

I text him back and suggest that we talk. Within seconds, my phone vibrates with a call. I answer it right away knowing that it's Oliver. "Hi."

"Hi, Samantha, are you doing okay?"

"Yes, I'm just hanging out with a friend."

"Oh?"

"Yeah, she's one of the reasons why I have decided we need to talk."

"Well, tell her thank you."

"Maybe you'll get the chance to meet her."

"I think I'd like that. Where do you want to meet?"

I proceed to tell him where I am. "I work at the little diner here and have to work tomorrow; can you meet me at the diner at eight?"

"That lake is beautiful. I've been there a few times when I've needed to think. Eight o'clock is fine; I'll meet you there." I click end on the phone and within seconds, it rings again. "Did you forget to tell me something?"

"Just that I miss you, baby sis, and I can't wait to see you again. I hear the lake is lovely this time of the year."

I drop my phone as if I had just burned myself.

"Sam? Sam, what's wrong? Sam, you're scaring me." Amber takes my face in her hands. "Sam, look at me." My eyes slowly drift to hers. "That's a good girl. Who is that?"

"Grady. It's Grady! He knows where I am."

"How would he know?"

"I don't know, but he always finds me."

"Maybe you should call Oliver back and let him know."

"I can't always rely on Oliver. He has his own life. He's not always going to be here for me."

"You need to at least tell him tomorrow when you see him." My head is spinning. I can't even think right now, so I just nod my head.

I slip my shorts and shirt on and hurriedly throw everything back into the basket. "I've got to go. I have to find another place to hide. He knows about the lake."

"You can't keep running. You said that Oliver always protects you; let him help you."

I turn and peer at her as I shove my towel in my bag. "This will never end until Grady is dead. I could never live with myself if he did something like that for me. I would rather live a life without him, than to live with the guilt of him killing someone for me. Because I know he would do anything to protect me, at any cost."

I throw my bag over my shoulder and pick up the basket as I start to walk back. Amber is on my heels trying to talk me out of leaving. "Hold on a second, I forgot the bag of garbage." I stop for a second. My mind is in hyper drive, trying to figure out what I need to do. Where am I going to go?

THE LOCKET

Out of nowhere, I'm grabbed. I let out a shrill as a hand clasps, over my mouth. "Feisty little bitch aren't you?" Kicking and fighting my captor, I try to see who has grabbed me. I don't recognize him. "We're going to have fun with this one," he says as another man approaches.

"So this is she? I'm surprised they didn't have more security on her." I kick at him, struggling to get away. Suddenly, he backhands me. A whimper escapes my lips as the pain radiates across my face, and heat rises to the surface as darkness takes me away.

CHAPTER FOURTEEN
OFF THE GRID

OLIVER

Reynolds and I proceed to Grady's last known address but the place is empty. As we search the house, we come to an attic door. I open it and feel around the wall for a light switch. Not finding one I pull my phone out and turn on the flashlight. I shine it to the ceiling and see a string hanging from a light bulb. Not paying attention, I reach for the string.

"Boss."

"Yeah, Reynolds,"

I turn to glance at him and see what has captured his attention. My stomach falls and my gut twists as I feel the blood drain from my face. The walls are covered with pictures of Samantha at all ages; Middle school promotion, Halloween, Thanksgiving, Easter, Christmas and of course graduation, there are hundreds, years and years of them. They are plastered everywhere. As I examine them closer, I realize some of them are recent, as in Seattle recent. Then I see the panties and scarves hanging. A candle with her picture behind it lies on a little table with another pair of lace panties. He had a fucking alter to her. "Fuck," I say under my breath. I glare over to Reynolds and shout, "This motherfucker never stopped! He's been stalking her this whole goddamn time."

We search the rest of the house, but there is no sign of Grady. I call up my best trackers to find him.

We stay in the area for about a week hoping he is still here and just hiding out, but he's off the grid. To top it off, I still haven't heard from Nicolas with an answer yet either. I hate the idea of leaving without confirmation either way.

I continue to text Sam everyday around the same time, letting her know I am still thinking of her and want her back. She texts me the same response every night… that if I'm not able to tell her who I am there is no relationship and no reason to come home.

A month has gone by and I feel as if Sam is slipping through my fingers. Although I know where she is, she's never been distant with me before. I'm feeling desperate, and I don't like this feeling.

When I text her today, she agrees to meet with me tomorrow. A sense of relief washes over me. Finally, I will get to see her without sneaking around in the shadows. I call her as soon as I get her text. I don't want to wait twenty-four hours to hear her voice, hell I don't want to wait to see her, but it's better than not at all.

Not long after my conversation with Sam, I feel anxious, uneasy, and I can't concentrate. I even try running, but there's something wrong. I feel it, but I don't know what it is.

It's eight forty-five in the evening when my phone rings and my stomach rolls even before I pick it up, "Drake."

"It's Reynolds. Sir, they have her."

"Who has her?"

"Di Fonzo."

"What the fuck do you mean he has her? What does he expect to gain from this? And how does he even know about her? Where are Gonzalez and Reese?"

"Dead, sir, they took them both out."

"FUCK" I yell. "Do Perrotti and Nicolas know?"

"No, sir, not yet, I wanted to tell you first."

"Are you sure it's Di Fonzo?"

"Yes, he left his calling card on Reese."

"This never would have happened if Nicolas would have let me have her. I want to leave in ten minutes."

"Yes, sir."

I call Perrotti and Nicolas conferencing them together. "Sorry for the late night call, but Di Fonzo has Samantha."

"What the fuck do you mean he has her," Nicolas screams.

I try to keep calm. "Well," I start, trying to sound calm when I'm actually dying inside not knowing what they are doing to her, "They took out Gonzalez and Reese."

"I thought you were watching her."

"With all due respect, sir, I told you that she didn't want contact with me until I could tell her the truth. As of today, I am still waiting. I lost two of my best men watching her. This wouldn't have happened if she were in my bed where she should have been. God only knows what kind of hell she is going through now. She has no idea what she is even up against because you wanted to keep the fucking truth from her, Nicolas."

"Oliver," Perrotti barks.

"I apologize for the disrespect, sir; however, I have been waiting patiently for an answer. My hands have been tied. You don't know her the way I do. She is a strong-minded woman, but nothing she has gone through in life will prepare her for what might be waiting for her. Sir, if you could see what your contacts know, I would appreciate any help trying to get her out alive."

"I'll contact you within the hour."

"Thank you, sir."

I end the call and get dressed after splashing water on my face. I pull a couple guns out of my safe then meet Reynolds downstairs.

"Go to the lake. I want to see if there's any evidence or anything that can tell us where they might be going."

"Yes, sir."

The first place I stop is the diner. The owner is just closing up for the evening. She hasn't heard anything. "She was with a friend when I called her earlier. Do you know who that might be?"

"Yes, it was Amber. They went to the lake together for the day." She calls Amber and hands me the phone.

"Hello?"

"Is this Amber?"

"Speaking."

"Amber, this is Oliver."

"Oh my God, Oliver! Thank God you found me."

"What can you tell me about what happened after I talked to Sam this afternoon?"

"Right after you both hung up, she received another call. She thought it was you again, but it was her stepbrother. She freaked out and started packing to leave. She was going to find another hideout. We were walking back to the car when a couple of guys grabbed her. They took her, Oliver."

"Did they say anything to you?"

"No, they didn't see me. I forgot to grab our bag of garbage and went back for it. When I came back, she was fighting to get away and one of them backhanded her and pushed her into the car."

"Did you call the police?"

"Yes, they said they would check it out, but I haven't heard from anyone but you."

"Do you know anything about the car, make, model, or license plate number?"

"Yes, it was a black Chevy Tahoe with dark tinted windows." Then she tells me the plate number.

"Are you one hundred percent sure on the plate?"

"Yes, the numbers were the date before my birthday. Find her, Oliver."

"I intend to. Thank you for your help, Amber."

I search for the information on the Tahoe and locate it on GPS. They're moving south on I-5, but they're several hours ahead of us. At this rate, we'll never catch up with them. We can't even take the jet because we don't know where they're heading. We're going to have to hope they stop somewhere and hold up for the night. However, if they stop, they could do anything to her. *Fuck*. I rake my hands through my hair furiously, trying to come up with a solution.

"Sir?"

"Reynolds."

"I have an ex-marine friend that might be able to intercept them. He's in Portland and owns a security company. He just pulled off a rescue from a biker gang. I know it's not much, but he's on the other side of them and might be able to get his eyes on them faster than we can."

"Do it! Call him. I'll deal with the repercussions of Perrotti later."

Reynolds pushes a couple buttons on the phone and it connects to the Bluetooth of our vehicle. "This better be goddamn good, Reynolds, and not just another drunken prank," he chuckles.

"Mitch, it is. I have a situation that might be right up your alley."

He clears his throat, "Speak."

"I have a girl that has been taken by the Di Fonzo family. They're heading your way. We're a few hours behind them, and we don't know what their destination is so we can't fly to get ahead of them. They should be making the Oregon border within the next thirty minutes. We have GPS on their vehicle so we can track them for now, but we need eyes on them."

"Got it, let me get my team together. I want as many eyes on them as possible so they don't feel the tail. Tell me about the girl."

I hear him rustling around. "Baby, get up, we have a job," I hear him say.

"She's twenty-two. She doesn't know she has ties with the Perrotti family."

"How do you not know you have ties to the mob?"

"It's a long story, but she has no idea."

"Well, if she doesn't now, she will soon. Does she have a cell phone? If so, I have a computer app that can track her. Send me over the number, and I will see if it's in the vehicle we'll be tracking."

"It's on its way. Thanks, Mitch." Reynold's says as he ends the call.

I glance over at Reynolds. "Tell me about him. Can we trust him to stay quiet, and what about his men? I'm not wild about him talking about this in front of some slut he's with."

"Sir, I understand your frustration, but Mitchell is a good man. One of the best. I wouldn't have mentioned him if I didn't trust him with my life. The slut… as you referred to her… is his wife, and she was very instrumental in the rescue at the biker's compound. She's wicked with a bow and arrow. Took out a couple bikers when a few of their men had guns to their heads. Mitchell was in the Marines until he was injured saving a buddy in an ambush in Afghanistan. He will do whatever it takes to save her."

"Point taken. We won't mention the slut comment."

"No, sir."

Fifteen minutes later the phone rings on the cars Bluetooth. "Drake."

"Mr. Drake, this is Mitchell, I've located the cell phone GPS, and it is tracking with the vehicle. How well do you know her and where she keeps her phone?"

"I know her very well. She has her phone either in her back pocket or in her bra. Why?"

"Because as soon as they find it on her they'll toss it, and I want to get as close to her as possible. We have eyes coming from the south and also heading north so we will be able to intercept them from both directions. What is your plan? Do you want us to stop them or just follow them?"

"Follow them for now. Keep in contact with us. If they stop, just watch them. Stand down unless she is in emanate danger, and then protect her at all cost."

"We will, Mr. Drake. Sir, I have just received confirmation that one of my men has a visual on the vehicle. They are still heading south on I-5. Unfortunately, due to the heavy tint on the vehicle windows, they are unable to get confirmation that she is inside the vehicle, but that is where her phone is."

"Thank you, Mitchell, I appreciate your quick response time. This won't go unnoticed."

"Thank you, Mr. Drake, that's my job. Nothing extra needed."

We continue tracking Di Fonzo's men. We haven't had contact with Mitchell for the last hour or so. I try to think of how I want this to play out. I can get my computer techs to shut off the engine to their vehicle, or I can wait until they stop somewhere to eat, sleep, or get gas.

The car phone rings pulling me out of my thoughts. "Drake."

"Mr. Drake, Mitchell. I wanted to keep you informed of what has been happening. The vehicle is taking the Albany exit, probably to fuel up and maybe get some food. We have five sets of eyes on them at any one time so no one is spotted."

"I want to try to get a message to her if they let her out. How trusting is she?"

"After this afternoon, probably not very."

"Is there anything that you can think of that would let her know that you are watching her?"

I think for a moment and it hits me. "Yes, yes there is, but, it won't go over well if a man talks to her."

"My wife Raven is here, and she can catch anyone's attention."

"Samantha wears a silver locket. Inside has an angel and a blue and pink birthstone I gave it to her when she was thirteen. She never takes it off."

"Is there significance to it that no one would know about," Raven asks.

"Yes, she lost her baby girl, and that's when I gave it to her."

"That's great. I'll use that then. Thank you, Mr. Drake," Raven replies.

"Drake, they're pulling into a gas station just off the freeway. I'm going to fill up and hopefully they will let her go to the restroom. Raven is heading to the restroom just in case. Can you give us a description of her?"

"I'm sending you a picture of her as we speak."

"Roger that, Drake. I have received it and sent it off to the team. I have eyes on four men getting out of the vehicle. One of them is escorting your woman inside. She appears as if she put up one hell of a fight. Raven is on her way back out. We're taking off and the next team will pick them back up."

"Drake, Raven here. She's okay, just bruised and roughed up. She understood the message. Her escort isn't chancing anything. He came into the restroom and wouldn't allow her to close the stall door."

"Thank you, Raven."

"Anytime, sir."

We drive for what seems like forever. Mitchell checks in with us every hour or so, or if they have deviated from the freeway. I'm still trying to decide what would be our best plan of attack. Obviously, a surprise would be ideal, but that's only if they stop for the night.

CHAPTER FIFTEEN
PROOF OF LIFE

SAMANTHA

I take a calming breath. I don't know who she is, but somehow she's working with Oliver. Of course, Oliver is on my trail, he's the one who always protected me. So why didn't I trust him? Why didn't I wait to hear him out? Why did I fucking run? I'm such an idiot. That brings up the next question; who these people are and what they want with me. I can't imagine that this has to do with Grady. He would never do something this elaborate. Maybe human trafficking? I can't imagine that either. They would be better off going to downtown Seattle and snagging homeless teens. Then who and why?

I shift in my seat as a sharp pain shoots through my face and stomach from where one of the men hit me as I was fighting them off. Although he hasn't done anything to me, I knew he was trouble, but this isn't about me sneaking out on him at the club, this is something more, way more.

"Where are you taking me and why?" Silence. "Who are you and what do you want with me?" Again, silence.

Maybe if I feign sleep I can catch them talking. I pull my feet up onto the seat and carefully I lean my head on my knees. Shit, I feel like I've been hit by a truck, my head is still hurting, and my face is already turning colors. I got a peek at the shiner fat ass gave me. Why is it that guys always hit a girl on the cheek? My whole face radiates heat and is swollen.

I can't comprehend why someone would kidnap me. I'm nobody, but I have four men watching me. It's a tad bit overkill I would say. It isn't as if I'm a fighter, well not a street fighter. I did take a couple self-defense classes in college, but when my class load got heavier, I didn't have the opportunity to take more. I close my eyes and just listen. TDD is driving, fat ass is in the passenger seat, pox is sitting to my right, and the kid is sitting to my left. All of them are in good shape except fat ass, and my name for him says it all. He thinks he's hot shit. Think again, fat ass.

I pretend to breathe heavy as if I'm asleep and the conversation starts. "What are we going to do with her," pox asks.

"Anything we want. We were hired to grab her; anything after that is fair game." Fat ass says with an evil chuckle in his voice, "And I plan on getting everything I want out of her."

"What about Perrotti," TDD asks.

"The wheels are already in motion. Once we get to the location, they'll inform Perrotti and Nicolas and to let them know where to pick her up," he laughs again, "At least what's left of her." Another laugh, "Then when they get there, Di Fonzo will get his revenge on both of them," fat ass says.

"What about proof of life? You can't tell me that they won't ask for it," the kid asks.

"They can have their proof of life, but that doesn't mean we can't take our turn with her. I mean, fuck, did you see her body? Fucking hell, her legs could wrap around you twice, well, maybe not you, Frankie."

"Fuck you, Eugene."

I don't know what's going to happen, but it's not looking good. I don't understand why they would think someone would have any interest in me.

"So why Reno? Why not Vegas," kid asks.

"It quieter, smaller and there is less of a possibility to be seen." TDD answers.

Reality hits me when we pull into a dive hotel in Reno, and I know there is a good possibility that I will be brutally raped once inside. I bite the inside of my cheek to keep me focused as the metallic taste of blood settles over my tongue.

CHAPTER SIXTEEN
CAVALRY

OLIVER

"Mitchell, Drake, what are you thinking? We need to brainstorm what we're going to do."

"I think we need to see what's around us first. At this point, we only have to deal with four men. However, we don't know if there are others waiting for them. I don't want to go in blind, get ambushed, and have someone on our team hurt, or worse, killed. We need to play it smart. If I have to guess, I would say he is heading to Reno," Mitchell says.

"Why would you say that?"

"There's still a lot of loyalty to the Di Fonzo family there. It isn't as heavily populated as Vegas, and there are several old, vacant buildings that are owned by the family. You could have an all-out war there and no one would be the wiser. What do you know about what's going on with the two families?"

"Actually, not much. My main purpose with the family was to protect Samantha. They took two of my men out to get to her."

"Didn't her parents raise her to be aware of what could happen?"

"No, Nicolas never let them know. He thought by leaving his wife and child when the rumors of a family cleansing were going to start would be best. No one knew he was married, and he had changed his name. He thought the family would keep them safe. He didn't realize he was trading one impending danger for another. Sam was never safe," I say under my breath.

"Drake, you have to be prepared for what they might do to her. Are you going to be able to endure that? I can't have you going in like a one-man army. If you can't, I need to know now, then all communication of where they are will end until we get her out."

"The hell you will," I roar.

"Drake, you're emotionally involved. This is a situation where emotions CANNOT get in the way of the mission. There are too many lives at stake."

"I understand. What do you need from me?"

"I need to know if Perrotti and Nicolas are coming, and if so, how many men they are bringing. I also need to know if we are to stand down and let them handle this, or are we the ones getting her out. This will determine if we are getting her out now or if we are going to have to wait for the big gathering."

"Let me get that information, and I will get back to you. And Mitchell?"

"Yes?"

"Thanks for your help."

CHAPTER SEVENTEEN
MY HAPPY PLACE

SAMANTHA

I'm slapped upside the head by fat ass as we pull up to the motel. It appears to be a place out of a 'B-Grade movie, including boarded up windows and the sign missing lights so the name flickers. "Bitch doesn't have a clue what we have in store for her once we get her inside." He glares at me with an evil smirk then chuckles. The kid takes me by the upper arm and leads me into the room.

I have to figure out where I can hide my phone. If I can escape, it'll be my only connection to get help. "I need to use the toilet." I peek up at the kid hoping there is still a little compassion in him. He takes me to the door of the bathroom and stands there waiting. "Can I have just a minute of privacy? I'm not going to go anywhere, there are no windows."

He peers into the room, and then steps out. "You have one minute."

"Thank you." I gaze up at him with a shy smile then close the door. I had already seen the tissue holder that was built into the front of the vanity. I quickly remove my phone from my bra and stuff it behind the empty box of tissue then sit and pee. Suddenly I hear fat ass holler at the kid for letting me close the door. The door flies open as I'm just pulling up my shorts.

"You won't need those tonight," fat ass laughs. He grabs me by the upper arm and yanks me into the room, shoving me on the bed. I let out a scream. "Scream all you want, bitch, no one's going to hear you, and if they do, they're not going to care." He reaches down and grabs my tank top, ripping it.

"Not now, Frankie, we have business to attend to," TDD says. "Mattie, stay here and watch her while we go next door and order a couple pizzas."

"Okay, Pauli."

The three older men leave the room. I hear them knock on the door to the room next to us and hear them greeting each other.

Mattie opens the old, marred desk drawer and pulls out a phone book. He dials a number then waits. "What kind of pizza do you like?"

Surprised that he asked me my opinion, I shrug my shoulders. "I don't think it matters. I really don't think they're planning to feed me, but thank you." I glance over to where he is sitting. "Can I ask you a question?"

He turns and stares at the door, "Sure."

"Why? Who am I to them, and what are they going to do with me?"

"Leverage, that's the only reason why they take family members."

I stare at him, and my brow furrows. "I don't know what you're talking about. My family is dead."

"Your father isn't."

"I don't even know who my father is. He left my mom and me when I was small, and I haven't seen him since."

"Your father is Nicolas Perrotti. He's Perrotti's son, his second."

"My last name is Hunter."

"I don't know a lot; I just know that they said your father is a Perrotti."

I peer down into my lap, my fingers twist and pull on each other. Shaking my head at the revelation of who my father is, I realize that I'm not going to get out of this. He doesn't care about me. If he did, he wouldn't have left my mother and me alone. A tear drops onto my hand and I quickly wipe the remnants of it away. It's not that I'm afraid of dying. It's the dark road to death that terrifies me. The agony…the torture I'll endure just to gain clout over my father. It's the suffering that scares me. I try to remember what my instructor would say. *'It's when you panic, that you are going to get hurt.'* And *'Fear is not real. It is a product of thoughts you create. Danger is very real, but fear is a choice.'* I will face my fears head on. I will not let fear defeat me. I will fight. I will fight for me.

I had only recently started to take a martial arts class. I hadn't even come close to being proficient in it. However, I have remembered what he had said, and maybe that's what will help me get through this.

Is this the secret that Oliver was afraid to share with me?

There's a knock at the door. Mattie peeks out the window then opens the door to the pizza deliveryman. The night breeze whispers past me bringing the smell of hot pepperoni, sausage, and basil. My stomach growls in protest. I haven't eaten in hours. I place my hand on my stomach as if it will quiet it down. Mattie pays the driver then takes the boxes of pizza and sets them down on the desk. He opens the lid, and curls of steam billow from the box.

As he hands me a slice, the door flies open and Frankie grabs it out of his hand. "Hey, Frankie, that was her piece of pizza."

"I don't think she'll need anything soon; we have plans for her." He stuffs the pizza into his mouth and wipes his mouth on his sleeve. "In fact, I need to get a little workout after indulging on pizza." He glares at me, an evil glint in his eyes, and I know what's coming. "Lay down, bitch." I stare up at him with narrowed eyes. I might not like what's going to happen, but it's not as if I haven't been to this part of Hell before. "I said lay down, BITCH!" He backhands me across my cheek. The pain radiates out over my face as the burning heat and swelling start. I raise my hand to my cheek, feeling something trickling down it, and when I glance at his hand, I see the ring. He has split my cheek open. I will not cry. I refuse to give into them. *'Show no fear, never back down.'*

I lay down as he pulls out a knife. The blade gleams off the ceiling light as he swirls it from side to side. I watch him as he cuts my tank top off, then flicks it again cutting my bikini top off, nicking me at the same time. I flinch but say nothing as I feel the warmth pool and settle on my chest.

He gropes my breast and starts to moan. "God, nothing feels better than real tits." I close my eyes, trying to find that old familiar spot, the spot that I always went to when Grady would come into my room. Suddenly, I feel something being taken from around my neck and my eyes fly open, "Please not that. Do what you want, but please don't take my necklace."

He continues to take it off and places it over his neck. I try grabbing for it, but he swats my hands away. "Well, well boys, she speaks," he says with a low, gruff voice as he chuckles a sinister laugh.

"Please, it's the only thing I have left of my baby."

"Where you're going, bitch, you won't need it. You'll be there with it."

I close my eyes again as he pulls my shorts off. I feel the cold steel of the blade slice my bikini bottoms, and I am bare for everyone to see. Mattie walks out the front door, as does Pauli. The drapes are wide open. Anyone walking by can see me naked and sprawled out. I retreat into my mind where no one can hurt me. I feel the bed dip down, and I prepare myself for the assault that is to come. I try to block everything out of my mind, but all I can do is smell BO, bad breath, and pizza. I feel my stomach roll as I swallow back the bile creeping up the back of my throat. I try to refocus. Closing my eyes, I see him. Oliver. His reassuring gentle smile accented with that one dimple, and beautiful indigo blue eyes. A single tear rolls down my face as Frankie rams into me, tearing through my dry, delicate tissues. I bite my lip to keep a whimper from slipping out.

"That's right, bitch, I'm going to show you what a real man feels like."

I keep my mind's eye trained on Oliver's face. *'It's okay, baby girl, I'm right here, I will always be right here. I'll get you out of here, just hold on, be strong, and show no fear.'* Frankie continues to ram into me, moaning as he pulls out and ejaculates all over my torso.

"It's my turn now," Pox says, and I hear him unzip his pants.

I pinch my eyes closed tighter as Oliver continues to talk to me, *We'll get them. We'll make them pay.* Eugene then thrusts into me, letting out a groan. He picks up my hips and continues to thrust into me. He's bigger than Frankie and not only do I feel like my tender tissues are being ripped further, he's longer and rams me hitting the inside wall, not giving me a chance to adjust to his size. Tears burn the back of my eyes as I squeeze them tight to keep them from falling. That would only show them my weakness. He pants over me as he leans forward and bites my nipple. I scream out, unable to hold back any longer. This isn't about fear this is about pain. He takes my breasts and mashes them in his hands as if he's kneading dough. Then he lets out a high moan as if he were a girl, as if someone is squeezing his balls.

Time elapses, they have been tag teaming me over and over. I am so exhausted and want to sleep.

I jump when the door bashes into the wall from being thrown open. I'm laying completely naked for anyone to see. Frankie is fucking me again, when an older man walks in. What I can see of him through my swollen eyes is that he's tall, and although he's wearing a suit, he appears as if in good shape, especially for his age. He has salt and pepper hair and blue eyes. He seems strangely familiar. Maybe I had seen him before in passing and just didn't know who he was. As he walks over to me, there is a fierceness to him, but for some reason, I'm not afraid.

"What the fuck are you two doing? She wasn't supposed to be touched." I see a flash of a dimple as he talks.

Frankie pulls out of me and backs away then, zips up his pants "She was asking for it boss. Look at her, who could say no to that?"

"And I said hands off. Now get her covered up."

Mattie rushes over and throws the bedspread over my naked, shivering body and gives me a sympathetic smile. I slowly start to sit up. The old man, takes my chin in his hand as I repeat my mantra *'Show no fear, never back down'* over and over in my head.

"Do you know who I am?"

I stare up into his intense blue eyes. Shaking my head, I say, "No."

"Your father hasn't taught you much then."

"I don't have a father," I say with a growl.

His eyes flash to mine as if I have revealed a dark secret. "Oh? And why would you say that?"

"My father abandoned my mother and me when I was a small child."

"I see, well none-the-less, he is still very much alive and still your father. I think he will pay quite well to get you back," he says as he flicks one of his brows up.

I jerk my chin out of his hand and glare at him through my swollen eyes as I square my shoulders. "Well, you better get ready for disappointment, because I am dead to him."

"If that's so, that puts me in an unusual predicament. I would have no use for you then."

"So kill me now and be done with it."

His eyes once again flash to mine. Maybe because I'm not showing a fear of death, maybe because I'm not pleading for my life; I don't know. He pulls out his gun and places it to my forehead. I close my eyes and say a prayer. I think of Oliver, he's my only regret. The only one, I will be sad to leave. The only one, I wish I had told that I loved him. The only one, I ever wanted a life with. BANG!

CHAPTER EIGHTEEN
KNIGHT IN SHINING ARMOR

OLIVER

We finally make it to the motel where they are holding Samantha. It's a quiet area littered with junky little motels all around. We are across the road where there's a hedge, which makes the perfect cover for us.

The drapes are open as I watch in horror, knowing what Mitchell said earlier was true, if I had gone over there, I wouldn't have realized that they have several men that occupy most of the motel. There is one thing for damn sure and it's that those two bastards will pay for what they are doing to her.

Mitchell and his men are ready for anything. His men are scattered around and everyone knows their job. Each of them has headsets and mics so they will know exactly what's going on.

Perrotti and Nicolas arrive, and I fill them in on what's happening as the two motherfuckers rape Samantha again.

All I can do is pray that she comes out of this with her sanity. I talk to her in my head, telling her to stay strong and that I'll get her out of there, but I think it's more for my peace of mind. Slowly, Perrotti's men start to pull in. Mitchell explains what his plans are and how to recognize his men so they are not collateral damage.

Raven... What a spitfire. She has a pink compound bow and is the female version of Robin Hood. C-4 is attached to the arrows that she shot around the motel as a distraction. We're all in position when a town car pulls into the parking lot of their motel and a man steps out.

"That's Di Fonzo," Perrotti says.

Di Fonzo peers through the window at the fat bastard who has his dick in my woman. By the expression on his face, he's not very happy.

A young kid covers her up as Di Fonzo talks to her. I don't know what he's saying to her, but she doesn't like it. Di Fonzo pulls his gun out and has it aims at her forehead. She doesn't even flinch. *FUCK!*

"Raven, it's your shot." Raven positions herself and aims, then shoots the bow. With a precise eye, the arrow makes contact with the gun, effectively knocking it from Di Fonzo's hand. It falls to the floor and fires, hitting the fat motherfucker in the leg. He screams like a little girl as everyone tries to figure out what happened. BOOM! A C-4 explodes. Mitchell's men are securing every man they can get to. BOOM! Another charge ignites. Then another. Samantha is on the floor scrambling for the gun. She clutches it in her hand and aims it in front of her. All of a sudden, one of Di Fonzo's men pulls a gun. "Raven," is all I hear before seeing the man fall down face-first.

As I stand there and witness this well-orchestrated plan come together, I realize everyone is secure. I glance over at

Mitchell, as if asking for permission. "Go get your woman," he says with a smile. "I love when a plan comes together," I hear him say as I race across the road.

I stand at the door to the room. It smells of sex, sweat, and pizza. Sam is in the corner like a frightened mouse. Her blanket had fallen in the struggle for the gun, dried blood is splattered all over her body. She appears as if she's in a trance, but I'm sure she is in shock. "Samantha," I call out softly, not wanting to spook her. "Samantha, it's me, Oliver. Look at me. Bring your eyes to my voice." Her eyes slowly follow my voice. "Baby girl, look at me."

She slowly brings her eyes to meet mine. "Oliver? Is it really you?"

"It's really me. I've come to take you home. Can you put the gun down?"

I slowly walk towards her and she peers up at me, "Indigo blue."

"What?"

"Indigo blue." Her hand slowly lowers as her whole body starts to shake.

I stand in front of her and hold my hand out for the gun. "You are always saying that, but I don't know what it means."

I pick up the blanket and wrap it around her. "That first day of school, I was mesmerized by your eyes. I had to find out what color they were. When I got to my seat, I pulled out my crayons. Your eyes are indigo blue."

I gently take her face in my hands, pulling her to me. I kiss each bruised cheek, her black eyes, and forehead before taking her lips with mine. "Let's get you out of here so they can clean this mess up. Can you walk?" She nods her head. I place my hand at the small of her back as I start to lead her out of the room.

"Oh, wait," she says as she scurries in the bathroom, dragging the blanket behind her. She pulls her phone out of the tissue box. She then walks over to the fat motherfucker who is zip tied and sitting on the floor. She reaches for something around his neck. It's the necklace I gave her. He must have taken it from her. She slips it back over her head and pulls the locket to her lips kissing it, before glancing up at me. She gets a mischievous look in her face, and I'm trying to figure out what she's thinking. She whips back around hitting the fat bastard in the cheek then she kicks him straight in the balls as he lets out a blood-curling scream and doubles over. She shakes out her hand. I grab the little garbage can that is being used as an ice bucket, it's filled with melting ice. I want Sam to use it for her hand and she grabs the box of pizza.

As we walk past Di Fonzo, I stop and glare at him. "Well holy hell, the prodigal son returns. I should have known he had you all along."

Sam glances from me to him and back again. She cocks her head to the side as if trying to figure something out. I pull her toward the door.

"What's going to happen to them?"

I glance at her. "I really don't know, that'll be up to Perrotti and Nicolas."

I take the pizza box from Sam and hand her the ice bucket. "I'll trade you. Put your hand in there." She does as I ask, slowly immersing her hand into the ice water as she winces.

"I need to speak to Perrotti. I'm not ready to speak to Nicolas yet though." Sam says.

"Okay, give me a minute." I walk over to where Perrotti and Nicolas are standing. "Mr. Perrotti, Samantha would like a quick word with you if that is okay."

He follows me back to where she's standing. "Mr. Perrotti, I know we don't know each other, and I don't even know how I got in the middle of this or why I am of interest to you or how this business works. But the kid, Mattie, and that one," I point at Pauli, "were good to me. I don't want to see them get hurt. They didn't seem as if they are one of them, maybe they just got in with the wrong group. I would like to talk to you more about this, but I'm exhausted. Contact Oliver and we can talk."

"Good job in there, Samantha, you really kept yourself together. Most wouldn't be able to. I'm sure your father is very proud of you right now."

"I don't know what to think about that other than it's going to take time. He will have to be patient."

I peer down at my beautifully battered woman. "Are you ready to go?"

"Yes, please, I think I'll sleep for a few days."

As we walk away I hear a small voice calling out. "Samantha?"

We both turn as Raven comes running up to us, she still has her bow in her hand. She wraps her arms around Samantha pulling her into a big hug and quietly speaks into her ear. So quiet I can't hear what she is saying.

Then she turns to me and pulls me into a hug. "You and Samantha were made for each other. It will take time for her to heal, but with your help, she will recover with very few scars. She needs to move slowly when it comes to her father. He will give you permission to be with her, but he won't like it. You need to tell her everything. Get it all out in the open, and start clean with no secrets. Secrets of your past and of your family will soon be revealed. Your parents' love you and are proud of you and of the man you had to become at a very early age. You and Samantha will be blessed, although there is someone that is still out there that can hurt her. She'll love the ring so stop second guessing it." She pulls out of the hug and gives me a wink.

"How?"

"It's a gift.

"Go get some rest and maybe tomorrow we can get to know each other more," Raven says as she holds each of our hands and gives them a little squeeze.

Smiling down at Raven, I feel it and I know that everything will be all right. At least for now.

I take Samantha to the car where Reynolds is waiting for us. I don't even have to tell Reynolds where to go; he knows that we need a place far from here.

I have Sam in my arms when we finally get to our destination. Reynolds gets our key and drives us to a back door so Samantha doesn't have to go through the entrance in just a blanket. We take the elevator up to our floor. I carry her into the bedroom and sit her on the bed. I walk into the large bathroom knowing that Sam would want to get the stench of the men off her. I start to fill the large soaking tub and pour the small bottle of oil into the water infusing the air with vanilla and floral.

There's a tap at the front door. It's Reynolds. He had brought up toiletries, some clothes, and an ice pack for Sam's face. "Thank you, Reynolds." I walk back into the bedroom with the items that Reynolds had just purchased for me. I place the bag of clothes on the chair and the toiletries in the bathroom.

I walk to the bed where Sam is sitting and pick her up, carrying her into the bathroom. Standing her on her feet I let the blanket fall to the ground as Sam gasps and tries to cover herself with her hands.

I gaze down into her sad face and tears brim her eyes. I take her hands in mine, pulling them away from her bruised and battered body, "You're beautiful, Samantha. These bruises are superficial, and they can't change you or the beauty that you are in here," I slowly place my hand over her heart. "Never be ashamed of who you are and what others have done to you. You are a survivor, and you should be proud of that. It's this," I glance down at my hand on her heart, "which I fell in love with all those years ago."

Her eyes flash to mine as the first tear slips down her cheek. I lean down and kiss it away.

I help her into the tub. She winces as she starts to sit. "Are you okay?"

"I will be."

I strip down to my boxers and slide in after her. I take a glass from the counter and fill it up with warm water, then pour it over her hair. "Tilt your head up, baby." I sit on the edge of the tub and pour the floral shampoo into my hands before running my fingers over her long, blonde locks. Working it into lather, I massage her scalp, and eliciting moans from her. I do the same with the conditioner. Then I take the washcloth and pour body wash on it. I start from her shoulders and slowly wash as I go down her body. I get to the bite marks she had to endure. They are red and swollen, already starting to turn bluish purple. I wash each one then kiss them as I also do with the knife wound between her breasts.

I travel down her stomach, washing away the semen that sprayed over her body, to the apex of her thighs. I glance down at her making sure she is okay with what I am doing. She closes her eyes and nods her head. I start at her knee and slowly make my way up. "Look at me baby, I want you to see me, that I'm the one doing this to you." Her eyes meet mine as she nods at me again. "I'm the one touching you, no one else." I run the cloth over her swollen folds. She winces and I stop. Another tear falls down her cheek as she nods one more time and I continue.

I step out of the tub and slip my wet boxers off and wrap a towel around my waist. I reach my hand out for Sam's hand helping her out. I dry her off then wrap the towel around her body. Picking her up, I set her on the countertop, I pull a first aid kit out of the bag. I clean the cut on her cheek with antiseptic and she flinches. "Sorry, baby, but I want to make sure it's clean." I use a butterfly bandage to pull it closed. I hand her a toothbrush that I put toothpaste on for her to brush her teeth. I think that's the last thing she needs to do to try to erase the tastes and smells off her.

Pulling a tank top out of the bag, that Reynolds dropped off. I slip it over her head, and then help her into a pair of boxer shorts. Taking her hand, I take her to the bed and pull back the sheets for her to get in. I get the ice pack and hold it for her to use. She places it on her cheek as I turn to walk out of the room.

"Where are you going," a frightened voice, almost a shriek comes from her.

"You need to sleep."

"Please don't leave me, Oliver. I don't want to be alone."

"Let me make sure everything is locked."

I take a pair of boxers from the bag and slide them on before checking the doors. I crawl up the bed and slide next to her, pulling her into my arms. I lay there listening to her breathe as it starts to even out and she drifts off to sleep.

As I lay there with her in my arms, I realize just how lucky I am. I could have lost her forever tonight. If I had, I wouldn't have the chance to tell her how I feel, what she means to me, and my hopes for the future.

Raven's comments stick in my head. How does she know? And the ring? I haven't told anyone about that ring, not even Reynolds. Maybe if Samantha is feeling up to it we can meet up with her and Mitchell. I would like to get to know the man and his wife more.

I finally let my mind relax and I'm just about to fall asleep when Samantha starts to thrash and whine, *'NO! Stop! Why are you taking me? Let go of me! Oh God! Why are you doing this? Oliver! Oliver, help me. Please Don't! No, God, No! God it hurt, it hurts so bad, please stop. I can't show fear, No fear. Oliver, I love you, Oliver, My God he's going to shoot me. Bye, Oliver.*

I scoop her up in my arms as you would a child. Not wanting to scare her more, I whisper in her ear, "Samantha you're safe, it's me Oliver, and I have you now. You're safe, open your eyes, and look at me." Slowly I start to see the beautiful sapphire of her eyes as she opens them. Her eyes start to flicker. "That's it, baby girl, look at me. I'm right here. I'm not leaving you."

"Oh God, Oliver." She wraps her arms around my neck burying her face into it as if she's hiding. I lean against the headboard and pull her tighter into my lap.

"Shhh, you're okay, I have you now, and I'm never letting you go. You're safe." I move her hair from her face, rubbing her back. Her body shudders as she sobs. I rock her like a baby. "Shhh, I have you. Shhh." I don't know how long I rock her for before she eventually falls asleep, but I don't want to let her go. I almost lost her today, and I don't ever want to forget this feeling, us being one, so I just sit and hold her.

I wake with a start as I hear my phone vibrate, but not as scared as I am when I realize Sam isn't in bed. *Shit!*

I reach for my phone as I scramble out of bed. I walk to the living room. "Drake. Yes, Mr. Perrotti. Yes, I know she will. I don't know if she is ready to meet him. I'll talk to her. At one? We will see you there."

I'm just about ready to hang up the phone when I hear Nicolas. "What do you mean she's not ready to see me? She's my daughter," he says in a stern voice.

"She not only just found out she has a father, but that he's in the mob. She needs time to adjust to the idea. My God! You are one of the reasons she had to go through what she did last night." Nicolas rants on the other end of the phone. "I don't give a fuck, Nicolas. I love her, and my priority is to protect her. She wouldn't have been placed in this situation if you had answered me a month ago when I first approached you about my feelings for her. She would've been safe, not in some secluded area where anyone could take her. I lost two good men because you didn't tell me that they knew who she was."

Sam slowly walks and wraps her arms around me. I glance down at her. I feel the anger radiating from my body, but she doesn't let that stop her. She pulls my face to hers and kisses my cheek. All the anger and resentment I've been feeling for Nicolas starts to melt away... for at least right now... and is replace with a look of love and devotion for the woman standing in front of me. I take a deep cleansing breath and kiss the top of her head. My heart skips a beat with the love I'm feeling for her. "Samantha's awake. We'll see you in an hour."

I take another deep breath. The last thing I want is to upset Sam after the night she had. Taking her hand, I lead her to the couch and cover her with a blanket. I bring her a steaming cup of coffee and set it on the coffee table. I gaze at her and sigh. She's so beautiful, even battered and bruised she makes my heart skip a beat.

"Hi."

"How are you feeling this morning?" I know I shouldn't ask, but I need to know what her mental state is. I go to the kitchen and fill another bag with crushed ice for her face to continue to help with the swelling.

"I'm fine."

I tilt my head to the side and shoot her a *'really'* look with a smirk on my face. "I think you know me better than that. We both know what *'fine'* really means*."*

"I don't know what you're talking about," she says with an innocent look on her face but a hint of a mischievous gleam in her eye.

"*Fine* for a woman means: freaked out, insecure, neurotic, and emotional."

She stares down at her hands holding the cup of hot coffee then back up to me. "What am I supposed to say, Oliver," she whispers.

"Tell me how you really feel."

She shakes her head and shrugs. "There's just so much that's happened in the last twenty-four hours I don't even know where to start."

I walk over to the couch handing her the ice and sit down facing her. "Then start with me."

"I don't know what to feel," she peers up at me. "I'm so confused with everything that just happened and what I think

I just found out." She sets her coffee and ice down on the table in front of her as she stares down at her hands that are twisting in the blanket that covers her. "Not only about you, but about my father, a father I didn't even know I still had. Add on top of that that I was kidnapped and repeatedly raped after getting the shit beat out of me. And let's not forget I had a gun pressed to my forehead."

"Then ask me what you want to know."

"You'll tell me?"

"Yes." I continue to watch her.

Tilting her head to the side, she asks, "Then why wouldn't you tell me before?

"I had to get permission."

"So did you get it?"

"No, but I think it's a little late for that now. You already know most of it and you shouldn't have to wait any longer. Plus, you deserve to know what I know."

"Then start from the beginning."

CHAPTER NINETEEN
THE STORY OF MY LIFE

OLIVER

"Do you know the story of my childhood?"

"No, not really, you never talked about your family," she says as she shakes her head, gazing up at me.

"That's because I didn't want you to know what I did. Well, didn't do."

She tilts her head to the side and narrows her eyes. "Go on."

I glance down as her warm hands twine with mine. I start to talk, but the words don't come out. She doesn't say anything as I try to formulate what I want to say. "This is very difficult for me. I've never told anyone about this before."

"Oliver, of all people, you have to know I would never judge you. Look at all the shit I went through as a child. I knew that out of anyone, you would be there for me, and I knew you wouldn't judge me for what I did."

"This is different, Sam."

"Then tell me and let me make my own decision."

She peers into my eyes with those beautiful blue eyes that have always given me a sense of hope.

Taking a deep breath, and holding it for a second to help relax me, before I exhale. "It was the year before I met you. I was one of those kids that couldn't get out of school fast enough. I was always the first kid busting through the front doors of the school when the bell rang to head home. School bored me. This one particular day, I had stayed after school to talk to a teacher about computers. We had just started using them. They intrigued me, and I wanted to know more about them. My teacher saw that I finally had an interest in something and took the time to nurture those feelings. I knew I would be in trouble when I got home because I was at least an hour late in leaving. When I got close to the house, I could hear my mom screaming. My parents' never fought so I knew something was wrong. My heart was pounding so hard in my chest. I was so scared. As I ran for the door, I could hear flesh hitting flesh. I stopped dead in my tracks, my stomach twisting as I watched through the front window I saw a man backhanding my mother. She fell to the floor. Blood was dripping from her lip. My dad was home too... he was never home that early... but he was pleading with one of the men." I peer down and my hands that are twined with Sam's. I glance up at her, tears brim her eyes and she bit her lip in anticipation.

"I stood there watching through the window as though I was frozen in time, as if I was watching a movie on the television. I was holding my breath hoping that it would stop everything that was happening before my eyes. I watched as my parents' begged for their lives. My father glanced up and saw me, one of his eyes was swollen shut, and there was blood dripping from his nose and lip. With his eyes, he told me to run… no, it was more as if he begged me to run, but I couldn't. I couldn't move to help them either. I tried, but my feet felt as though I was wearing cement boots." Samantha grips my hands tighter as the first of her tears roll from her long lashes. "They were both executed as I watched." Sam gasps as one of her hands rise to her mouth and she tries to stifle a sob from escaping. "If I would've come home on time, they would've shot me, too."

"Oh God, Oliver, why didn't you ever tell me?"

"What was I going to say? Besides, I didn't know if they were going to come back after me."

"Did they catch the men responsible?"

"No, not until last night." I glance up at her as realization hits her.

"The man last night? You mean the one that was going to shoot me?"

I nod my head at her, "Di Fonzo."

"Oh," she whispers.

"What did they do to him?"

"Nothing yet, but we've been requested to go to meet Perrotti and your father. They want you to decide the fate of the men who raped you."

"Why? Why would they want my opinion?"

"Because you are Nicolas's daughter."

"I might be his daughter, but he's just a man to me. He lost the privilege to be my father the day he walked out on my mom and me. I don't know anything about him, and to be honest, I don't know if I want to."

"Either way, we have to go."

"How did your adoptive mom find you? Is she family?"

"No, my parents' were my only family. I ran to my neighbor's house and she called a friend that just happened to know Mr. Perrotti. Savina Baldini's late husband used to work for him. He knew from what I told him about how they were killed, that it was a mob hit."

"Was your dad in the mob?"

"No, he was a garbage man. What I was told was that he saw something that he shouldn't have. They were afraid he would go to the police, so..."

"Oh God, Oliver. I am so sorry."

"Anyway, because I saw the man that pulled the trigger, Perrotti somehow pushed the paperwork through and Savina became my foster mother, then she adopted me and raised me as her own."

"So what does this have to do with me?" She gazes up at me with furrowed brows.

"After the hit on my parents,' Di Fonzo started searching for me. There were rumors that he was going to start cleaning out the Perrotti family unless they gave me up. Your father had lived a quiet life, and no one knew about you or your mother. Your father changed his name for his home life, essentially living a double life. His real name is Nicolas Perrotti, but his alias was Tristian Hunter when he married your mother. He left her and you when Di Fonzo started to investigate the Perrotti family."

"So Mr. Perrotti is..."

"Your grandfather."

"Oh my God." She shakes her head as she tries to absorb what I had just told her. "And you?"

"I was in bad shape, blaming myself for my parents' death. I was seeking penance and redemption. Mr. Perrotti got me to see a shrink. You were going to go to my school, so a favor was asked of me."

"What kind of favor?" She peeks up at me through her dark lashes.

I lift her chin with my index finger so she looks me in the eye. "He asked me to watch after you. To make sure that if any adults came searching for you, to let them know. He knew I was too young to do anything, but I could notify them if I saw anything that didn't seem normal."

"So this whole time the only reason you were around me was because of loyalty to the family?" She pulls her hands out of mine and turns her body away from me.

"It might've started that way, but I liked you. I could talk to you, and you were my only friend, but that all changed when you turned thirteen; the day I picked you up in my car. The day you came back to school..."

"After they took my baby," she says in a whisper."

"Yes." I reach for her necklace and roll the locket around my fingers as if it were a coin, staring at it as if in a trance. "It was then that I knew." I gaze into her face, wanting to see her reaction. I stare into her glimmering blue eyes, then lean forward and kiss her forehead.

"You beat him up didn't you?"

"I would have killed the motherfucker if it wouldn't have drawn so much attention to you."

"So where does that leave us?"

"What do you mean?"

"Look at me, Oliver, I'm a mess. I don't know that I'll ever be the same again. What they did to me..." She puts her face into her hands as starts to weep. Her shoulders shudder violently as her cries take her over.

I pull her onto my lap, and she buries her face into my neck as she continues to sob.

"Let it out, baby," I whisper as I rub her back and stroke her hair. "What happened last night hasn't changed the way I feel about you; if anything, it has made me love you more."

She pulls away tilting her head. Her brows furrow as she peeks up at me through her damp lashes.

"I don't understand."

"You're such a strong woman. Most people would've cracked at what they did to you, but you didn't back down. You showed no fear even when Di Fonzo held a gun to your head. I'm so proud of what you did."

"Really?" She peers up at me, surprise written on her face.

"That's why I know you'll get through this, we'll get through this. That's if you want me to help." I run my knuckles down her soft cheek. "This happened to you because of me. I haven't done a very good job of protecting you. I didn't know they had found you or figured out who you were. I'm sorry I didn't get to you in time." I stare down at my hands then slowly glance up at her. She's just staring at me. Fuck, if it hadn't been for me this wouldn't have happened to her. I screwed up. She'll never forgive me for what she's gone through.

"I'm the one that ran away from you."

"Maybe so, but I always knew where you were. Di Fonzo took out two of my men to get to you."

"You had me watched?"

"Yes. I needed to make sure you were safe and even then I couldn't do it."

"How did you find me after they took me?"

"I tapped into your phone with the help of Mitchell, the man that helped get you out last night." She glances at me as if she's trying to remember. "By the time I realized you had been taken, you were a couple hours ahead of me. Reynolds knew of Mitchell and suggested I call him. He lives in Portland, and I thought he and his team could intercept your location faster than I could. He has a great team that tracked you all the way, not to mention his wife."

"His wife?"

"She's the one with the bow and arrow."

"Oh my God, now I remember, I couldn't figure out what hit the gun out of Di Fonzo's hand. That was amazing."

"They want to meet up with us tonight for dinner before we drive back."

"That will be great. I can't wait to get to know them." She smiles up at me with excitement I haven't seen in her for a while. She places her soft, delicate hands on my face, lifting it to look at her. "You did all of this for me, why?" She stares at me confused, "You could've been killed."

"Because I love you," I whisper as I raise my eyes to meet hers. "I've loved you for more than ten years."

"You have?"

I nod.

"But you never said anything."

"I couldn't, or, at least, I didn't feel like I could. I was supposed to protect you, not fall in love with you. I tried to distance myself, to turn my feelings for you off, but I just couldn't." I tuck a strand of hair behind her ear.

Then, as if there is a plasma ball in the room, electricity is all around us, and a strange current filled the atmosphere. She stares me in the eye. Neither of us move as we sit there mesmerized by each other. She studies me as if she can see my deepest wants and needs. Her eyes darken to a lapis blue and I can't turn away. I'd never seen eyes that color before. We are locked together.

Her eyes shift to my lips as she strokes my cheek with her soft hands. Her fingers sink into my hair, and she pulls me to her soft, supple, moist lips. My gut twists as my balls tingle, and my dick strains against my zipper. A groan resonates from deep in my chest as I wrap my arms around the woman I have loved for a lifetime. I place one arm around her lower back, pulling her close into me as I feel her breasts firm against my chest. I thread the other hand through her hair at the roots, angling her head for better access. It starts slow and sweet, almost, as if we were exploring and learning each other. I run my tongue over her bottom lip, tasting her. She opens for me as I slide my tongue in to meet hers and they weave and twist together. She sucks my tongue into her mouth, and a moan vibrates through her. I breathe in her scent, drinking her in, feeling every curve of her sumptuous body. My heart beats erratically through my chest and I'm sure she can feel it. As she lets go of my tongue, I take her bottom lip and nibble on it. Another moan escapes her as I run my tongue across it again. I slowly slide my hand up her ribs to her breast, taking one into my hand. I whisper light kisses up her jaw line to her ear then take the lobe into my mouth, sucking it. Little moans and mewls escape her kiss-swollen lips. I run my tongue down behind her ear to her pulse point, kissing and sucking it, finding her erogenous areas. She grips my hair tight with her fingers as I walk my lips across her face and neck.

I pull back to gaze at her. Her eyes are still closed. I slowly glide my hands down to her butt and lightly squeeze as I kiss her collarbone. "Oh God, Oliver." Her breathing accelerates as she moans louder. She tightens her grip on my hair, grabbing it by the roots as she draws my mouth to hers once again. This time she is voracious, as if she's a hungry animal devouring her prey. Pulling me hard to her, she takes over, fucking my mouth with her tongue. *Oh, Fuck!* She growls as she ravages my mouth with hers.

I lift her up and she wraps her legs around my waist. I start to carry her to the bedroom then stop before reaching the doorway. What the fuck am I thinking, I can't do this, not now, not after last night. I pull away from her kiss and stare into those dark blue radiant eyes. She gazes at me longingly. "Please, Oliver, make love to me. Make me forget. Show me what love really is." I stand there a moment longer debating what I should do versus what I long to do. "Please, Oliver, only you can make me forget."

I peer down into her beautiful face, and even with the bruising, she's the most beautiful woman I have ever seen. "As much as I want to make love to you, baby, I want you to be able to relax and enjoy everything I'm going to make you feel. I want your body healed first, and I don't want to have to worry about being anywhere. I want to be able to take my time with you. I want to make love to you slowly. At which time I will make you forget everything but me. I love you, Sam, but I want to do this right. I'm not going anywhere." I kiss her forehead as I set her down. I cradle her face with my hands and brush my lips over hers as a soft moan escapes her lips. I rest my forehead against hers as I stand there attempting to stay restrained. My eyes are closed as I inhale deeply trying to control my breathing. Taking a deep cleansing breath, I open my eyes and gaze into Sam's sapphire blues. I kiss the tip of her nose as I endeavor to pull away.

"Okay, Oliver, I know your right, I just..."

She stares down and her fingers start to worry. I lift her chin, and she slowly glances up into my eyes. "Samantha, nothing is going to change the way I feel about you. I have waited ten years for you, another few weeks is nothing compared to that."

Her eyes go wide. "I don't want to wait that long, Oliver."

"Baby, we'll know when the time is right, but this is something I don't want you to worry about now." I pull her back into a hug, kissing the top of her head. "Let's get ready to go see your grandfather."

"Okay."

CHAPTER TWENTY
PAYBACKS

SAMANTHA

Oliver takes my hand and leads me into the old warehouse, squeezing it as if reassuring me that everything will be all right. "These are the good guys, they're with us," he says. However, that isn't what I fear.

I cling to Oliver's arm as we enter the building. It smells of old rancid car oil and musty rags, with a newer smell of sweat and urine that sends a shiver down my spine.

We're greeted at the door by two giant men, both with metal detector wands. They run them up and down my back and front as well as Oliver and Reynolds.

Walking toward us is Mr. Perrotti and another man who appears vaguely familiar. As he gets closer to us, I realize it's my father. He's of course older, but I remember his eyes. I don't remember a lot about him, but what I do remember is that he was very kind and loving. When he was at home, he would always read me a bedtime story. I surprise myself at that memory. I thought I had pushed all those memories away. He not only hurt my mother, but he also hurt me. I never could understand what I did to make him leave. I know he said he was trying to keep us safe, but he should have given my mom the chance to make that decision herself.

Oliver takes my hand as we walk past the giants. Mr. Perrotti has a friendly smile on his face as he holds his hand out and Oliver takes it, greeting him. Then he peers to me, his smile grows wider and he opens his arms and pulls me into a big hug.

"We have much to discuss, and you have decisions to make." He pushes me back, holding my shoulders studying me. "How are you feeling today?" He takes my chin and turns my head from side to side to see the bruising on my face. "You are a very strong woman; I am proud of how you conducted yourself last night." He kisses my cheeks and runs his hands down my arms until he gets to my hands. "My granddaughter," he says with pride as he lets go of my hands. He then turns and walks past my father.

My father walks up to me, sadness fills his eyes as he pulls me into a tight hug. I don't respond back, but my body rigid as he says, "You will decide their fate as they would have decided yours. You were so courageous last night. I wish I could've stopped them."

"I don't think this is the time to be talking about that now. There are a lot of things we need to discuss, but now isn't the time," I say curtly.

"Yes, you're right, now isn't the time."

Oliver comes to my side and takes my hand as we follow my grandfather and father further into the warehouse.

The rank smell of feces and urine hit me harder as we walk. My stomach churns as the smell gets stronger and infiltrates my senses.

There are five chairs sitting in the middle of the room. Five bodies strapped down at the wrists and ankles. Each one has a black hood over their dangling heads. Their shirts are stained crimson from the blood that has dripped down from their face and head. Clear plastic covers the cold concrete floor under each chair, blood splattering it. My heart pounds violently in my chest as my breath hitches, and although what they did to me was cruel torture, this sight is still hard to witness. Oliver's grip on my hand tightens.

I glance up to him and whisper, "Have you ever been to anything like this before?"

His glimpse tells me he has, but he shakes his head. I think he's just as nervous as I am. I have no idea what to expect.

We walk closer to where my grandfather is standing. As we do, I notice a table with some items sitting on it, pliers, knives, a torch, and an ice pick. I have to work hard to swallow the bile creeping up the back of my throat.

There's another man standing by the table watching us. He's of average height, but you can see the outline of his muscles as his black shirt hugs every curve and valley. His biceps are so large they stretch the armhole of his shirt. Black pants, shoes, and leather gloves finish off his attire. His black hair is disheveled as if from his earlier exertion. His azure eyes that appear empty could have been beautiful at one time, but it's as if what he's been doing has left him an empty shell of a beautiful man.

My grandfather refers to him as Bobby. He glances up at me, and for just a fleeting second, I see a glimmer of life in his eyes, but as grandfather starts to speak, it dissipates like the morning mist.

Bobby walks over to the line of chairs and removes the hoods as he does. They appear to have had the shit beat out of them; however, I can still recognize them. The kid, Mattie, is on the end, his head drooping, battered and bruised but not as bad as the others are.

Pauli is next to him. His once beautiful face is marred with cuts and bruises, a busted lip, broken nose, and swollen eye round off the damage to him. Like Mattie, he doesn't seem as bad as the others.

Eugene and Frankie definitely have seen better days. They are hardly recognizable, but there is no mistaking Frankie's gut and Eugene's pocked face even swollen and bruised.

Di Fonzo sits at the other end. He has been beaten, but I think they have something else in mind for him.

Bobby walks back behind each chair as Perrotti speaks of their crime against the family and me.

Grandfather knows everything about each of the men. However, of course, he would know these things; it's his job. If he didn't this could happen to him, and who knows, maybe one day it will.

He starts with Mattie. Bobby hands his wallet to grandfather. He starts with his name, then his age. Shit, he's only nineteen. He joined the family because his brother did. He was trying to get his brother out according to the information they'd gathered about him. He lifts his head and glances at Pauli as a tear slides down his cheek. My heart breaks as I realize Pauli is his big brother. One of the giants cuts Mattie loose and drags him into another room as my stomach falls. A few seconds later, BANG! I jump and gasp as the gunshot scares me. My stomach revolts as I desperately search for something to throw up in. I shake loose of Oliver's grip on my hand and run to a box sitting on the floor as I expel the contents of my stomach.

Oliver is at my side in seconds. He holds my hair to the side and rubs my back. Tears burn my eyes as they slide down my face. "He was fucking nineteen," I say as I glare up at Oliver. Out of all the people that are up there, he tried to help me. He and Pauli weren't like the other three.

My father brings me a bottle of water. I had asked for mercy for Mattie, and my words weren't listened to. Now I'm pissed. Pissed that my family is a bunch of monsters, no better than the ones battered and bruised, waiting to die. What the fuck, this is my legacy?

Oliver helps me up as we walk back over to where my grandfather is standing. Next is Pauli. I wonder what got him to join this family of men that he would risk his life and family for. In another world and another time, I could have seen myself with him. I remember the night at the club. I could have easily gone home with him. Maybe we would be in this same place although he isn't the one that grabbed me, Eugene and Frankie did that. I'm brought back from my thoughts. Something shiny catches my eye as grandfather opens his wallet. My eyes go wide as reality hits me. I peer up at Oliver then to Pauli. He's a cop. He glances at me with sadness in his eyes then at grandfather. He squares his shoulders and defiantly says, "You might as well just do it, you have taken the only thing I care about."

Grandfather nods his head. The giant cuts him free and drags him to the back room, and I wait for the infamous sound. BANG!

I blink back the tears. He was a fucking cop! What kind of people are they?

Eugene is next. He glowers up at me as his crimes against me are spoken. My mind is instantly taken back to the brutal rape by him and Frankie. How they beat me, and ultimately their order was to kill me.

Eugene laughs at the charges against him, as Frankie joins in. The scowls on their faces are malicious, callous, smug, and vindictive, almost inhuman as they laugh and joke about their torture and abuse of me. Bobby throws a right hook at Eugene, and blood spurts from the obvious break of his nose as he screams out profanities.

Bobby then throws a left to Frankie, and something flies from his mouth and bounces on the floor landing by my foot; a tooth. I can see why Bobby has dead eyes. I would too if this is what I had to do. Blood flows from Frankie's mouth as he too yells his profanity, his head lifts as his eyes meet mine. "You're just a used up cunt. Only good for a quick fuck."

He laughs and Eugene joins in. "You deserved every second of it. You enjoyed it, you didn't even fight back. Your cunt was begging for my dick."

Bobby hits them both again. Grandfather pulls a gun from inside his jacket and holds it out to me. "This is your choice," he says, "You can do what you want to them. It's your right as a victim and as my granddaughter."

I peer down on the gun and think back to the days when Oliver took me shooting. He said he wanted me to know how to use and handle a gun in an emergency. We would go out into the woods, set up cans, and shoot them, not that it ever did me any good, and I never had a gun. There was no reason for me to have one. Well, that's what I thought anyway.

I take the gun, release the magazine, rack the slide to empty the chamber. I reinsert the magazine and hand the gun back to my grandfather. His face is etched with pity and disappointment.

Eugene and Frankie continue their verbal assault on me again, both laughing and sneering at me, taunting me with the gross details of everything they did to me. Then Frankie says, "Once a whore always a whore. Learned how to whore yourself out to your brother at an early age."

Eugene adds, "At least they got rid of the kid before it grew up to be like her mother." They knew, they knew about Grady and my baby. I can't think or feel. Blood pulses through my ears. Everything happens so quickly, and I don't even register my actions as I grab the gun from my grandfather. BANG! BANG! I don't even flinch. I release the magazine and rack the slide to release the live round then drop the gun on the table. It clanks against the wood with a heavy thud as the smell of the gunpowder hits my nose. I turn and walk out the door.

CHAPTER TWENTY-ONE
MY FAMILY

SAMANTHA

Fresh air, I can't get enough. I keep drawing it in, but it doesn't seem to fill my lungs. BANG! I jump at the sound of the gun going off again. How the hell am I going to go on with my life now? I'm no better than they are. I let my anger take control.

I slide down the side of the building. The smell of gunpowder and death still lingers in my nose as my mind flashes through the events of the last twenty-four hours. I try to rationalize everything, but my mind keeps going to Mattie and Pauli. Two innocent people that were caught in a horrible situation that is now my life. I wonder about their family, their parents. How am I going to live with myself? I'm a murderer. This might be something my father and grandfather are accustomed to, but not me. I don't want this kind of life.

Tears burn my eyes as I think about Oliver. Although he hasn't been in the family as my father or his henchmen, he's still in it, and I realize that as much as I love him, I can't live in fear like this.

I think about running, but really, where am I going to go that they can't find me. Not to mention Grady is still out there.

Taking a deep breath, I gather my resolve and stand up. I walk over to the car and see the keys are still in the ignition. I quietly open the door, and I'm adjusting the seat when there's a knock on the window. I hang my head as my grandfather opens the car door. "I think we all need to sit down and talk."

"No disrespect, but I don't even know you. I didn't know you even existed until last night. What is there to discuss?"

"Please, Samantha, please come back inside and talk to us."

I shake my head not wanting to go back to see the dead bodies and smell death. "I can't go back in there with it smelling of death." I glare up at him. "I'm not you or my father. This isn't the life I want to live."

"I understand that, but yet you are and have always been a part of this family. Let's go inside, and we can talk. The warehouse is clean. There's an office that is comfortable for us to sit in." He holds out his hand to me. I take a deep breath and reluctantly place my hand in his.

We walk through a different door in the warehouse and into a fully furnished office. I sit on the couch. Grandfather and I are alone. I'm wondering where Oliver is, then I remember the conversation he was having with my father this morning and the last gunshot that I heard. I begin to panic; my heart pounds hard against my ribs, my stomach twists and I pant for air, unable to catch my breath. I know I have fear on my face. "Oliver, where is he," I say almost like a demand, but grandfather is silent.

The door finally opens and Oliver and my father walk in. Oliver's head is bowed, and he won't look me in the eye. I run over to him and throw my arms around his neck, but he doesn't reciprocate. "Oliver?" I peer up into his sad indigo eyes. He closes his eyes and turns his head slightly to the side as if shunning me. I glare over at my father and drop my arms from around Oliver's neck. I walk over to where my father is standing. "What did you do? What did you say to him?"

"I don't know what you're talking about."

"Like hell you don't." I feel my face flush and my fists clench as I square my shoulders, and glare him in the eyes. "Tell me what you did or I will walk out of here and you'll never see me again." My voice is low and controlled.

"Don't you threaten me. I can find you anywhere, just as I have done all your life."

"You're doing a damn good job at it too, Dad," I say sarcastically. "Not only did you leave my mother, your wife devastated when you left us, but then I was sexually abused in my own house for four years. I got pregnant and then my baby, your grandbaby, and your great grandbaby," I say as I stare at my grandfather. "Was killed and ripped from my body. Shall we talk about the last twenty-four hours?"

"That's enough," my grandfather shouts, "We need to sit and talk about this calmly."

I turn and peer at my grandfather. I calmly say, "Neither of you has ever been a blip on my radar until yesterday. Oliver has always been the constant in my life, the only constant, and if you don't allow us to be together, then you won't have me either. Neither of you," I say sternly.

"How do you think you can do that." My father asks.

"I'm a kid, I grew up with computers and know how to stay off the grid. If that means I live on the streets, then that's what I'll do. You should know after last night that I'm not afraid of a lot of things."

"You wouldn't last?"

"Really? You're going to go there. Living on the streets is a hell of a lot easier than the life I've had to live. Why is it that you have trusted him to watch over me, but you won't let us be together?"

"Because I want better for you. I don't want you to be involved in the family business," my father says.

"Don't you think it's a little late for that? I just put bullets into two men. It's a little hard not to be involved with the family now." I peer up at my grandfather. "I'm asking you to see that Oliver and I belong together. He's my best friend, I love him." Tears fill my eyes blurring my vision, and I take his hands in mine and blink the tears away. This isn't the time to be emotional. "If you don't want me involved with the family, then let Oliver out, and I'll never ask you for anything else."

"You already asked for something last night," Grandfather says as he nods his head at one of his men who promptly leaves the office.

"Well, that didn't go the way I had asked. They were innocent men and you..." The door opens as the bright sunlight shines through the door. All I can see is the silhouette of the men in the door. As the door starts to close, and the glare of the sun is shielded, I can start to make out the faces. "But... I thought... I heard..." I glance up at my grandfather then to the two men standing in front of me. I walk over to them in almost disbelief as I take Mattie in my arms. "Thank you for your kindness to me. I knew you were never one of them. This is your second chance. Make something good out of it."

"Thank you, Samantha, and call me Matthew. Thank you for saving us."

I then peer up at the man that I first met at the club. "Call me Paul. If you wouldn't have run out on me that night, I would have told you what they were planning. I'm sorry I couldn't warn you before this happened. Thank you for saving us. To be honest, I didn't know what was happening until I saw Matthew standing in the back room. Words can't express my gratitude for sparing us, but especially him." He pulls me into a tight hug, kissing the top of my head.

I step out of the hug. "I knew you weren't monsters like Frankie and Eugene," I gaze up at my grandfather, "Thank you for listening to me."

"Samantha, I'm not a heartless man." He places his hands on my shoulders. "You will learn in time that all we want is the best for you."

I back out of his touch and walk over to where Oliver's standing. I take his hand in mine. I don't know what they threatened him with, but we both need to stand united right now. "Then you're the ones who have the choice to make," I say to my father and grandfather.

I glance up at Oliver, and as if it gives him the extra strength he needs, he squares his shoulders and takes me in his arms, kissing the top of my head. Releasing my hand, he walks over to my father and stands in front of him. "Mr. Perrotti, I am asking again for permission to date Samantha." My father's face turns red as he starts to walk away shaking his head. "I've loved your daughter most of her life. I've tried to be there to protect her, care for her, and comfort her. I'm asking you out of respect. Your family found me a home and protection when I needed it. However, I've paid that debt by caring for her and protecting her as she's grown up. My job was to watch after her for three years, my final years in elementary school, but I never stopped, nor will I ever. In fact, I cared for her through her college years, and I've been supporting her since her mother passed when she had no one or nothing."

I stare up at him, surprise written on my face. "What," I say.

"Samantha's smart, and she's good with a computer. That's one of the reasons I hired her to work for me at my company. If she decides to go off the grid, she will and can do it. And if she's off, so am I, because there is no way in hell I'll let her be alone again. I have more than enough cash stashed away to live off of for a very long time. I am a very patient man, Mr. Perrotti; I have waited over thirteen years to have Samantha. I've not only grown into a respectable business owner, but I've repeatedly proved how much I love your daughter. You came to me as a child to help you with Sam. If I were good enough then, I should be good enough now. If this is just a matter of not being good enough for her and that you'll never agree, then just shoot me now, because I WILL NOT STOP loving Samantha," he states, emphasizes his words.

My father reaches into his suit jacket pulling out his gun and brings it up to Oliver's head. But Oliver doesn't flinch. I move quickly between them. Glaring my father deep into his eyes I say, "If you kill him, you might as well kill me too. You might not put the bullet in my head, but you will kill me all the same. Because whatever happens to Oliver, I will do the same to myself. I've tried to be respectful and listen to your reasoning to why you don't want Oliver and me together, but you haven't given me a valid reason." I turn and peer at my grandfather for some sort of insight.

"Grandfather, you asked me to come in here to talk, but we're getting nowhere." Grandfather motions to father, and he holsters his gun.

Grandfather glances at Paul and Matthew, who have been a witness to our beyond heated discussion. "One moment Samantha," he says as he takes a step over to the brothers. "Have you two decided what you want to do, now that you have new lives?"

"Yes, sir, Matthew and I have decided to accept Oliver's offer to work security for his company."

"Good, that's a good decision; I know he'll get Matthew the training he needs. We'll get your new identity paperwork by the end of the week."

"Thank you, Mr. Perrotti." Paul reaches his hand out to him, shaking it, and Matthew follows suit. "Mr. Drake, we look forward to your call," Paul says.

After Paul and Matthew leave, grandfather motions for us to sit around the small table to the side of the room. It isn't in great shape, and you can tell it was just left here, one leg is gone and being held up by a broken broomstick, but it's somewhere I can sit and hide half of my body as I worry my fingers in my lap as I try to stay stoic. Oliver sits beside me, taking my hand in his. He knows. Maybe he sees my shoulders or arms moving, but he knows. Just his touch on my hands sends a sense of calm through my body, and I can gather my strength from that as we sit side by side, united, strong, resolute. Grandfather and my father are sitting across from us.

I stare at my father, hoping that he can see how I feel. The emotions and events of the day catch up to me as the realization of what I have turned into is starting to take its toll. I just shot two men that brutally raped me and I don't feel anything. No sadness, no happiness, nothing. I'm numb.

THE LOCKET

Am I supposed to feel something? I'm so tired. I just want them to see how I feel for once. It's hot out, the heat from the concrete and steel building is stifling, and the sun beams through the unshaded windows. Rivulets' of sweat run down my back and down the valley between my breasts.

When I finally speak, it's quiet, barely audible. "When I was a small child, I dreamed about my fairytale life, where I was going to live, what my castle would be like, the tiara I would wear for my wedding and who my prince charming would be." I stare down at my hand now joined with Oliver's. Then I gaze into his face, into those indigo eyes that I fell in love with so long ago. "I used to dream that my prince would be just like you." I glance at my father as sadness fills his eyes. "In fact, I would pray at night that you would be my prince charming just as you were for mom. However, you left us alone and broken. Nothing was ever the same again. Then Oliver came into my life, and even though bad things happened to me, he was always there to help pick up the pieces.

"You see, my prince changed. You might not have known it at the time, but you're the one who made me think of him as my prince, since the only other man that I had trusted and loved walked away from me. Oliver became that man. I know he will always be there for me because he *has* been there for me. He's never turned his back on me. You must have seen something good in him for you to ask him to watch over for me. What has changed?" I tilt my head to the side searching deep into my father's eyes. "Father, I love Oliver that will never change. I'm asking you to please reconsider. You walked out of my life seventeen years ago. You lost the right to tell me what I can and can't do back then, but you're the only family I have left, and I would like to know whom my father and grandfather are. However, I will walk away, just as you did to my mother and me if I have to. This isn't a threat, I have lived my life without you, and I can do it again. But I will not stop loving Oliver." Oliver squeezes my hand as I gaze at his beautiful face, then back between my father and grandfather.

My father glares grudgingly at me then at Oliver. "Alright, you have my blessing."

Oliver squeezes my hand, but I'm not done yet. I fight the smile that is begging to come out, but I need other reassurances. "So we're clear on this. If anything happens to Oliver, as in, if he disappears, dies, or stubs a toe, expect the same consequences for me. Because I will not live without him. He's not to be harmed, so if you're just placating me and plan to get rid of him, then you will be doing the same to me too." I stand and extend my hand. "Deal?"

"You love him that much?"

"With all my heart and soul."

My father reluctantly reaches his hand out, "Deal."

I move my hand in front of my grandfather as he stares down at my hand. "This is between you and your father."

"No, this is between the family and me. If I have your word, I know that no one will cross that promise."

He takes a deep breath, then slowly releases it, "You sure you don't want to go back to school to be a lawyer?" I shake my head as he takes my hand in his. "Deal."

A big smile breaks across my face. I feel as if I won the fuckin lottery. I turn to Oliver, who still appears a little apprehensive. My father rounds the table, pulls Oliver into a hug, and whispers something in his ear that I can't hear. I watch as Oliver shakes then nods his head. "Yes, sir." I wonder what he says to him.

My grandfather interrupts my thoughts and with a cocked brow he asks, "Where did you learn to shoot a gun,"

"Oliver showed me how to handle a gun and shoot when I was thirteen."

Grandfather places the gun in my hand and orders, "Show me how you take it apart."

I take the gun; peer up at my grandfather then to Oliver as he nods his head. I stare at the gun. It's a little different from the Glock G17 that Oliver had taught me to shoot. But I release the magazine, setting it on the table. I rack the slide making sure there's not a round loaded. Pulling the trigger, I dry fire the gun. Gripping the gun with my fingers over the slide and my thumb wrapped around the grip with one hand, I pull the slide back slightly as I press down on the two slide locks releasing the slide to pull off the receiver. I peer up at my grandfather and shrug my shoulders. "Did you want to test me at my target shooting, too?"

"No, I already saw that first hand."

I flash back to earlier today when I murdered two men. My heart starts to pound hard against my chest, as my breath hitches and my eyes start to sting with unshed tears. I quickly blink them back, not wanting to show my emotions as I try to swallow the lump in my throat. I have to get out of here. I need air. I set the rest of the pieces to the gun on the table and walk out the door. I hear Oliver's voice as the door closes behind me.

CHAPTER TWENTY-TWO
TO NEW FRIENDS

OLIVER

The drive to the hotel is in near silence. Samantha sits with her hands worry in her lap as she stares out the side window.

"Are you up to dinner with Mitchell and his wife?" She appears in deep thought. I run my fingers through her hair, placing a strand behind her ear so I can see her face. "Baby?" She peeks up at me through her long dark lashes. They're damp as the first of her tears start to roll down her cheek. I unbuckle her seat belt and pull her into my lap as she buries her head in the crook of my neck, weeping quietly as shudders sweep through her body, leaving a tear-dampened spot on my shirt.

I sit there rocking her, soothing her, and running my fingers through her hair. "Shhh, we'll stay in tonight. I'll call Mitchell and cancel, I'm sure they will understand."

She desperately peers up at me, shaking her head, "No, I'll be alright. I want to go... please." Her sad expression melts me.

"Alright, but only if you're up to it."

"I'll feel better once I have a shower and get some clean clothes on. Seattle and Portland aren't that far apart, only a few hours. I would really like to find some friends. Kassidy's so far away, I haven't had the chance to settle in. I was only at work for a week before I... oh." She stares up at me. "I don't have a job. I've been gone for the last month."

"You let me worry about that."

"But Lucas already thinks I slept my way in, oh shit." She frowns at me with a distressed look, "I slapped him then kneed him in the groin."

I laugh, "Yes, I did hear about the 'crazy bitch' night." Her eyes light up as realization sets in at the hilariousness of the situation.

"Oliver?"

Her tone now serious, "Yes, baby." I run my fingertips over her cheeks and down the middle of her lips. They are so soft, and I long to kiss them, to taste her again. My jeans strain at the thought of my lips on hers. She's going to feel me soon if she stays on my lap any longer. "You should get in your seat and get belted back in."

She starts to slide off my lap. "You said that you'd been taking care of me and that you've been supporting me since my mother died. Mom's lawyer contacted me and said he would take care..." Realization finally hits her as she tilts her head to the side and gazes at me. "He's your lawyer, isn't he?"

I pause, "Yes, Mr. Costa was hired by me." She stares down at her hands sitting in her lap.

"Mom didn't have a lawyer?"

"No." I glance over at her to gauge her reaction. I know the bigger questions are coming.

"The house?"

"Your mom took out a loan after her cancer went into remission to pay off the medical bills. When the cancer came back, she had no way of paying the mortgage."

"Oh," she says her voice quiet, "Mr. Costa said he sold it."

"He did."

"Oh. I didn't even get the chance to get my things out of the house."

"All your things are still in the house baby. I bought the house; it's in your name. I wanted you to have a place to stay if you had decided to stay there."

"You bought my mom's house?"

"It was your family home. I couldn't just sell it without talking to you first. I asked Kassidy if she would like to live there with Derek. They moved in just after graduation."

Her head snaps up to look at me in shock. "What?"

"I asked her not to say anything to you about it until I talked to you. She's caring for it while you're here. You can decide what you want to do with it later.

"But it isn't mine," she says as she peers up at me, a range of emotions written on her face.

"But it is; your name is on the Deed."

"But why? Why would you do all of this for me?"

"Because I love you. I knew you wouldn't be able to afford the house, and I knew you wouldn't be able to get the time you needed to empty the house and sort through yours and your mother's possessions. This was the best answer."

"Should I ask what else you have done," she asks as she tilts her head to the side.

I smile at her, if only she knew just how much I would give up for her. The threat her father gave me before walking into the office, I know he isn't happy with us being together, but she's my drug and I haven't been able to break this habit for over thirteen years. "What do you want to know?"

"Tell me," she says.

"Financially?"

"For starters, did my mother have a life insurance policy?"

"No."

"Did I really get scholarships from the school?"

I pause, gazing down at her beautiful face eager to absorb all I tell her. "Yes, but they were from me."

She gasps and tears brim her eyes as she turns to gaze out the window.

I take her hand in mine and speak in a whisper. "I love you, Samantha, and I always will. I had the means to help you and I did, and I will forever. There were several things that I knew were very important to you, your education, your family home, and a nice place to put your mother to rest."

Her head whips around and the tears finally breach the brim of her eyes, rolling down her cheeks. "You were the one that picked the plot under the willow tree that faced the lake? The cemetery said she had picked it. And the headstone?"

I nod my head. "I knew from talking to you what you wished you could have for her, I also knew how much you loved her and what you would want on the headstone."

"I don't know what to say," she whispers. "That's exactly what I would have done if I had the means to do so. Thank you, Oliver." She leans in and softly brushes her velvety soft lips over mine making me long for more.

We're meeting Mitchell and Raven downstairs in the lobby of the hotel. It's early evening. Sam wants to spend as much time getting to know them as possible. She wants to make a good bond with both of them since they saved her life. I keep thinking about what Raven whispered in my ear and what she said to Samantha. I never did ask her what Raven said.

We had stopped in one of the shops downstairs and picked up some more clothes after returning from the warehouse, sending ours out to be cleaned. I just grabbed another pair of jeans and a T-shirt. "Wow!" Samantha walks out of the bedroom in a flirty little backless, pale yellow sundress. The color on her makes her glow. She turns in a circle as the soft flowing skirt rises and floats with the air movement. "You look amazing, Sam."

Her face flushes as if she's embarrassed. "Thank you, Oliver," she says as she peeks up through her lashes and a shy smile illuminates her face. She covered most of her bruises with makeup as her face is still slightly swollen, but I don't care, she is still beautiful.

I don't know why she is acting so shy tonight. Maybe it's the thought of what she has gone through the last couple of days. All I want is for her to relax, have a good time, and enjoy herself tonight. "Are you ready to go?" I hold my hand out to her. "Our official first date." I raise my eyebrows in jest. "So, if I'm good tonight and I ply you with liquor, do you think I'll get lucky?" A big smile stretches across her face as her eyes light up. She appears so carefree right now, as if she doesn't have a care in the world. "God you're beautiful when you do that."

"Do what?"

"Smile like that."

She places her hand on my chest, tilts her head slightly as she gazes into my eyes. "I love you, Oliver."

I pull her into me, kissing her soft pouty lips.

CHAPTER TWENTY-THREE
MY FUTURE

SAMANTHA

I try to remember the events of what happened after Oliver got me out of the motel room, but I think I was in shock and can only pick up fragments of what happen just after. That is until I see Raven.

I didn't remember what she looked like the night before, everything is still a blur, but as a glimpse at her, I am amazed at what this woman can do.

She's pixie short at five-feet-tall with raven black glossy hair. She has such a presence about herself. Then it hits me. I remember her whispering in my ear. *"You and Oliver were made for each other, and he will be there for you as you heal; not only from tonight, but from your past. You two will be blessed, and the child that was taken away is and will always be with you. Anastasia will come back to you."*

My body shivers and goosebumps instantly cover my body with the memory of Ravens whispered secrets.

"Are you alright," Oliver asks as he turns and studies me.

I didn't realize it was noticeable. "Yes, I just felt a little chilled." Oliver furrows his brow, and then I see the temperature gauge on the bank sign across the street as it reads ninety-three degrees.

Mitchell and Raven walk up to us, Raven pulling me into a hug as Mitchell reaches for Oliver's hand. "I knew it would take you a while to remember, but I see you have. I also see he's told you everything."

I pull away and stare at her. I know I must have a confused look in my face, "I don't understand."

"I know it's hard to understand, but I'll fill you in tonight," she says. She leans back into me. "Just know that he's loved you for a long time and will do anything to protect you, and no, you're not."

Again, I pull away from her, giving her a quizzical look. "No, I'm not what?"

She leans into my ear. "A cold-blooded murderer. You did what needed to be done, and if the fat one hadn't been shot when the gun fell I would have taken him out first. But just as I was going to take the shot, a car drove by. When the other man pulled his gun, I had to wait a half second longer than I wanted. He moved and I missed my mark or he would have died last night, too." She takes my hand in hers as we walk into the restaurant and she continues to talk. "I never thought I would be comfortable doing what I am doing, but when it comes to saving an innocent life, it's totally worth it."

"How long have you been working with Mitchell?"

"I actually don't work for him. I work for a computer software company. My best friend was kidnapped and we went to save her. No one even knew I could use a bow and arrow," she laughs, "You should have seen their faces when

I mentioned it. That's a picture in my mind I will never forget."

As we're seated, she proceeds to tell us a little about herself, how she was a runaway from the Seattle area, and that's where her mother and father still live.

"I have to know..."

"... It's Toby Mitchell, I call him Toby, but everyone calls him Mitchell, it's a military thing," Raven cuts me off, shrugging her shoulders. She knew exactly what I was going to ask.

"So, Raven, tell us about this little gift that you've used on us," Oliver asks

She smiles up at Mitchell. "This is the most bazaar story you will ever hear," Mitchell says.

The server comes over to our table to take our drink order as we sit and talk.

She tells us her story of how she met her maternal grandparents. They showed her, her gift as she calls it, and how to utilize it.

"But you know things that no one else knows, you know what I'm thinking or concerned about," I say.

"My best friend was kidnapped not too long ago. If I had listened to my instincts instead of hoping they weren't true, she wouldn't have been put into that situation. So now, every time I feel something, I tell the person that it deals with, just as I have told both of you.

Mitchell and Oliver are in a discussion about security and each of their businesses as Raven and I continue to talk.

"Raven, how do you get over the guilt of killing someone?"

"I try not to think about it. I had trained in martial arts and I learned that you have to protect yourself in order to help others. When Charlie, my best friend, was kidnapped, I knew what the kidnappers were capable of. They had killed her fiancé the year prior. He was also a good friend of mine, too." She tells me that if it weren't for Charlie begging her, she would have killed him the night he killed Charlie's fiancé. "Other than working out in the gym, I never had to use my martial arts skills until that day."

"How did you get into using a bow and arrow," I ask.

"When I was younger, I would go hunting with my father. I didn't think it was fair to the animal to use a gun even though we were hunting for food, so we started to bow hunt. It had been a long time since I had used one, but I had been pretty good as a child. I was just out of practice. The week we rescued Charlie, I practiced a lot with the new bow system I bought. I knew going in that I might have to kill someone, but I also knew that if I didn't, one or more of my friends could die. The choice was easy. Samantha, you made the choice initially to spare them. You need to know that if you had decided not to kill them, Oliver would have. This was closure for what they did to you. You'll never have to look over your shoulder for them." She lays her hand on my arm, and a strangely calming effect comes over me as though a weight has been lifted, and I realize that she's right, I needed to know that they would never do that to another woman again.

"Raven, you said something about my baby. How do you know?"

"I wish I could tell you, but it's just a feeling or thought that I get. It's like seeing a picture in my mind. I see it and focus on it as the story is played out. I see what she wants me to see and she's going to come back to you."

"But you called her by her name."

"Can you tell me how you came up with that name?"

"After I found out she was a little girl, the name came into my head and never left. I have been obsessed with it ever since."

"Do you know its meaning?"

"No, I just love the name."

"Well, Anastasia's name origin is Greek and means 'resurrection.'"

"You're joking right?"

I don't think her face could be any more serious. "No, I'm not joking."

I contemplate what Raven has just revealed to me. I place my hand over my chest gripping my locket. A sense of calm washes over me as I realize she has once again placed her hand on my forearm.

I stare up at her as the thought of my baby coming back into my life. My Anastasia. I'm filled with an emotion I've never felt before.

The rest of the evening, I sit in a haze. Fading in and out of conversations as I think of what my future will now hold.

I'm in awe of the life that both Raven and Mitchell have lived and their life story together.

It's the middle of the night. I keep thinking we're going to be kicked out of the restaurant, but then I remember we're in Reno and almost nothing closes here. As we say our goodbyes, I'm grateful and blessed that Raven and Mitchell came into my life. Raven pulls me into a big hug whispering into my ear. "You'll have a blessed life with Oliver. However, you will have to be strong for him just as he's been for you. He's going to meet with trials of his own." She kisses me on the cheek then takes Mitchell's hand as they turn and walk away.

CHAPTER TWENTY-FOUR
WHO AM I

OLIVER

T aking Samantha's hand, I glance down at her. "Did you have a nice time tonight," I ask

"Yes. There's just so much I need to process." She pulls herself closer to me, almost hugging my arm. "Are you and Mitchell going to work together?"

"I'm sure there might be times that we will. We deal in different types of security. I never would've been able to pull off what he and his men did last night. He has a great team that is almost all military trained. Whereas I have the software and computer type security."

"It seems as though there are a lot of possibilities for both of you to work together. Him being the brawns and you being the brain."

"You appeared as if you were in a deep conversation with Raven. What did you think of her?"

"Where do I start? Her gift is unbelievable. I like her a lot, and she doesn't live too far from Seattle, so it will be nice to see them as friends."

I take Sam's hand in mine as we take the elevator back up to our floor.

There's still a lot that I'm trying to sort through from the last twenty-four hours. Not just the words that Raven whispered in my ear, but what Di Fonzo said to me. He referred to me as *the prodigal son* twice. What did he mean? What did he know about me? Maybe that was his way of thinking I wouldn't put a bullet in his head for what he did to my parents'? I don't know, but my mind is racing.

I send a text to Tiffany letting her know that I want to see her in my office first thing Monday morning. I have to find the underlying cause of this or I'll go crazy thinking about it.

I toss and turn all night. At one point, I slip out of bed and start a search on my computer. I find a few things, but not enough to sink my teeth into. I don't have the patience to wait, but I don't really have an option.

I'm sitting on the sofa with another cup of coffee in my hand as the sun peeks through the blinds. I don't know how many cups I've had, but it's not helping now. I'm exhausted and I'm not looking forward to the long drive home. But maybe I can get some rest on the drive.

CHAPTER TWENTY-FIVE
PRODIGAL SON

OLIVER

"Samantha, we're home. Baby, wake up." Samantha has been sleeping for several hours now. I know she has to be exhausted, having not slept but just a couple hours the last several days. I'm sure the days have passed in a blur, filled with torture, torment, pain, emotions, and distress. Not to mention the revelation of her father and grandfather.

Although Samantha never asked what happened to Di Fonzo, I know she knows. I had told her that he executed my parents'. What I did to him was my vengeance and redemption for their murders.

My mind is still tormented. I keep going back to what he said right before I took his life:

So the prodigal son returns. I wondered where they hid you. It's ironic that this story has now come full circle. Did they even tell you who you are? It's fucking Romeo and Juliet all over again, son.

Those last words play over and over in my mind as if it were on repeat, never stopping, over and over.

What does this have to do with Romeo and Juliet? Was he talking about Nicolas and how he didn't want me in a relationship with Samantha? Moreover, how would he even know I wanted a relationship with her? How would he even know anything about that, they were enemies.

But there was something about him that seemed so familiar. Was it because I remember his face from my childhood as he executed my parents? Have I seen him in passing and just not realized who he was? Then my mind goes back to what he said to me once again.

I need to investigate more into Di Fonzo when I return to work tomorrow. What he said disturbs me; it doesn't make since. As a kid, I was always good at putting puzzles together, but this one has me mystified. It's gnawing away at me. Consuming me. It's there, but I'm so goddamn tired from not sleeping I can't reach it. I feel as if I could grasp it right under the surface, but then it slips away.

I carry my sleeping beauty to the elevator. Her arms are wrapped around my neck and the delicate fragrance of her perfume awakens my senses, not to mention the feel of her body against mine.

Punching the code into the panel, the mirrored doors open. I step in and the doors close behind us. I gaze at my sleeping beauty in the mirror doors, then glance at my tired face and eyes. I look as though I've aged ten years. My face falls. It's there, I just can't grasp it. Fuck, it vanishes again. We quickly ascend to the top floor of my building. I open my front door and I'm greeted with two balls of fluff at my feet. I carefully step around and over them so as not to trip with Samantha in my arms. Carrying her back to the bedroom, I lay her down and slowly start to remove her clothes. Taking one of my T-shirts out of the drawers, I finish taking her jeans and socks off. As I get to her shirt, I stand there frozen, blindly gazing at my angel. My Samantha, lying innocently in front of me, and I'm reminded of how close I had become to losing her.

My eyes burn and I bite my lip to stop the tears from falling. Men aren't allowed to cry. I've never cried. I didn't even cry at my parents' funeral. But the emotions of the last several days have caught up with me. As if the weight of the world is on my shoulders, and I know I'm losing it. I'm so emotionally and physically exhausted; I have to step away. I finish putting the T-shirt on her, then go to the spare room after grabbing clean clothes.

I stare at myself in the mirror again as little pieces start to come together. Fragments of memories flick through my head, but are little flashes that I can't grasp. My pulse spikes every time a memory flashes as bile creeps up my throat. I step into the steaming shower as a torrent of scalding water numbs my skin, wishing it would numb my mind. I know it's there, I don't know how or what. Maybe because I just don't want to admit it. Maybe if I just don't think about it, it won't be true. The reality of what I remember Raven saying comes back to me hitting me full force. As if someone slapped my upside the head. My heart is hammering in my chest as the emotion I feel from witnessing Samantha's torture and brutal rape along with the last eighteen years flood me. I stumble back against the shower wall, hitting my head against the edge of the tiled soap niche as my body crumbles to the ground and eighteen years of anguish and emotion escapes in a roar of sorrow and grief.

CHAPTER TWENTY-SIX
REALIZATION SETS IN

SAMANTHA

I jolt awake to the horrible sound. It takes me a few minutes to recognize my surroundings and I think I am just hearing things when I again hear it. This time so loud that Maxx and Levi leap from the bed and scamper away. "Oliver?" I feel for Oliver in bed, but he's not there nor has he been in bed. His side of the bed is cold and decorative pillow haven't been removed. I get out of bed and try to locate where the sounds are originating, following the source of the noise. I end up in the spare bathroom, and what I see in front of me is something I never would have expected to see.

Oliver is huddled on the floor of the steaming shower. The water is so hot it's as if someone poured water on the hot stones in a sauna. Dense steam billows out of the shower. Stepping closer, I see his face is buried in his arms which are wrapped around his knees. I don't know what happened, but

I've never seen him like this before. He's always been so strong, but right now he resembled a small child as a soul retching wail escapes him.

I quietly slip through the shower door kneeling in front of him, and the scorching hot water rains down on my back scalding me. He still hasn't noticed me, his skin bright red from the water. I wrap my arms around him as I whisper in his ear, the way he has done for me so many times before.

He releases his arms from around his knees and pulls me into him, and burying his face in my water soaked T-shirt. His grip is so tight I can hardly breathe. His body shudders as he tries to control emotions. "I killed him."

"Killed who, Oliver?"

"I killed him, Sam, I killed him," he repeats as he continues to sob.

"Oliver, honey, let's get you out of here," I say after some time has passed. I break the hold he has on me to study his face. He appears as if he is a lost little boy, his eyes red and swollen. I run my hand over his cheek. "Oliver, whatever this is, I will be by your side." I gaze into his weary indigo eyes making sure he really sees and understands me. "I love you, Oliver."

He clings to me as if I'm his lifeline. Finally, he takes a deep steady breath and loosens his grip on me. I help him stand, then I shrug out of my wet T-shirt, letting it pool at my feet as I turn off the water. I grab two big white bath towels, wrapping one around my body and the other around Oliver's waist.

Taking his hand, I lead him to the master bedroom. I pull back the covers on the bed as he slips on a pair of boxers. He slips under the covers as I pull on a tank top and shorts. Just as I walk out of the bedroom. His voice cracks with panic. "You're not going to stay in here with me?"

"I'm just going to turn off the lights and make sure the doors are locked, Oliver. Okay?" He slowly nods his head. I don't know what happened, but this is a total role reversal. It wasn't but a couple days ago that I was the one in the fetal position. As I lock the front door, I wonder what happened in the short amount of time that caused Oliver to crash as he did.

I walk into the bedroom, Oliver still resembling a scared and lost little boy. I crawl in next to him in the bed as I lay my head on his chest, listening to the rapid beating of his heart.

"Do you want to talk about it," I ask reverently.

I lay there waiting for him to answer. "I ... I think I ..." he starts then roughly clears his throat, "I think I was related to him."

Unconsciously running my fingers through the dusting of chest hair, I ask, "Who Oliver?"

"Di Fonzo."

CHAPTER TWENTY-SEVEN
MEMORIES

OLIVER

I toss and turn most of the night, making a laundry list of things I need to do when I get to the office. I must have finally drifted off because when I open my eyes again, it's seven thirteen and the smell of coffee, bacon, and toast fills the apartment. I jolt out of bed and rush to the shower.

Walking into the kitchen, I'm greeted with the most beautiful face in the world. She gazes up at me with the biggest smile I have seen in a long time, yet there is a touch of sadness in her eyes.

"Good Morning. Are you hungry?"

I wrap my arms around her, her back to my chest. I lean my head into her hair by her ear, inhaling her scent as my soul is recharged with determination. "I love you, Sam, thank you for last night. I'm sorry I..."

She turns in my arms and places her fingertips over my lips as she peers deep into my eyes. "Everyone needs to show they are human sometimes. If we're going to be together, then I want us to be whom we are, no hiding behind walls. If you're upset or sad, I need to know those things so I can help you. I want to be your comfort, always, just as you've been for me all my life." She cradles my face pulling it to hers, softly brushing her velvet lips over mine. I close my eyes and bask in the love I feel for her and think about how lucky I am.

"What did you want to do about work?"

"I know I need to start back up, but I need to get things at the lake taken care of. I also need to pick up my car," she says.

"I'll have Reynolds drive you there and help you pack, and then you can visit with Amber and Val and let them know that you're alright. I know they were extremely worried about you."

"You met them?" A look of surprise crosses on her face.

"I actually only met Val, but I did talk to Amber. She's the one that gave us the license plate number for the car that took you."

"Oh. Yes, I am sure they are both worried sick. It'll be nice to see them again. I would love for you to meet them under better circumstances; maybe have dinner at the diner. Val is an amazing cook."

"I think that's a great idea. What about this weekend?"

"Really!"

"Yes," I chuckle. "And maybe we can spend the weekend there and relax, I think we both need a little R and R."

She throws her arms around my neck as she jumps up and wraps her legs around my waist, planting kisses all over my face then squeezing me tight in the best embrace ever.

"You are going to love them," she says as she slowly slides down my body.

Feeling her on me that way makes me want her so badly, but before I take this any further, I need to find out who I am and why Di Fonzo said what he said. At least, I had the guts to look into his face when I took his life, unlike what he did to my parents', shooting them from behind, like a coward. My mind drifts back to that horrible day. A memory flashes through my head, just long enough to know it was a memory, but not long enough to know what it was exactly. I try to get it to come back but all thoughts melt away as I hear Samantha.

"Oliver, Oliver? Are you alright?" She touches my cheek softly.

I gaze down into her worried face. Clearing my throat, "Uh, I'm sorry, yes, I'm sure I'll love them. Do you want to make the arrangements while you're there?"

"Are you sure you are okay?"

"Yeah… yes, I just have a lot on my mind."

Once at the office, I start my search on my parents' and Victor Di Fonzo. Tiffany had my security team pull everything they could find, and the boxes were waiting for me beside my desk when I got in. They brought not only the banker boxes that I've been accumulating information in but anything that was current as well. There isn't a lot of information that I didn't already know. I spend the day pouring through everything I've got on both families. Piece-by-piece, page by page I scour and study them. Papers cover my desk as I painstakingly sift through them trying to find anything that will piece them together. I come upon my parents' marriage license, which brings a smile to my face even though it's bittersweet.

My memories have faded a lot since their death, and I'm trying hard not to forget. I sit and try to remember the good times we had. Mom would take me out on 'dates with mom,' and dad would take me on 'men's night out.' Sundays were our family time. We would all decide on a movie and we would have a movie night, complete with popcorn, candy, or whatever. I smile fondly at the memory. Laying it aside, I pull out the family portrait we had taken the Christmas before their death. It's funny that although my facial features are like my mother's, I don't look anything like my father. Both my parents' had blonde hair, but Mom had brown eyes and Dad had green. I know there is a recessive gene in there somewhere; I just don't know that much about them to understand how they work. They always told me I resembled my grandfather, but he had died when I was a baby.

I see the edge of another photo and pull it out. I sit there paralyzed. I'm staring at myself, but it isn't me, it's someone younger. Maybe in his late teens early twenties, and he even has my dimple. My breath hitches and my heart pounds hard in my chest. I taste the bile crawling up the back of my throat as the realization hits me.

My mind flashed to that day all those years ago. That memory that I've been trying to grab. *Di Fonzo stood in front of my mother. He said something to her, and she shook her head no. He backhanded her. My dad tried to protect her, but one of Di Fonzo's men hit him and he fell to his side. Mom cried out and Di Fonzo's voice got louder. I remember getting closer to the window to see if I could hear anything.*

"I warned you that if you left, this would happen. He belongs with us. He's part of our family; he's a Di Fonzo.

He is Victor's son, my grandson, and you took him away from us. First, I lost my son then my grandson. I'm here to take back what is mine. I'll ask you one more time, where is he?"

"I told you, he's not here. I don't know where he is. He's always home by now."

"You're wasting my time." Di Fonzo nodded as the big man grabbed my father by the hair to set him back on his knees.

It was at that moment that I looked in my father's eyes for the last time. He pleaded with his eyes to leave, and then he mouthed, "I love you." He knew what was going to happen next, and he didn't want me to witness the gruesome event. I tried to move, but I couldn't. My feet were glued to the porch. "This is your last chance, tell me where he is."

"I don't..." my mother started to say.

BANG!

Something hit the window, startling me, making me jump. I peered up, a big glob of blood slowly slid down the glass collecting in a pool of red on the once white windowsill in front of me.

"NO," my mother let out a cry.

BANG!

I clasped my hand over my mouth as if to keep the scream inside of me as the beige carpet of the living room floor slowly turned to red. I stared at the man that pulled the trigger, imprinting his face in my mind. It wasn't until I heard the door handle rattle that my feet became free again and I could move. I ran around the corner of the house and hid in the camellia bush.

The big man carried two rolled up pieces of the carpet out to a waiting van as the man with the gun got into the back of a big black car a few minutes later. I stayed there in the camellia bushes until it was dark. I was numb and shaking, but not from the cold.

Staying in the shadows, I ran to Mrs. Martin's house. She pulled me inside the house and retrieved an afghan from the back of the couch wrapping it around me as she put a pan of milk on the stove, then she called someone. I just sat there at the table trying to figure out if what I saw was real or not.

I vaguely remember someone knocking at the door. I heard them quietly talking about my father, then when I glanced up, there were two men sitting at the table. Mrs. Martin set a mug of steaming hot chocolate in front of me. It even had marshmallows in it. She said the men were friends of hers and to tell them what I saw.

They introduced themselves as Nicolas and Alonzo Perrotti and that they were friends of my parents'. They said they would take care of me.

That was the night I met Savina Baldini. A few months later, she became my new mother and they changed my last name to Baldini. It wasn't until Savina died and I became an adult that I changed it back to Drake. She had done so much for me. I didn't want her to think I didn't appreciate what she did. She was a wonderful mother, but there was always something missing.

I pick up the picture turning it to see if anything was on the back. I see what I already know to be true. Victor Di Fonzo, Jr. January 2, 1970 - June 2, 1991. I start throwing papers around looking for my parents' marriage license. I stand and push everything off my desk and the desk lamp crashes to the floor. Within seconds, Tiffany is at the door. "Mr. Drake," she asks with a concerned tone.

I don't even look up. I finally find the marriage certificate. "Get Ms. Hunter on the phone for me."

"Yes, Mr. Drake." She turns and quickly closes the door.

I look at the certificate as I slowly sink down into my chair.

I jump when my phone buzzes. "Mr. Drake, Ms. Hunter is on the line."

CHAPTER TWENTY-EIGHT
DIVINE HELP

SAMANTHA

Reynolds is driving me to the lake to pick up my car and belongings. I am so consumed with thoughts of Oliver and what happened the night before I don't even talk to Reynolds the whole way to the lake.

Although I am excited to see Amber and Val, there is a sense of foreboding that floods me and I can't shake it.

He pulls in front of the boarding house, next to my car. Stepping out of the SUV I check my purse for my spare key and send Reynolds on his way. I walk into the house, and speak to Mrs. Golden, the owner, and make arrangements for the weekend with Oliver.

I load my things into my car and then go to the grocery store. Before I can even get to the door, Amber is on me in a huge hug. "Are you okay? What happened? Where did they take you? Did Oliver find you or did they just let you go?"

She touches my still bruised and swollen face. "Oh my God, Sam, what did they do to you?'

"Slow down," I say as I pull away. "Can you take your lunch anytime soon? I want to sit down and fill you and Val in, but I can't stay long."

"Let me get Drew from the back and I can go." She runs to the back room and within seconds is back out and pulling me out the door.

We walk over to the diner where Val runs out to meet us. She has a girl training as a cook so she's able to sit with us for a few minutes before having to get back to the stove. I tell them what had happened and how Oliver found me and saved me. I didn't tell them about me shooting Frankie and Eugene though. Shock and disbelief are written all over their faces as I tell them who my father and grandfather are. I also let them know that both Oliver and I are coming back for the weekend and make plans to go out for the evening so he can get to know them.

Apprehension fills me and I can't eat, I just nibble at my sandwich. I decide I need to head back to Oliver. I know he needs me. I say my goodbyes and start back for Seattle.

Still feeling uneasy, I pull my phone out and locate Raven's number then call her. I figure that if anyone knows what is going on it will be her.

The phone doesn't even ring when she answers. "Sam, he's going to need you soon."

"Raven, what is it? Last night..."

"I know. He is going to find out some shocking information in the next hour or so, when are you going to be back?"

"How...? Never mind. I'll be there in an hour. Please tell me what's going on Raven, tell me what you know."

She proceeds to tell me how Oliver started remembering the conversation with Di Fonzo before he killed him. "He's going to learn that the father that he loved wasn't his real father."

"What do you mean?"

"His mother and real father fell in love. She got pregnant and shortly after found out who he was. She was scared and started to run. He went after her but was killed. Being pregnant and alone she went to an old friend and he agreed to marry her, hoping that the real father's family wouldn't find her."

"Who was it, Raven? Who was his father?"

"Victor Di Fonzo, Jr."

"Oh Fuck. He killed his grandfather."

"Yes he did, and his grandfather killed his mother and the only father he knew."

"Why would he do that? Why would he kill his mother?"

"Victor, Sr. had lost his only child. She was hiding the only part of his son that was left, and when Oliver didn't come home that afternoon, he thought she had sent him away somewhere."

"Do you know how he and my father and grandfather got together?"

"This goes real deep, Sam, real deep. All I know is he is somehow related to the Perrotti's." She explains that my grandfather and father knew who Oliver was all along.

"Is that's why my father didn't want Oliver and me together?"

"Yes, but there's more, I just don't know what it is. It's the ultimate Romeo and Juliet. Two rival family's children come together and fall in love."

"But with Di Fonzo dead, is this something that we're going to have to worry about?"

* * *

"No, anyone that knew about Oliver is dead."

"Oliver had all the information he has gathered on Di Fonzo brought to his office. His plan is to go through it all. Oh my God!

"What is it?"

"When I was leaving the motel, there was something familiar about Di Fonzo, but I was too exhausted to place it at the time. Oliver has his eyes."

"And his dimple," Raven says.

"I think he realized it last night and that's why he had the breakdown. Thank you, Raven, I didn't mean to pull you away from your job."

"Take care of yourself and Oliver. Things will work out."

It doesn't take too long to get to Seattle. I park in the garage under the building, stopping at David's desk to get my pass. My phone rings as I'm getting on the elevator. It's Tiffany, and I have her put me through to Oliver.

"Samantha?"

"Oliver, are you alright?"

"Samantha, I know you're probably still at the lake, but is it possible for you to come home early. I really need to talk to you." His voice is weary.

I step into his office. He looks like shit. His eyes are red-rimmed. I don't know if it is from the strain of going through the mounds of papers and files that stack his desk and floor or just the stress of his discovery.

He stares up at me with surprise on his face, but within seconds he's standing in front of me. "How..." I give him a sympathetic smile, "I thought you were at the lake?"

He takes my face in his large hands, slipping his fingers through my hair. "I had a feeling you needed me so I came back early."

"I was right, I killed..."

I place my fingers over his soft lips.

"I know. Shhh," I wrap my arms around his neck pulling him to me, "I know. Let's go home."

As we make our way out of his office and to the elevator, I see Lucas out of the corner of my eye. The look on his face goes from happy to disdain instantly. I grip Oliver's hand tighter as he peers down at me then over to Lucas. "This has gone on long enough," Oliver says sternly. He tries to pull his hand from mine, but I refuse to let it go.

I turn to him, placing my other hand over his. With a smile on my face and all the love I have for Oliver coursing through me, I say, "I'm okay; I can be the bigger person here and play nice with him. If he has an issue with that, then I'll take it up with Mr. Dunthorpe. If I'm going to work here, then I can't have you fighting my battles."

"If? What do you mean if? And yes I can, this is my goddamn company."

Stepping into the elevator, I turn to him and say, "Oliver, people already think I'm sleeping with you... Okay, well, I guess I am, but I wasn't at first."

"Sam, I have waited far too long to give a shit about some snot-nosed asshole that thinks he's the best. You have more talent in the tip of your pinky than he has in his entire being. If I want you to have that office and be his superior, then dammit that's my right."

I stare up at him in shock. "Do you really feel that way? I mean, honestly. You're not just doing it because we grew up together?"

"Sam, have I ever said anything that wasn't true just to make you feel better?"

"No, you've just told me that we would get through it."

"That's right. I would never say something to you unless I mean it. You're a very talented woman, Samantha Hunter, and I would be honored if you would stay on with my company and help me run it."

CHAPTER TWENTY-NINE
SECRETS

OLIVER

On our way home, we stop by Pike Place Market to pick up some fresh shrimp and sourdough bread for dinner. Samantha said she wants to fix dinner tonight.

I tell her that we need to talk about what I found out today and if and how it could affect our relationship. She doesn't seem to be worried, but now I see why Nicolas was so adamantly against us being together. After all, each of us was born into two of the largest crime families in the state, each vying for total control.

I don't know how many know about me, but I know several will know about Sam. Not that I am afraid for myself, but it would be nice not to have to worry about looking over our shoulders all our lives. Not to mention if we are to ever have a family.

After dinner, we sit on the sofa. Maxx and Levi jump up and lay down between us. "Now I know why your father didn't want us together." We sit facing each other as I peer down into her beautiful eyes of blue. "After reading everything I have today on my family, I think he might be right." My chest tightens, my eyes sting with tears that are trying to escape, and my heart feels as if it's being ripped to shreds as it's pulled from my chest, but I know what the right thing to do is. The look on her face is one of terror as her lower lip quivers and her eyes fill with tears. I glance away, not able to bear the tortured look in her eyes. As much as I love her and as hard as it will be, I have to let her go. I will do anything to keep her safe, and if that means walking away from her, I'll do it.

The terror that was once on her face is replaced with anger. The tears are gone, and the scared little girl is replaced with a woman possessed. Shit, she's never shown this side of herself to me before. She squares her shoulders and her back is ramrod straight. This defiant, strong Sam keeps her calm. The one who isn't terrified or intimidated by Di Fonzo. She jumps up suddenly, frightening the kittens and they claw at anything to escape the fury of wrath that is coming.

"If you think for one goddamn minute that I am just going to walk away, or let you walk away, then you forgot who the fuck you're dealing with. I don't give a fuck about who your family is. Let alone mine. We…," she motions her hand between us. "Are no different than who we have been all of our lives. I realize that you have known who my family is, but no one has known who yours was except my family, and they protected you. That is unless you're too afraid to be with me." She glares me dead in the eyes. Her eyes are squinted and her lips pursed.

She starts to taunt me as I leap from the sofa and we are standing inches from each other. "Stop," I say in a quiet voice.

"What is this Oliver? Did my father or grandfather get to you again? Or is this because now that you've found that it was your family that had me brutally raped, you don't want anything to do with me anymore and you think this is the easy way out," she says as a sob escapes her throat. She turns away from me trying to hide her emotions that are starting to come out.

I grab her shoulder and swing her around to face me as she quickly swipes at a tear that slipped. "You know that isn't true," I say in a stern voice but still quiet, trying to control my own emotions.

"Do I, Oliver? All this time you've kept secrets from me. My whole life is a lie."

"And what is mine, Sam? My grandfather killed my mother, and let's not forget I just blew his brains out less than seventy-two hours ago. My God, Sam. It's in my blood. I'm no better than they are. I don't want to have to worry about something happening to you again. I carry enough guilt about what just happened to you, if they come..."

She covers my mouth with her hand. In a barely audible voice she asks, "Oliver, do you love me," Her hand slides down and rests on my chest.

"More than life itself baby."

"I understand you're scared, I'm scared too, but are we going to let this rule our lives? I fought with a man that used to be my father to allow us to be together." She takes a step closer to me again and we are inches apart as she stabs me in the chest with her finger. "Are you telling me that you're willing to just walk away from me that easily? If so, then you're not the man I thought you were. This time it's all on you. You say you love me, then prove it."

She has me so riled up. My emotions are about to snap; I don't know how long I can keep this up. Can't she see just how much I love her, how this is killing me. Yes, I'm scared. I don't want to see her hurt again. My God, she almost died because I couldn't protect her.

I wrap my hand around the nook of her neck, startling her and pull her face to mine as my lips claim hers. There is no gentleness to my touch as I devour her mouth, fucking her mouth with my tongue. Our teeth clash, and I'm sure I'm bruising her lips. I hold her body tight to mine as my dick presses hard against her lush body. I crave her, she is my addiction, and I don't want to quit her. I want to drink her in, get drunk on her taste, and get high on her scent. I'll never get my fill of her. She moans as I thread my fingers through her long locks, pulling it tight at the root. She wraps her arms around my neck and her legs around my waist squeezing me tight. I feel her hot, body and the smell of her arousal makes me strain even more against my zipper.

She pulls away, our lips still touching as she asks, "What do you want, Oliver? This doesn't feel like a man who wants to walk away."

"God, Sam, don't you see how much I love and care about you?"

She twines her fingers through my hair, and this time, it's her taking what she wants as she consumes me. Our tongues dance in an erotic tango, and her hands roam my body fervently.

Taking a deep breath, I know I need to slow this down. She's still healing. I have to stop. As much as I want her, the timing needs to be right. I pull away staring her deep in her eyes. "Sam, we can't…I can't. You're still healing. I want our first time to be something so special. I love you and I want you to only feel me, not the soreness from what has happened to you." I whisper kisses on her cheek and then forehead, to the tip of her nose, and ending at her lips.

"Are you telling me that you don't want me, Oliver?"

"Hell no! Dammit, Sam, close your eyes and think of me. Think of everything we've been though. Now tell me that you think I'm saying no because I don't want you."

I watch her. Her eyes are closed and I recognize the moment she finally realizes I'm right. "Okay, Oliver. It's just that now I know you feel the same way as I do, I want more. I always thought I was a patient person, but when it comes to you…I've waited so long and I feel so insecure…"

"Sam, baby, look at me." She opens her sapphire blues to me. "I'm not going anywhere, ever. Because I've loved you for so long. I just want our first time to be without any outside distractions." I draw my finger along her jawline, to just below her chin and pull up to softly kiss her wonderful mouth.

CHAPTER THIRTY
OUR LOVE

SAMANTHA

I awaken to the smell of coffee. I reach for Oliver, but his side of the bed is cold. There isn't a trace of warmth at all on the sheets. I stretch, my muscles are sweetly sore, and wipe the sleep from my eyes just as Oliver brings me a large mug of coffee. I sit up in bed as he hands it to me. He climbs on the bed with me as I take a sip and close my eyes at the taste, it's perfect. As I open my eyes, Oliver takes hold of my mug with one hand, while in the other is a little black velvet box. I gasp as I gaze up at him then at the box. It's a good thing he took my coffee because I'm a shaking mess. I know we briefly talked about it, but that was only briefly.

"I know this isn't the most romantic way to do this, but I want this ring on your finger when we go to meet your father and grandfather."

"What, we're going to see them? When?"

"We leave within the hour. I promise I will make this up to you."

"Are you not even going to ask me?"

He set my coffee on the nightstand and the box between us as he takes my hands in his. A song comes on over his Bose speaker on his clock. I don't recognize it. I'm too preoccupied with what he is doing. "Samantha, I have loved you almost my entire life. I have dreamed that one day you would be my wife. All this time I have waited for you. I want to love and protect you, and for once be a family. Please agree to be my wife so I can prove to you every day just how much your love means to me."

Tears stream down my face as he pulls his hands away from mine and opens the box. Sitting inside is a stunning black band, inlaid with pink tanzanite and diamond begets, and a matching wedding band, the center stone of the engagement ring is a heart-shaped diamond. I've never seen anything so beautiful. I stare up at Oliver, speechless. I just nod my head. Then I hear the words to the song that's playing on the speakers.

All this time, we were waiting for each other, all this time I was waiting for you, we got all these words, can't waste them on another, so I'm straight in a straight line running back to you. The song is by One Republic.

It's so true; we have been waiting for so long.

He pulls the engagement ring out of the box and takes the hand that is currently covering my mouth, and he slips the ring onto my finger. Peering down into my eyes he says, "I wanted something just as unique as you are, Samantha, and I felt this design was perfect for you."

He cradles the back of my head as he pulls me to him, brushing his lips over mine and we're once again lost in our love.

CHAPTER THIRTY-ONE
LEAVING ON A JET PLANE

OLIVER

As we board the jet, Reynolds hands me a file. "Is this the file we have been waiting for?"

"Yes, sir, it just came this morning. I thought you'd like to view it on the way."

"Thank you, Reynolds. Yes, I would like to see how he's progressing."

"He's doing well, sir."

"Good," I say dismissing Reynolds to take his seat in the cockpit with Meyer's, the captain. Reynolds' was a pilot in the military so it works out great when we have to fly that he can be the co-pilot if necessary.

The Gulfstream G280, although not the largest of jets, accommodates my needs. With the comfort and safety it offers, it's perfect for me. I lead Sam over to sit in the luxurious cream leather chair and I move to the other side across from her and set the file on the table. As I set up my computer, Piper, the flight attendant comes back to great us.

"Good morning, Mr. Drake, is there anything I can bring you before we take off?"

"Good morning, Piper." I glance over at Samantha as she glowers at Piper. Piper is pretty, but doesn't compare to Sam's beauty. "This is my fiancée, Samantha Hunter." I keep my eyes locked on Sam's face. I don't want her to think that I'm interested in anyone but her. As I introduce her as my fiancée, Sam's eyes dart to mine. This is the first time I've referred to her that way.

"Oh my goodness, I didn't know, congratulations, should I bring out some champagne to celebrate?"

"Yes, that would be nice, thank you. Also, two coffees with cream and some fruit and pastries please," I say as I continue to gaze into Sam's eyes.

As Piper retreats to the galley, Sam says, "She's very pretty."

"Yes, but there's only been one woman that I've wanted to worship, adore, love and keep me warm in bed at night."

She smiles flicks her right eyebrow in a sexy way, asking, "And who would that be, Mr. Drake?"

Tilting my head to the side, the corner of my lip curls up in a playful manner. "Well, Ms. Hunter, if you have to ask that question, I must me doing something wrong."

As I reach for her hand, Piper returns with our champagne, a strawberry sits at the bottom of the flute. I lift my glass to hers as we tap the rim. A beautiful tone rings out. "To you, my love, thank you for making me so happy."

We take a sip of our champagne as Piper returns and carefully sets a tray brimming with fresh fruits and pastries down on the highly polished wood table. "We will be taking off in just a couple minutes, please make sure your seat belts are fastened."

"Thank you, Piper." I glance up, acknowledging her. As Piper leaves, I hear Meyer's over the intercom announcing our preparations for takeoff. The engines roar as we slowly taxi toward the runway.

I've never been a big fan of flying, but the information I need to obtain can't wait. I glance over at Samantha, her head is leaned back and her eyes are closed. I see she isn't a fan of take offs either. The engines start to whine and the wheels grip the runway and the centrifugal force pushes me forward. I force myself to push against it by leaning my head back. I feel the bump of the tires leaving the runway as the noise of the landing gear doors close and silences the sounds of the outside. As we climb to our cruising altitude, I open my eyes. Samantha's eyes are still closed. "Are you okay, baby?"

She nods her head and slowly opens her eyes. "Yes," she says in almost a whisper. "I'm always nervous on takeoffs."

I open the file Reynolds gave me and glean through the information that he's gathered. I'm very pleased with what I see, and I'm excited for the future and what it has to bring with this information.

"What are you going to do when we see my father and grandfather?"

"I need to know what they know. They obviously knew about my father and grandfather, which indicates they knew who I was from the very beginning. Why were they keeping me from them? Was this just some cruel plan they had to try to destroy my family; well, my grandfather? That can't be it. If it were, then they would have used me as a pawn, but all they have done is help me and keep me safe. I remember the look on Mr. Perrotti and Nicolas's face all those years ago in Mrs. Martin's house. They appeared distraught, as though they were truly upset with what had just happened. I just need to know, I need closure."

As happy as I am for the day, I am still torn with the secrets that have been kept from me. I now see just how much Samantha's and my life parallels each other's.

She glances down at her engagement ring. "What do you think they'll say?" she asks.

I reach across the table and run my fingers over the top of her hand. She slowly brings her eyes to meet mine. "I know this is the reason your father didn't want us together, but with my grandfather out of the picture, I don't know what his problem will be. I guess we'll find out when we get there."

Sam pulls a book out of her bag as I continue to study another one of my files and follow up on my email correspondents.

I've just hit the send button when Meyer's voice sounds over the intercom announcing our approach to the airport. My stomach rolls with the thought of what's to come. I'll be walking into the Perrotti office as if I have every right, when in all actuality I'm nobody to them. Yes, I love Nicolas's daughter and I've asked her to marry me, but I am a Di Fonzo; the enemy.

Reynolds has arranged for a car to meet us when we land. I see it through the oval windows of the jet as we taxi to the hanger.

We travel to the office in utter silence. I take her hand in mine as I run my thumb over her ring. "I love you, Samantha, and I hope you'll always remember that."

Sam's eyes flash to mine. "Why are you saying it like that? Is there something that you know and are keeping from me?"

"No, but now that I've found out who my family is, I don't know what your family will do."

"But they knew who you were all this time. Why would that change?"

"Because they didn't know I knew. That could make all the difference in whether or not they will accept me. Not to mention let me marry you."

Sam's face turns ashen and her breath hitches. "Do you really think they will do something like that, to keep us apart," she whispers.

I grip her hand tighter, it feels clammy due to nerves I'm sure. "I don't know baby; your father wasn't happy."

CHAPTER THIRTY-TWO
THE STORY OF MY LIFE

OLIVER

I drag the back of my hand over my lip, wiping away the beads of nervous sweat. I have no idea what the Perrotti's will say to me, but I have to show them that my feelings for Sam are true. I have always been loyal to the family. They're my family too, even though I'm not blood.

We pull up to the office building owned by the Perrotti's. Although they do deal in illegal businesses, they have reputable ones as well.

The sun beams off smoked mirror façade of the building as we walk through the huge mirrored glass doors. You can't see inside until the doors open. Sam grips my hand tighter. Although I've been here before, this is her first time to her family's office. Reynolds opens the door and we walk inside and up to the security desk. We're handed visitor badges and wait to be escorted back.

* * *

It's not more than five minutes when I see Nicolas striding towards us. His hand outstretched in greeting. "Oliver, it must be very important to get you to fly out here and bring my daughter with you. Samantha." He leans in and kisses her on the cheek before pulling her into a hug. He leans Sam back studying her closely. "I see you're healing well."

"Yes, nothing that time won't take care of."

He skims his hands down her arms to her hands. As he runs his hands down to her fingers, I can see the recognition on his face as his thumb slides over her ring finger where her ring is seated. His brows furrow as he glares from Sam to me then down at her hand. Rage flashes across his face as he glares at me through squinted eyes. He lifts her hand glancing down at the ring. "Is this the reason for your sudden trip?" He peers down at her belly. "Or are there more surprises that you're planning to spring on us?"

Before I can even get a sound out of my mouth, Sam is in his face. She rips her hand out of his grasp. "How dare you? You have no right to tell me what I can and can't do. You lost that privilege eighteen years ago when you walked out on my mom and me." People in the lobby of the building are starting to stop and stare at the commotion Samantha is drawing.

"Sam, this isn't the place to be doing this," I say to her.

She doesn't even turn to glimpse at me as she continues. "He's the one who started this in the lobby, not me. He should have thought about that before he implied that I'm a slut," she says, her eyes shooting daggers at Nicolas.

I step to her and gently place my hand on her shoulder and lean into her ear. The scent of her perfume distracts me briefly, but when I feel her relax under my touch, I whisper in her ear. "Baby, I know how mad you are, but you can't show disrespect to him in front of everyone. Wait until we are behind closed doors." She turns peering up at me, and her eyes start to calm. I kiss her on the forehead then rest mine against hers. "I love you, Sam, we'll get through this." She slowly nods her head.

"Of course, I'm sorry, father, for the disrespect."

I take her hand in mine as we both turn and look at Nicolas. His face is stoic as he rakes his hand through his hair and turns. We follow him to the elevators.

Once upstairs, we're led down a hall into a big office. I haven't been in this office before. There is a large desk to the right, to the left there are two black leather sofas facing each other and two upholstered armchairs at the end, a hounds'-tooth rug sits between them and a large black ottoman centered between the sofas acts as a table. A tray with a steaming French press and China cups sit waiting for us. "Please be seated, and I'll let Mr. Perrotti know you are here."

The outside wall is floor to ceiling glass and the view is spectacular. We sit with our backs to the window and Sam pours coffee from the carafe.

I stand when the door opens and Mr. Perrotti and Nicolas stride in. Anticipation, anxiety, nerves, hit me all at once, but I stand tall as I reach my hand to Mr. Perrotti and greet him. He then approaches Sam. She stands, and he pulls her into a big hug. "I hear congratulations are in order," he says in a gentle voice. He holds up Sam's hand and gazes at the ring, then glances up at her.

She smiles. "I'm happy, grandfather."

"Good, that's all we want for you." He turns and cocks his head to the side and raises an eyebrow.

"Grandfather, please. I love Oliver and have for many years. Please be happy for us."

He kisses her on the forehead then peers down at her. "Of course." He motions back to the sofas, "Please sit. What brings you both here on this surprise visit?" He fills his coffee and takes a sip.

I start to speak, but my words don't come out. I know the power they have and they can crush me with the flick of a finger. The last thing I want is to piss them off. I try to speak again, and this time, I sit up and square my shoulders. Sam takes my hand and twines her fingers with mine. Taking a deep breath and clearing my throat I say, "I know who I am. I put it together yesterday. I've been going over what Di Fonzo said about the prodigal son and then I searched through all the information I had on the Di Fonzo family…I found the picture of Victor, Jr. I know that Di Fonzo was my grandfather." I glance down at my hand that is joined with Sam's. I stare at Nicolas then at Mr. Perrotti. "Why did you do what you did? Why did you take me away? Why didn't you tell me who I was?" I start rambling off questions as they strike my tongue, not giving them the chance to answer them. "My God, I murdered my grandfather." My breath hitches. Not that I approved of what his thugs did to Sam, but could there have been another way?

I sit there waiting for some sort of explanation, glancing from one Perrotti to the other. Mr. Perrotti clears his throat as he peers over to me. "Your mother was my daughter."

Silence fill the room. The air thick. "Oh Fuck!" *Oh my God, oh my fucking God!* My eyes dart to Sam. No wonder they didn't want us together. She's my cousin. *Oh my fucking God.* This is so much worse than anything I could think of. I pull my hand away from Sam's as if I were burned. My heart is racing. The realization of the situation is just hitting Sam. *Fuck, I'm in love with her…she's my cousin, I've touched her, kissed her. Fuck I asked her to marry me. Oh, Fuck.*

"What," she questions shaking her head. "Why then didn't you tell us back in Reno? You knew how we felt about each other. You both just stood there and you didn't say anything. Why? You knew we wanted to get married, but you never told us why you didn't want us to." Sam stands up and starts to pace. Tears fill her eyes.

"Samantha, please come and sit. We will talk, and everything will be fine."

"Fine? Fine," she yells. "Do you know the acronym for fine? *Fucked up...* well I think we've crossed that line. *Insecure...* If I wasn't before, I sure as hell am now. *Neurotic...* Well, that goes without saying. And *Emotional...* Holy hell! Can my life be any more fucked up? I'm in love with my cousin."

"Please, Samantha, let's talk," Mr. Perrotti says.

"Talk? What's there to talk about? You can't change blood," she says. Samantha slowly walks over to the sofa. My eyes are burning from the unshed tears that I blink away. My heart has just been torn out of my chest as the weight of this revelation strangles me. My gut is twisting and my body has forgotten how to breathe. How the hell am I going to go on? I love Sam, how am I going to live without her. She is the only constant in my life.

I feel so alone, so empty, so numb. I never thought I would ever feel like this, but this revelation is just too much. I've always been strong, but the thought of never seeing Sam again, never holding her, being just out of reach of me is such a heavy burden to bare. The feeling in the pit of my stomach right now is as if all the butterflies that once fluttered with excitement just died and lay heavy in my stomach.

Mr. Perrotti starts to speak and pulls me back from the anguish and hopelessness that I am drowning in. "First off, I have no problem with the two of you getting married." Our heads snap up to stare at Perrotti's including Nicolas's.

"How can you say that? It's incest," Sam whispers.

"Actually, no it's not."

"Father, don't. It's best this way," Nicolas says in an angered voice.

"Nicolas, I've watched you for the last eighteen years. You walked away from the only woman you loved. You can't even think about looking at another woman because of the love you had for Jill. I'm not going to let your daughter do the same thing."

"I don't understand," Sam says. "You loved my mother? Then why?"

Nicolas starts to speak in a quiet voice, a loving fatherly voice. "Samantha," his voice breaks, "you might not believe this, but I loved your mother with all my heart and soul." Nicolas turns and walks to the window, peering out at nothing as he continues to speak. "When Di Fonzo got word that I was married and had a child, I couldn't risk anything happening to you or her," he says in almost a whisper. He turns back to us sliding his hands through his brown curls. "As much as it killed me to walk away, I knew it was for the best. Well, that's what I told myself, thinking it would help me sleep those lonely nights. I know now that I was wrong."

I can't believe it, for the first time in my life, there's a human side to Nicolas. His eyes glimmer with unshed tears as he proceeds to tell Sam his story. I honestly don't know how this will change for the better with Sam, because we are still related.

"Your mother didn't know who I was. I had changed my name when we met. I thought it would be a way to protect her, and then you after you were born. I did what I thought was best. I never told her who I was, if I had, it would have put you both in danger. So I left."

"You should have told her. She had the right to make that decision for herself. You broke her. She was never the same after you left."

"It was better that she was broken than to have both of you dead. I could barely live with what I had to do, but I would have died if they would have gotten to you or your mother. Even with what happened to you as a child... as much as I ache and am tormented about it, it was still better than death," Nicolas says.

I take Samantha's hand in mine offering her my support, but still not understanding how this could help us.

"I don't see how that changes anything though. We are still cousins."

"Your grandmother was the love of my life," my grandfather confesses. "When we got married, she wanted babies, lots of babies. But God had other plans. We got lucky when we got pregnant with Nicolas, but that was after years of trying. Your grandmother would volunteer at the hospital, rocking drug babies and unwanted babies that had no families. She came home one day, all worked up. She told me about this little baby that she'd been taking care of, a little baby girl. She was surrendered to the hospital and was found to have traces of drugs in her system. The hospital had a new policy that you could surrender a baby and walk away. Anyway, she fell in love with her. She knew she would have a hard time being adopted because of the drugs and they were going to discharge her and send her to an orphanage. Your grandmother was so upset. She didn't want her to be ignored and she didn't want her to be all alone. She had fallen in love with her. I loved your grandmother so much, I called and arranged to adopt the little girl. She had already been named and we kept that name, Sallyann."

Mr. Perrotti glances at Sam then to me. "My mother?"

"Yes, your mother. She wasn't blood, so it isn't incest. Yes, you are related in a sense, but not blood." I take Sam's hand in mine again and squeeze it. I think I breathe for the first time since hearing the word cousin.

"So what happened?" I'm almost on the edge of the sofa, wanting to drink in all the information, all the knowledge of my family that I had never heard before.

"Your grandmother, God rest her soul, died. Sallyann was fourteen when she passed. Sallyann had such a hard time with her death. Her mother was her world. They were so close. The bond they shared was different. Maybe it was because of how Sallyann came into the world, but whatever it was, it was strong. I couldn't give her the attention she needed so she started to act out, getting into trouble, and hanging with the wrong kind of kids. She met Victor, Jr. at a club. They hid their relationship for a long time. When your mother found out who Victor was, she knew she had to leave him. Victor went after her, but was killed in a freak car accident. It wasn't until a couple months later Sallyann told us she was pregnant." Perrotti peers up at me, chewing on his lip. He stands up and paces the floor as he begins telling the story. "Somehow, Di Fonzo found out she was pregnant and was gathering information on when she was due and who her doctor was." He talks with his hands, as they're moving and gesturing he continues. "He was trying to get his hands on his only heir; you. Thomas Drake was a friend of the family and a close childhood friend of Sallyann's." He peers into my eyes. I can see and feel the love in them. "Thomas loved your mother, he had for years. I knew he would love you too, that was just the type of man he was. He offered to help, so they got married right before you were born. I moved them away so they would be safe, and I cut all ties so Di Fonzo couldn't find them. That is until you were eight. Somehow they found your family, and well, you know the rest."

He comes back over to the sofa and sits down. "You're my grandfather."

He nods slowly. "Yes, that I am," he said in almost a whisper. A small smile turns up his lips, but it doesn't reach his eyes. "That's why I hid you after the death of your parents.'" He curls his fingers and sets them over his mouth as his thumb rests under his chin. "I didn't want them to make an example of you. I wanted you to grow up as normal as possible. My God, Oliver, you're my grandson and you watched him murder your mother and father."

"Why didn't you tell me any of this before?" I get up and stride over to the window as I run my fingers through my hair out of frustration.

He gently sets his hand on my shoulder as he stands behind me. "Do you really think you would've been ready to hear that your grandfather killed your parents'?"

I peer over my shoulder at him as I run my hand across the back of my neck. I shake my head. The tears burn my eyes again and I quickly blink them away. "Probably not," I say barely audible. I glance over at Nicolas. "What do you have to say about all of this?"

"I think you know how I feel, but obviously, my opinion doesn't matter. I know you love Samantha; that's never been in question." He stands and walks over to where we're standing as he rakes his hands through his hair then shoves them in the front pockets of his slacks and turns to me. "I always knew that this was a possibility, and it's nothing against you, Oliver. I..." He shakes his head and turns away from us.

Samantha stands and walks caringly over to where he's standing. "Father." Nicolas turns to look at her. "You have tried to protect me all my life," she says in a soft voice, "But things still happened no matter how hard you tried to protect me." She places her hands on his forearms, sliding her hands down to his. "I love Oliver, and of anyone I know, he can and will protect me with his life. He has proven that time and time again."

"I think it says a great deal that you both care so deeply for each other after all these years." I glance over to my grandfather and take in his comment.

Sam tilts her head to the side. "Father, I know we don't know each other well, but I do want you to be happy for us."

I can physically see his body relax. "Oh, Samantha, it's not that I'm not happy." Nicolas glances over at me, then back to Sam. "I've known for a long time just how much Oliver loves you, I've known for years, but... you're my only child, the only piece of Jill I have left." Tears roll down Sam's cheeks at the mention of her mother. "I left you and your mother because I didn't want you being dragged into this life. I know it's too late for that now, but that's what I wanted."

"And now," Sam asks.

Nicolas's face, which was once somber and held no expression begins to relax as a smile breaks across his face, and his shoulders let go and his body language changes. "Well, it sounds like we're going to have one hell of a wedding."

It was as if a light switch was flipped on with the change in Nicolas's demeanor.

Sam's face lights up as she realizes what he's just said. "I'll accept this on one condition," I walk over to where Sam is standing next to her father. "If I can throw you the best wedding this city has ever seen." A big smile breaks across his face as a look of hope flashes in his eyes.

"I just have a couple friends. We don't need anything elaborate. Small and quiet is fine." Sam glances over at me and I just shrug my shoulders. I don't care as long as she is happy, and although I am concerned about the safety of Sam and our guests. I know the Perrotti's will have high security, and while this isn't the way I wanted to get married, it will be something that she and I can talk about in private.

Lifting Sam's chin to look him in the eye, Nicolas says, "But we do, and I want to show off my beautiful daughter. Have you set the date yet?"

Shaking her head, she says, "No, to be honest, we haven't talked a lot about it yet. Oliver and I felt that it was more important to take care of the current issues first."

"You just let me know, and I will hire a wedding planner that will take care of everything for you."

"Thank you, father." Sam reaches up placing a kiss on Nicolas's cheek.

"It's time to celebrate," Mr. Perrotti says. "Oliver."

"Yes, sir."

"I'm your grandfather, and I don't expect you to be so formal with me any longer."

"Yes, sir... grandfather."

We spend the rest of the day celebrating with family. Grandfather and Nicolas tell me stories of my mother and grandmother, and Sam is able to get to know her father and grandfather a little more. I never thought I would ever feel this way. Never thought I would have a family outside of Sam and me, but it's nice to finally feel this way again. It's been far too long.

CHAPTER THIRTY-THREE
FAMILY

SAMANTHA

I never thought I would feel this way again after mom died. I knew I would have a family of my own one day, and while I look forward to that, there's always something different about having a parent's love and support. My father and I have missed a lifetime of memories and we both vowed to rectify that along with my grandfather. I know Oliver feels the same way.

We say our goodbyes as we promise to visit each other every few weeks, especially since my father wants to help with the wedding plans, including helping me find the perfect dress.

I feel as though I'm floating on a cloud. Things are finally starting to turn. I'm in love with my soul mate, we're getting married, and according to my father, it will be the wedding of the century. I have found my father and grandfather and I'm getting to know and love them both as I learn more about them and my family. I live in a beautiful apartment with two kittens that I have always wanted and have a dream job. There isn't much more I could ask for. I don't know if the smile will ever fade from my face.

I yawn as we board the jet. I hadn't realized just how exhausting this day has been. Oliver takes my hand as we walk to our seats. "How are you feeling about things," I ask.

"I think I'm still in shock." He glances over at me as he runs his finger over my ring. "After discovering the secrets of my family and then the confirmation of it followed by the bombshell about my mother and Victor, Jr., I'm a little overwhelmed and a lot surprised." He gazes down at our hands. Shaking his head, he peers back up at me. His beautiful blue eyes filled with uncertainty. "Never in a million years would I have guessed just how deep those secrets were. Then when Grandfather said that my mom was his daughter..." He peers down again as if trying to shake the thought from his head. "I thought I was going to get sick." He gazes back at me as tears fill my eyes. "Not only that, but I felt lost, a wave of hopelessness came over me as I saw my whole world crumbling around me." Holding both of my hands in his, he says quietly, "Sam, I don't know what I would have done. I've been in love with you for so long and then after last night. Sam, I don't know that I could go back to being just friends." His eyes glisten with unshed tears. "I felt as if all my dreams were right there and as I was grabbing them they were ripped out of my grasp, just as a sick and cruel joke."

I get out of my chair and crawl into Oliver's lap. "I know, baby." I cradle his face in my hands. "The world as I had known it shattered, too. The way Grandfather was so nonchalant about us being together... I just didn't understand." I gaze up at him and say, "We don't have to worry about that anymore." A smile spreads across my face. "Oliver, you have made me so happy." I shake my head, my hair whipping around as I wiggle and shake my body in a happy dance. Oliver laughs, a deep belly laugh, so carefree and happy. I don't know if I've ever heard him laugh like that. "We're getting married," I yell as I wrap my arms around his neck.

CHAPTER THIRTY-FOUR
BITCH, YOU'RE A FAN

SAMANTHA

I'm nervous. Today will be my first day back at work in over a month. There has been so much that has happened, not to mention that Oliver and I are engaged. A month ago, I didn't even know he owned the company I work for.

I rummage through the half-folded pile of clothes looking for my favorite pink blouse.

I need to stop living out of a suitcase. I had only been in the apartment less than twenty-four hours before I left. I hadn't unpacked, and I guess that's a good thing since most of my things were still in suitcases when I left, but now, I need to spend a day ironing all my clothes and get them hung up and put away.

I finally find something and then head to the kitchen in search of Oliver. I stop in the doorway and get caught up in the vision before me. To see Oliver in a suit and tie, working diligently at his computer…well, there are no words. He takes my breath away. He's so gorgeous, with his beard precisely trimmed, giving him a rugged, masculine sexiness. I don't know if I'll ever get used to him in his business attire. He's male perfection.

He takes a sip of his steaming coffee, and his tongue slowly swipes across his upper lip, licking the remnants of his coffee away. My tongue mimics his. God do I want to be that lip right now. He curls the fingers on his left hand, resting them on his mouth as he stares at his computer screen. Lust consumes me as I feel myself getting wet and my clit starts to throb.

"Keep looking at me like that and we'll never get to work." Oliver smiles, not even looking at me, but knowing I have been staring at him.

"How long have you known I've been standing here?"

He tilts his head slightly, a mischievous smile playing on his lips. "Baby, I always know where you're at. I have watched you from a distance all my life."

I walk over and wrap my arms around his neck, leaning down to whisper in his ear. "I'll have to show you my thanks later," I say as I nibble on his ear as he lets out a growl from deep inside his chest.

Oliver takes my hand as we walk to the office together. "So how many people know who I really am?"

"As in Nicolas' daughter, or as in you are the reason I started this company?"

I stop, shocked at his admission. "You started this company because of me?" My brows knitted as my eyes dart to his. Then I remember the comment that Dunthorpe made about the owner protecting a young girl in school. Holy hell.

"It's what I know. I'm a protector by nature, and I'm good at computers so I mixed the two. I want people to feel safe so I've been trying to make security affordable for everyone. There are a few people that know my story about watching you as a child."

"Dunthorpe?"

"Yes, he was one of my first hires."

"I figured he knew, he told me about you protecting a young girl when you were younger, but I didn't put it together because of the name."

"My father was a loving and caring man. He never treated me as if I wasn't his own flesh and blood. I remember him seeing me and mouthing that he loved me right before he was murdered."

"He saw you?"

"Yes," he whispered.

"I am so sorry, Oliver. What a horrible thing you had to witness."

"Anyway, I wanted to honor him by taking his name back. Savina was a wonderful mother to me, but there wasn't a bond. Maybe because I was so closed off after my parents' murder, I don't know." He gazes down at me, sadness and maybe regret fills his eyes, then a flash of hope. "It was you that brought me back. You made me feel again, made me want things that I never thought I would ever have again." He cradles my face in his hands. "Thank you, Sam. Thank you for showing me that I can love again and have the family I once had."

"Oliver, loving you is easy. You've shown me what real love is. Unconditionally."

Oliver leans down, taking my lips with his in a loving, gentle kiss.

We walk into the building and up to David's desk. Surprised, his eyes flash from me to Oliver and back again. "Ms. Hunter, welcome back, I'm sorry for your loss."

I don't know what Oliver told everyone, so I just play along. "Thank you, David," I say as he hands me my new ID card.

As we turn to walk toward the elevators, I glance up at Oliver and the corner of his lip starts to curl up. "I guess I should have told you that you lost a family member."

I smile up at him raising my eyebrow. "Oh really? And who was I supposed to have lost that has kept me away for the last month?"

"I didn't identify anyone in particular as that wasn't important," he says as we walk onto the elevator. "Your office is just as you left it."

"What? You said...?

"I know what I said... I lied." He confirms with a smirk. "I was willing to tell you anything to get you to come back to me. I was desperate, I wanted... no, needed you back." All signs of his smile are gone as he pulls my hand to his mouth and kisses it.

"I'm here now, and I'm not going anywhere," I say as I bat my lashes at him.

"Yes, you are." The smile is back. "And we need to talk later about dates and lists."

A big smile spreads across my face as I remember we're now engaged.

The doors open and I am so preoccupied with my thought of getting married, I walk straight into someone as I'm exiting the elevator.

"Oh shoot, I am so sorry, I was so pre..." I glance up and Lucas is staring down at me.

"Ms. Hunter, I see you've finally met Mr. Drake or did you not realize that's who you're standing next to." His eyes drop to Oliver and my intertwined hands. "Do I need to introduce you to him," he says in a contemptuous tone.

"Mr. Masters..." Oliver's voice is low, authoritative, and fierce.

I cut Oliver off. This is my battle not his. I drop my hand from Oliver's taking a step closer to Lucas. In a quiet voice, I say, "I told you this was between you and me. If you don't like my work, and you think you are better than I am, prove it. If you don't like me, for who I am, have a seat with the rest of the bitches waiting for me to give a shit, but if you still watch everything I do..." I take Oliver's hand again in mine as I start to walk past Lucas, "Bitch, you're a fan," I say as I stare straight ahead and walk past him. My face stoic, my eyes focused. Oliver squeezes my hand in silent support. I know what is happening with Lucas isn't over, far from it. That's his issue, and as I said to him, he will have to prove me wrong.

CHAPTER THIRTY-FIVE
THE BENCH

OLIVER

I thought I was going to bust out laughing hearing Samantha's comments to Masters. She's so quick witted, and the expression on his face was priceless. I know she wants to handle him on her own, and I commend her for that. But I won't allow any of my employees to be bullied, no matter who they are. I'll keep my eye on him to make sure it doesn't get out of hand.

Dunthorpe approached me about a marketing campaign. During a marketing meeting earlier this week. Sam and Masters got into another heated debate. Sam came up with the idea that if we could double our budget for this marketing event, it would prove, once and for all, whose marketing strategies would serve the company better. Sam even threw in her office, so in essence, if Sam loses, she'll give up her office to Masters. If she wins, Masters can no longer essentially harass Sam about her marketing style.

It was agreed that I was not to know the identity of the owners of the ideas, and all analysis was to run through our accounting department. Both projects were to be presented to Dunthorpe and unmarked by the author. I come into this by approving the budget.

The contest will last a month; at which time we'll name the winner. I saw both projects, and know the one that I like the most, and I can almost guarantee that it's Sam's. It's fresher and something new, not seen before. It identifies with the demographic that I'm trying to target, as well as cross-markets on different social media sites. The other one is good too, but it doesn't catch my attention as much as the other.

As the end of the day draws near, I find myself getting more excited and anxious. I've been working on what I hope will be a wonderful surprise for this weekend. Sam and I have spent a lot of time talking about the last month since her graduation. She told me about her time at the lake and her new friends. Little did she know, once I found where she was at, I checked both Val and Amber out. I figured that if she was going to be spending that kind of time with them, I wanted to make sure there wasn't anything in their past that could hurt her.

I have so many things planned for the weekend, and I have no idea how they'll come together, not just meeting and getting to know Sam's new friends, but a couple of other things that have to be timed just right. Reynolds texts me to let me know that everything is on track for my surprises.

The closer we get to the lake the more Sam fidgets. I can't keep the smile off my face as I glance at her squirming in her seat. "What," she asks.

My smile gets bigger with her question. "What, what?"

"What are you smiling at?"

"Really? You're sitting over there... Let me take that back, because you're not sitting, you're squirming around like a child needing to pee." She breaks out into a laugh.

"How would you even know what a child acts like when they have to pee?"

"It's my job to observe. I see all different types of things, storing them away in case I need to remember what it looks like, and you... look like a toddler that has to pee." She laughs harder.

"I'm just so excited for you to meet Val and Amber. I know you'll love them and they will love you too.

"I know I'll like them, too. After all, they did take care of you while you were here. So tell me a little bit about them."

"Well, Amber is the first person I met when I arrived. She knew I was running from something, but I didn't tell her what until the day I was taken." She tells the story about Amber's husband and how his addiction to steroids ruined their marriage. Then she tells me of how she met Val. Wow, I would not ever picture the woman that I met, that cold.

We pull in front of the B and B. Sam checks in and gets our key while I bring our luggage in. "Is this the room you stayed in while you lived here?"

"Yes, and it has such a wonderful view of the lake. Oh look, there are little boats on the water that are all lit up. Can we go down there first before we meet up with the girls?"

"Sure."

I take her hand in mine, lacing our fingers together as we stroll down to the lake.

"I've never been this way before," Sam says, as I take her to a special place I found when I had been here before.

"Oh my gosh, this is so magical, but it appears as if someone else knows this spot too." Her face lights up like a child on Christmas morning. There are twinkle lights in a couple small trees that bank a wood bench. The bench is exquisite, made from cut logs, and there's no conformity to it. It's amazing. It's dusk and the lights are getting brighter. "Wow, they even have a bench out here. Your spot isn't your spot anymore," she says teasingly.

I pull her close to me memorizing each moment. "Since you are here with me right now, it's ours." I kiss her temple.

"Oh, they weren't little boats they're floating candles, I wonder who put them out here, maybe we shouldn't be here, maybe someone has something planned." She peers up at me, raising her eyebrow.

"Well, we're here first, so, you know what they say."

"What do they say?"

"Possession is nine-tenths of the law. Let's sit and just enjoy the scenery." We sit on the bench, the back of which is intricately carved.

She turns to look at the carving as she runs her finger over it. "It's too dark. I can't read it." She fumbles for her phone then flicks the flashlight on, holding it up to read the inscription. She shines the light on the side of the bench where the detailed carving starts. "Oh my God, this is beautiful." She runs her fingers over the carving. Ivy and flowers twine together to make a border around the inscription. She slowly moves the light over when she sees the words that are framed in the middle of the bench. Her eyes light up when she sees there is an inscription. "Oh, look, there's something written on it." She adjusts the light. Her curiosity taking over now.

In you, I have found my best friend and my eternal love.
You are my constant, my always, my forever.
Dedicated to the love story of Oliver and Samantha

Her fingers cover her lips to hide the gasp that's hitched in her throat as she turns to face me, down on my knee in front of her. Tears swell up in her sapphire eyes and trickle down her cheek.

I open the velvet box that houses a black band with pink tanzanite and diamond begets inlaid in it. I take it out of the box and slide it onto her finger.

"I told you I would make it up to you. Samantha, you are and have always been my best friend and now my eternal love. I have loved you for more than half my life, and now I want to make you mine. Please tell me that you will marry me and be my constant, my always, and my forever."

"Yes, God yes! Oliver, there's never been anyone but you. I too have loved you for almost all of my life, you're my only constant, my always, and my forever."

I stand pulling her into my arms, absorbing this feeling of overwhelming love that saturates my soul. This amazing woman wrapped in my arms, the only woman I have ever wanted.

CHAPTER THIRTY-SIX
THE LAKE

SAMANTHA

My heart is still pounding as we walk back from the lake. I lift my hand up to gaze at the new addition to my finger. I don't know where he found them, but he knows me well enough that I don't always go for the usual and customary. "How did you arrange all of this?"

"I have friends all over the place." He intertwines his fingers with mine and then lifts them to his mouth. My body melts as his lips brush over my knuckles, sending goose bumps over my body. He squeezes my hand lightly and smiles down at me. I told you I would make up for the first proposal.

"The bench is amazing, aren't you afraid it will be stolen?"

He laughs, "If someone can actually get it out of the concrete that it is bolted to, then they can have it. But for now, this is our place. This is the place you came to find yourself, to find us. If I had my choice, this is where I would want to get married."

My eyes widen with surprise. "Really? Me too. I just don't think Dad will agree."

"As long as we can be married soon, that's all I care about now. I've waited long enough. I don't want to wait any longer."

I wrap my arms around his arm, hugging it.

We walk into the diner where Val and Amber are anxiously waiting for us.

They are both out of the booth and making their way across the diner before the door closes behind us. Amber squeals as she envelops me in a hug that has me gasping for air, and Val joins her.

"Val, I know you have met him before, but this is Oliver. Oliver, this is Val and Amber." I introduce them and they briefly shake hands.

"It's nice to finally meet formally. Thank you for taking care of her while she was here," Oliver offers.

"Let's go sit down. I have a place set up for us out of the way," Val says as she leads us to a corner spot. It's a slow night for the diner, so Val can sit and enjoy dinner with us while her staff tend to the patrons.

Oliver strikes up a conversation with Amber about her education, then somehow we get on the subject of Tyler. I'm surprised how she opened up to Oliver about him.

"Tell me about him," Oliver says.

As she talks about her life with Tyler, the love she carries for him is so clearly written on her face. It's obvious he's the love of her life, and I think even Oliver can see that. But as the story unfolds, her face falls into a sullen sadness. A lost love. It's heartbreaking.

"Do you still love him," he asks. I'm surprised he's getting so personal about this with her. Maybe he's feeling sentimental because of our evening at the lake.

"When Sam told me about you and how you were asking her every day to come back, yeah, I would do anything to get Tyler back if he was my old Tyler, but when he's on those pills or whatever it was that he was taking, he was a different person. Someone I didn't know. He scared me. Tyler is never far from my mind. I think about him all the time. I don't think I could ever love a man the way I loved him."

"What if I could help you with that," Oliver says as he punches something into his phone. "I know you were hurt, but if he were clean and had a job, would you consider it?"

"In a heartbeat. Yes."

The bell on the door rings alerting the staff that a customer has entered. Suddenly, Amber's face goes white and tears fill her eyes and see a young man with a slight Mohawk, a close shaved beard, and tattoos down his muscular arms. Amber peers at Oliver then back at the man, which I know now has to be Tyler.

He walks over to the table and reaches his hand out to Oliver. "Mr. Drake, it's nice to put a face to the name. I'm Tyler Ray."

Oliver stands and takes Tyler's hand. "It's nice to meet you too, Tyler. I've heard a lot about you, please, pull up a chair."

Tyler pulls a chair up and sits next to Amber, who hasn't said a word. Oliver proceeds to tell Amber about how he had found Tyler and got him the help he needed over the last month in a residential facility. Tyler knew he needed help, but didn't have the means to get the help he needed. Reynolds met with Tyler to see if he truly wanted to make the commitment to get better, and then he arranged everything up for him. Oliver has set him up with a job where he can get the training he needs as well as continued counseling. Although he will be randomly checked for steroids, he is on the path to a much better life.

"So what did you tell your family when you left all of a sudden," Amber asks.

"I told them the truth, that was part of the deal. I had to tell both mine and your family why you left me." He stares down at his lap. "It wasn't the hardest thing I have ever done, but it was hard to see the disappointment on their faces."

"If that wasn't the hardest thing you had to do, what was?"

"Coming here to see you, face to face, and to ask for your forgiveness. I know I was wrong, but I just couldn't see it. I'm so sorry, Amber, I know it will take time for you to trust me again, but if you will try..."

"And if I say no, that it's too late?"

I can't believe she is going to reject him after everything she said to me... to us.

Peering down at his hands folded on the table, doubt fills his face. "I understand. What I did to you was inexcusable. I'm very ashamed of myself that I would even think about taking drugs, I knew better. I'm sorry. I'll leave you to your dinner." He stands, stretching his hand to Oliver. "Mr. Drake, I will see you on Monday. Ladies, it was nice to meet you, too. Amber, I'll have the papers signed and ready on Monday."

Papers? Oh my God, the divorce papers that he never signed. Disheartened and dejected, he turns his back to us as he strides toward the door. I want to holler at Amber to run after him, but maybe there is more to the story that I haven't heard.

Amber's head hangs somberly and I see tears drop from her cheeks. The bell from the door dings his departure. Again, I want to kick her under the table. I want to yell at her, tell her life is too short to focus on the past, and that if she still loves him to go after him.

Amber glances at Oliver; her eyes are puffy and her cheeks tear-stained. "You set this up for him?"

"Yes."

"He finished the rehab program?"

"Yes. He's a strong man. He knows what he wants. It was hard for him to face what he did to you, but he wants more out of his life. He found the confidence to help him fight. It won't be easy, but I've given him all the resources that he'll need."

Suddenly, Amber bolts from the booth as the bell sounds. I watch as I see Tyler striding through the door with his head held high. They stop mere inches from each other, both gazing deep into each other's eyes as Tyler takes Amber's face in his hands and brushes her tears away with his thumbs.

"I can't just walk away without you getting to know me again. You loved me once. We said it would be forever. I know you tried, and I was an idiot. I am so sorry. Now it's my turn to fight."

"Tyler, marriage isn't a fifty-fifty split, we both have to give one hundred percent or it won't work. So if you're going to give less than one hundred percent, there is no need to try."

"Yes, I know that. I plan to give everything I have to fix what I broke. I was just going to carry you until you were ready to walk again," he tilts he head to the side, "Please let me show you."

Amber just stands there staring at him. I can see a battle raging through her mind. I know how much she loves him; it's written all over her face. After what seems like forever, she slowly nods her head yes.

A smile spreads wide across his face. You can see just how much he loves her. He leans down and kisses her softly on the forehead. "Thank you, I'll make you proud of me again."

Amber's glistening eyes light up with sheer happiness. Tyler links his finger around hers and brings her hand to his mouth, kissing it softly. "I'll let you get back to your friends, we'll talk later."

Amber's face falls with dejection as Tyler kisses her on the cheek. He lifts her chin to look him in the eye. "I'm not going anywhere. I have a place next door for the weekend and..."

"Tyler," Oliver says, "Come join us." God, I love this man.

"Thank you, Mr. Drake, but I don't want to intrude. This is your time."

"Exactly, it's my time, and I have invited you to come and eat with us, please." The smile that once had faded from Amber is now full of hope as she glances up at him.

Tyler runs his knuckles over Amber's cheek. "Only if it's alright with you. I don't want to intrude any more than I have this evening."

"I would like it if you stayed," Amber says as she peeks up at him through her damp lashes.

He nods his head as he places his hand on the small of her back and guides her to the table.

Tyler pushes in Amber's chair before seating himself. Wow, if this is the way he always was, I can see why she was never able to get over him. Amber places her hand on the table, and Tyler slowly runs a finger over each part of her hand. It's loving, endearing, and erotic in its innocence.

Oliver places his hand on the back of mine, which is resting on my thigh and slowly fingers my ring, and then interlaces our fingers together, his palm to the back of my hand with a soft squeeze. My heart skips a beat and goose bump rise over my skin at his touch. As much as I want to be with my friends, I would much rather be spending the weekend in bed with Oliver.

It's so nice to be able to just sit and get to know each other. It's something I haven't done in a long time, and really the first time with Oliver. Val talks about her plans for the diner and how my marketing strategies have helped bring in new business. Oliver, with his business sense that I never knew he had, shows her some additional ideas he has as well. He listens intently to every conversation and interacts as if he has known everyone at the table for years. He leans over, kissing my cheek as he wraps his arm around my shoulder, making little designs with his finger on my arm.

When our food arrives, he leans into me, and the scent of his cologne sinks deep into my core, tightening every muscle as he brushes his lips across my ear. "I hope our room has good insulation in the walls." There's a mischievous glint in his eyes as a searing heat settles between my thighs. I squeeze my legs together trying to quench the desire I long for. I lick my lips as he runs his hand from my knee to my thigh. I place my hand on his to stop his progression to my inner thigh as I try to pay attention to what Val is saying about her plans, but in all honesty, I haven't heard a word she has said once Oliver whispered in my ear.

"So have you two set the date?" I'm pulled back from my Oliver haze, to the question Amber has just asked.

I glimpse up at Oliver, shaking my head slightly then turn my focus to Amber "No, we've been so busy trying to find normal that we haven't even talked about it." I glance up at Oliver and suggest, "Maybe we can decide a date this weekend. This is the first chance we've had to relax."

"I think we can set a date, but I don't want to wait longer than necessary," Oliver says.

"But I wonder if we can even find a venue that will be available. With Dad wanting to have something big and flashy..."

"We'll set the date and they can work around it. It's simple," he says, "As long as we don't have to wait, I don't care where we get married."

The server comes out with our dinners. Steam rolls and twists from the plates as the smells mingle together. "Oh, Val, this looks wonderful," I say as I close my eyes and inhale deeply. We eat in relative quiet as we enjoy our delectable meals.

"We should go to the club after dinner," Amber says, her eyes gleaming with excitement.

"I haven't had the best of luck the last couple times I've gone clubbing." I say as I raise one of my brows, but deep inside I just want to get back to our room.

She smiles at me. "But you don't have to worry now, you have Oliver here to protect you." She peers at Oliver batting her lashes at him. Oh, brother. Please. "Say yes Oliver, I know she loves to dance and I know she's always wished it was you on the floor with her."

His indigo eyes shimmer with delight as the corners of his eyes crinkle and he gives me a lopsided grin that brings out his dimple. "Well, I did say we need to make new memories, and we've never gone dancing. I think it's about time, don't you?" I never went to any of my school dances, not even prom. I hadn't even seen the inside of a bar until Kassidy started dragging me along with her in college. There was only one person I ever wanted to share those special times with. Yes, it is time to make new memories.

"Dancing it is," I say quietly.

Val declines to come with us, and I think because she feels as if she would be the odd one out. Even though these days, you just get on the floor and dance, you don't need a partner.

As we start to walk out the door, Oliver turns to say something to her. Then he pulls his phone out and punches something on it then slips it back into his jacket.

Amber, Tyler, and I are standing outside in the moonlight. The sky is dark, lit only by the moon and all the twinkling stars. As I gaze up, I see the big dipper, then the little dipper, and finally Cassiopeia. This is the first time I have ever seen it. I remember studying about it in school, but to actually see it is cool. Out away from all the city lights the stars stand out so bright and clear. Suddenly I'm privileged with the flair of purple, blue, and yellow lights as a falling star streaks across the sky. I take in a deep breath. Inhaling all the summer fragrances of floral and pine; reveling in the beauty of this wonderful place.

I'm so engrossed with what I'm seeing I didn't even hear the bell on the diner door as Oliver steps out to join us. Not only that, but Reynolds is here and Val is standing next to him. Where did he come from? I didn't even know he was here.

Oliver slips his long slender fingers between mine and asks, "Are we ready."

"I was born ready," I hear Amber say behind me as she laughs.

Oliver squeezes my hand in a knowing gesture as we start to walk toward the club. "Where was Reynolds?"

"He was here checking on the security here and at the B and B. You might not see him, but he is always around." With that I relax a little more.

Walking into the club, I inhale sharply at the memory of the last time I was in here. I now know that Paul was a good person, but back then, I was scared and just wanted to get away. My pulse spikes as my mind replays the kidnapping.

The music is loud, and the beat vibrates through my body. Knowing Oliver is here to protect me allows me to take that deep breath that calms my nerves, but the shots of tequila also help.

There are only a few people on the dance floor. We easily find a table as a tall redhead strides over to us in her ripped jeans and low cut V-neck, black T-shirt. She bends down, placing her order pad on the table and staring straight at Oliver. Her shirt is so low her fake boobs are practically spilling out onto the table. I scowl at Val then Amber, tilting my head as if to say, *really.* But I have to say, our men pay no attention to her, not even Reynolds, who barely acknowledged her, not even to give her his and Val's order.

I don't want to wait to get our drinks; I want Oliver out on the dance floor. I place my hand on his well-formed thigh and slowly run my hand down his knee then back up. My hand travels further north, and I rub from base to head, his erection growing and straining under the tight denim of his jeans. I lean up into his ear, softly breathing into it as I run my tongue along the curl of it. I whisper, "The sooner you take me on the dance floor and make new memories, the sooner you can take me to our bed and make memories. The bed that I laid in night after night, wishing you were in it with me, holding me." I lick his ear again before taking the lobe into my mouth, nibbling on it.

With a mischievous glint in his eye and a smile on his lips showing off his dimple, Oliver takes my hand and pulls me out of the booth. My stomach flutters with anticipation as I bite my lower lip trying to hold off excitement I'm feeling.

Our server returns with our drinks just as we're stepping out of the booth. Closing my eyes, I toss back the shot of tequila, savoring the flavor and the burn as it travels down my throat warming it.

Oliver leads me to the dance floor. The music pulses through my body, immersing me with the rhythms that fill the room. I close my eyes and absorb, the energy as I start to move. Dropping all my inhibitions, I raise my hands in the air and dance. Letting the music permeate me, move me, relax me. I haven't felt this free in a long time.

Strong hands slip around my waist and for a fleeting moment, I panic. Soft warm words at my ear sooth me. "Yes baby, relax, and let it go. I have you now and will protect you." He pulls me into him, my back to his front. His body is hard and warm. His scent is so intoxicating.

I turn around throwing my hands around his neck, taking in everything that is all Oliver. This is what I longed for all those times, My Oliver. He leans down, whispering in my ear, "God, Sam, the way you move and feel. I am so lucky. I love you so much." My eyes burn with unshed tears as I feel consumed with the love I feel for the man that is holding me tight in his arms.

In our room, I excuse myself to the bathroom. I've planned and waited for this night. There's nothing in the way tonight. No threats, no demons, and no concerns. Just love. Our love.

I'd tucked a special little outfit into my bag and intentionally placed it in the bathroom. My stomach flutters with anticipation and the reaction I hope to receive from Oliver when I walk through the door. As the silk of the gown slowly melts down my body and over my curves, my ring catches the light, winking kisses at me. My pulse spikes, and I blink back the tears as I remember what he did for me earlier. The bench, the lake, and the proposal. It was amazing and perfect.

I glance at myself in the mirror, brushing away my unshed tears before opening the door. I pull the door open and search for his face, but I think my face is more surprised. There are candles lit throughout the room, and as my eyes adjust to the light, I hear the bubbles of champagne already poured into flutes, and see a plate of strawberries and whipped cream sit on the table. A small gasp escapes my mouth. My fingers cover my lips as the tears that I tried to keep from falling have now been released. I catch the look on Oliver's face as his eyes gaze up and down my body, landing back on my face again. His lips curl in a seductive smile that spreads across his striking face, releasing that beautiful dimple. Yes, that's the reaction I was hoping for.

Oliver is standing in just his jeans, no shirt and barefoot. God, he has sexy feet. I never thought of myself as a foot person, but there is something about him barefoot that makes my body burn. Desire shoots through me like a bolt of lightning as he steps toward me, drinking me in. The seductive gleam in his eyes tells me he's about to devour me.

He hands me a flute of champagne. My skin tingles at the touch of his fingers on mine. I inhale sharply, breathing in his masculine scent as it engulfs me, sending a warm pulse of need between my thighs. I squeeze my thighs together trying to stave off the heat burning amid them.

We clink our flutes together, "I have loved you for so long. I never thought I would be so lucky for you to feel the same way as I. Thank you for loving me." he says in a low tone. We maintain eye contact. I'm simply unable to look away. He mesmerizes me. He isn't just beautiful... he is entrancing. But even more than that, it's the connection I have with him, his inner self. Yes, I love his beauty with my eyes, but it's his heart I fell in love with; everything else is irrelevant.

We sip our champagne. He takes my hand leading me to the bed, taking my flute from me and setting it on the table with his. I shudder as heat rushes through me. He takes me into his arms, drawing me close. My chest heaves and my pulse is racing with anticipation.

His thumb brushes over my lower lip, my eyes raise to his as we stare into each other's eyes, communicating silently. His eyes are not the normal indigo; now; they're darker. Full of need and desire. I run my hands up the corded muscles of his back, feeling his hard body. I thread my fingers through his hair, pulling his lips to mine. Tasting him, wanting him, and needing him. He picks me up, and as I wrap my legs around him, I smell my arousal as wet heat builds in my core.

CHAPTER THIRTY-SEVEN
MAKING LOVE

SAMANTHA

Oliver carefully sets me on the bed, his eyes burning with desire, as the ache between my thighs grows stronger and deeper. I never thought I would want this, but as I fall deeper and deeper in love with him, I should have known he would be the only man I would ever want to make love to me, to show me what love truly is. He's the only one to make me forget. My Oliver.

I can actually feel my clit throbbing and pulsing with need.

Gazing down at me his eyes never leaving mine, "You are the most beautiful thing I've ever known. I've dreamt and fantasized of this day with you. I've envisioned this moment for so long."

There's a tightening in my belly, one that I've never felt before, radiates down to the apex of my thighs, damp with need. I wonder if that's normal. I continue to stare into his eyes, now midnight blue, the most perfect color I've ever seen.

He slowly takes the hem of my gown and pulls it up and over my head, dropping it on the floor in a puddle of silk.

He leans into me and takes my mouth with his. His soft, warm hands caress up my ribs to my breasts, gently massaging and making the nipples harden at his touch. Leaning down, he takes a nipple into his mouth, swirling his hot wet tongue around the tip then tugging gently with his teeth. Goose-bumps layer my skin as I let out a moan and my body shudders. He carefully rolls the other nipple between his thumb and finger. "Oh, Oliver," I say as he teases my nipples more.

"Baby, you are going to see what it's like to be worshiped like you should always be."

He slowly kisses his way down my belly. My inner muscles clench with anticipation. I've never wanted anything as badly as I want Oliver at this moment. My breathing harsh, my chest heaving as my head sags back with all the sensations I'm experiencing. Not from fear, but from all these feelings I've never felt before. He's so gentle. Making sure every touch is okay for me, showing me that *he* is the one touching me as I gaze into his mesmerizing eyes. I slide my hands up his broad, toned shoulders, then to his corded muscular chest. Just a dusting of dark hair clusters down his sternum. I run my fingers down his well-defined abs. I draw my index finger down his happy trail, that leads down to his jeans vanishing under the waistband. His well-defined *V*, starting at his hips points to the place I will soon see again.

He tenderly skims his hands up my thighs as he continues to kiss his way to my mound. I hear as he inhales a sharp breath, and feel the vibrations as he groans, "Oh baby."

My body shivers with anticipation. This feeling is more than I hoped for. My body clenches with excitement. I can hardly breathe with every sensation he's giving me. I feel moisture running down my inner thighs.

"Oh, Sam." He leans into me, drawing his tongue up my inner thighs licking the moisture that has slid down my legs as a low rumble from deep in his chest vibrates against me. My body trembles at his touch, and I let out a moan. My belly twists with anticipation for what I've never experienced before, for the love he's showing me. I peer down at him for as he gazes up at me for acceptance. His eyes are full love and caring.

He closes his eyes as he leans into me, running his tongue between my soft folds. I almost collapse as he finds my clit and rubs his tongue over and around it. I try to balance myself as I thread my fingers through his dark, thick curls. Whimpers escape my lips, and my head falls back. My breaths come in short pants as the sensation between my thighs builds. The muscles clench with each touch and each warm swipe of his hot moist tongue. I feel as if I'm going to explode. Then he is gone. A cry escapes my mouth at his absence.

I pull my head forward as a sense of emptiness fills me. I open my eyes. He is standing before me, staring at me. I gaze into big pools of blue, full of need, want, and desire, and then I see love as he blinks. Our eyes never leaving each other's as we keep this union between us. He reaches down, and slowly unbuttons his jeans and undresses. In only boxers, he gazes down at me. "Please, Oliver, make love to me."

He tilts his head to the side as he looks lovingly at me, "Lay on the bed, baby." I turn and crawl on my hands and knees to the middle of the vast king size bed, lying in the middle as I hear him groan from behind me. I clutch the silky sheets in my fingers as I wait with anticipation. "Oh, Sam, you are so beautiful."

I watch as he slowly slides his boxers down his legs, releasing his large, hard erection. *Oh my, God,* he's perfect. I can't stop staring at him. Adonis comes to mind.

He crawls onto the bed and I sit up, taking his length in my hands. I gaze up into his eyes, feeling his erection, imprinting this moment in my mind. There's a drop of dew on the tip of his broad crest, and I slide my thumb over the tip and to the sensitive ridge of the crown. I gently rub as Oliver's head sags back and moans escape his mouth. His erection jerks in my hand, and he somehow gets larger as I touch him. "Aw, Sam. If you don't stop..."

I slide my hands up his chest and goosebumps form on his body and his cock jerks again between us. I cup his face, pulling him to me as my inner muscles tighten. I long for him to be inside me, putting out the fire of desire that's burning deep inside me. We're both on our knees as he pulls me to him, and the once soft kisses are replaced with passionate ones, deep, raw, and intense. I slide my hands through his hair, pulling as he does the same to mine, angling my head so he can feed off me, kissing, nibbling, and sucking my neck. I can't breathe, but I don't care.

He slides his hand to the nape of my neck as he lays me down on the bed and positions himself over me. He's kneeling between my legs. I'm panting; I feel out of control. I want him, and I will do anything to have him inside. He slowly slides his body down, resting on his forearm. He stares deep into my eyes. Holding his erection in his hand, he positions it between my small wet folds, and rubs it along my opening, teasing it. Then he rubs it over my clit, making every muscle inside me dance with excitement and need. I don't know how much longer I can take this. I pull him closer to me; I feel as if I'm going mad. I take his mouth with mine, and draw his bottom lip between my teeth, He lets out a loud growl and pulls away. I wonder if he's mad as he glares down at me with dark, heavy eyes. His lips curl up and his lips crash against my own as he devours me. We've both waited so long for each other. It's as if we are addicted and bingeing on each other.

I reach down and take his erection in my hand and position him at my opening. I wrap my legs around him just under his ass and pull him in with the strength of my legs. I need him. Now. He breaks the kiss, but his eyes remain locked on mine. The look of ecstasy on his face is intoxicating. The feeling of him inside of me, filling me, stretching me. It's…Overwhelming. "Oh God, Oliver," I whisper.

I swivel my hips against him and he sets the pace. Our hips dance in unison. I reach my hands down to his ass, pulling him deeper inside of me. His balls slap against my ass. "Sam, my God... you feel... Oh God, you feel so good." We're absorbed in each other. Our rhythm, perfect as he hits every sweet spot.

He wraps his arms around me and rolls, pulling me on top of him. I grip his hands leaning forward and ride him. He feels so much longer this way, hitting my core as I feel a building sensation deep inside. I let go of his hands and lean back on him, my hands on his thighs as I ride him. My eyes flutter closed as my head falls back, and I revel in this feeling I never thought I would have. "Look at me, baby, feel me inside you." He groans out roughly as he clutches his hand tightly around my hip. Lazily, I peep through my lashes ant his request. He sucks his thumb into his mouth. Then places it on my clit, massaging small circles as my body explodes. I scream out his name and my body quivers as my orgasm rips through me. Stars flash in my eyes as I gasp for air. He continues to press on my clit and the sensation erupts again. "That's it, baby, feel me. Feel the love I have for you." He grips both of my hips and moves me back and forth, harder and faster. He rolls over, pinning me beneath him as he thrusts into me roughly. He hits a totally different area inside of me, and I raise my hips to meet his. I feel the building in my core again. Oh, this one is different. It hits everything. Oliver's cock swells and pulses as he exclaims "Sam, oh Sam, awe. I fucking love you so much. You feel so good!

"Oh, Oh, yes!" My body explodes again, and I feel a heat inside me as Oliver finds his release. Oliver collapses on top of me, trying to catch his breath. Both of us glisten with sweat as I run my nails down his back, and he kisses my neck and nibbles my earlobe.

"You are amazing. Your body is so responsive. I love you," he says as he gently kisses my lips.

I'm filled with emotion as I fight back the tears. But, Oliver sees the glimmer in my eyes as he gazes down at me. "Samantha? Did I hurt you?"

He gently kisses me. I can't speak, I try, but nothing comes out. Oliver rolls off me and pulls me to his chest. "I'm sorry Sam, I shouldn't ha..."

I lean up, still trying to catch my breath as I hover over him and cover his mouth with mine, taking him by surprise. When I pull away, I run my fingers over his lips. I gaze into his beautifully sad eyes. "I never thought I would feel like this Oliver. I never knew that making love was supposed to incite so much emotion." I lean over and kiss him again. I snuggle back down into the crook of his arm reveling in the love I feel for the man that has just shown me what love is.

CHAPTER THIRTY-EIGHT
THE DATE IS SET

SAMANTHA

I awaken to the touch of Oliver's fingers skimming over my body; up my arm, over my shoulder, down my back, then up again.

My eyes flicker open and I see beautiful pools of indigo staring back at me. They're so full of love. He's lying on his side, his head propped up on his hand as the other one explores me with its touch. "You look so beautiful when you sleep, so carefree and at peace.

I turn to my side facing him. "Good morning to you, too." I raise my hand to his face. I softly run it down his slightly dark stubble chin. Pushing a wayward curl out of his face, he takes my hand and kisses my palm. I gaze at his hard toned chest as a small moan escapes my lips. My eyes flash to his face, and a big smile stretches across his as his eyes light up.

"So I take it you like what you see?"

I bite my lip trying to stave off a giggle, but I'm unable to speak as I gaze into those eyes. I'm so caught up in him. I simply nod my head. My eyes widen, and I run my tongue over my bottom lip as if starving for what's in front of me.

"How are you feeling this morning," he asks, smiling down at me.

"How long have you been awake for?"

"For a while."

"Oh." I glance down, almost embarrassed. Shy, insecure…I don't know.

He again asks, "You never answered me. How are you feeling?"

He tips my chin up so I won't look away again. "A little sore."

"Oh," he says with a resigned voice. "I should have been easier on you. Taken it more slowly."

I shake my head. "No, it's a good sore, and if you hadn't asked, I wouldn't have paid it a lot of attention. How are you feeling?"

A smile slowly stretches across his beautiful face. His dimple deepening as his smile becomes larger. Sweeping a strand of hair over my shoulder, he traces the outline of my lips, my cupid's bow with his long tapered finger as his eyes raise to mine. "Amazing. Words can't express what I'm feeling, Sam. It was more, you were more, than I ever imagined, and the feelings I have inside are ready to explode. I love you, Sam, and making love to you last night has shown me just what I have missed all my life." He leans over me as I fall onto my back. His warm hands slowly feel up and down my body. I feel a tingle between my thighs. I need him. I want to show him how much I love him.

I wrap my arms around his neck, one hand threading through his hair and the other clawing at his back as moans emanate from his chest and escape as he opens his mouth, letting his tongue explore mine. He tastes of cool mint, but his mouth is far from cool. It is hot, and full of need and desire. I reach for him, taking his silky hard erection in my hand, gripping it as I slowly stroke him, making him roar with passion. "Oh God Sam, what you do to me, I can hardly contain myself. You're sore, we need to wait. I don't want to hurt you."

Ignoring what he's saying, my lust for him takes over. His cock still in my hand, I place him between my hot, wet folds, teasing not only me but him, too. I wrap my legs around him, and tilt my hips, he slides into me making me tremble. I moan at the feeling of him as he sinks into me. Stretching and filling every part of me as ecstasy consumes me.

I have so much going through my head about the wedding. I know my father wants to help, but I don't want to be bullied into something I don't want either. We already conceded to a big wedding back home when I would have preferred a quaint wedding here at the lake. Oliver and I are sitting at the diner writing down what we both would like to have for our wedding day.

"Okay you two, put those pads aside and get ready. I have some new recipes that I'd like for you to try." My mouth drops open with the amount of food Val carries to the table. All I had asked for was some fruit and coffee, but she is balancing two plates on her arms and one in each hand. "This is crème brulee' French Toast." She sets it down in the middle of the table. It looks amazing. The top is caramelized with burnt sugar, and the bread has to be at least two inches thick. "Biscuits and gravy, filet mignon, chicken fried steak, and Eggs Benedict." Not to mention the additional eggs and smashed baby Yukon gold potatoes.

"Val, you do realize there is only two of us, right?"

She eyes both of us with a wry smile. "Don't forget, I was at the club last night. I saw the way you danced together." She quirks a brow up at me. "I know you need to refuel. Besides, these are possible new items to the menu. So, tell me what you think. Enjoy." She winks as she turns and walks back into the kitchen.

Oliver smiles a playful smile. "What," I say as I tilt my head, loving his playfulness.

"You didn't get your fruit."

I close my eyes and shake my head, as if, I would be able to eat it if I had gotten it. I glance over all the plates of food. It all looks heavenly. The chicken fried steak and the biscuits are all smothered in homemade country sausage gravy. I dip my fork in and taste it. Oh God, I think I died and went to country gravy heaven. My mouth waters longing for more. It's my breakfast weakness. A moan escapes my lips. Oliver laughs at me. "Don't laugh until you try it."

He picks up his fork and slices through the thick piece of French toast and places it in his mouth. His eyes light up as a moan leaves his mouth. I giggle at his reaction then slice my own bite. It's like an orgasm in your mouth. The custard inside is amazing.

We eat until we're satisfied. I feel guilty for what we left, but there's just no way we can finish the bounty in front of us.

I flip the page of my legal pad and jot down some notes for marketing the new menu.

I would have loved to have Val cater the wedding, but I know there's no way she can with the wedding at home.

I glance down at my rings, admiring their beauty and how unique they are. "How did you find my rings?"

He peers up from his notepad tilting his head to the side as the light through the window cause his eyes to shimmer. "As you have told me on several occasions, you're not the typical woman, so I didn't want the usual and customary ring for you. I wanted something that reached out and grabbed me as you did with my heart all those years ago. The black is for the strength you have and the pink is for the soft feminine side of you. The heart diamond is for you to always remember you have my heart in your hands and that I will always be there to protect you."

His words stun me. He really put a lot of thought into picking my rings. I don't know why it surprises me so much, Oliver has always been attentive to my needs and always knows how I'm feeling. He has always been able to read me even when he wasn't around me all the time. I think back to all the times he's been there silently standing in the shadows. That first day at school when I was thirteen, my mom's funeral, graduation, my first week in Seattle, and so many other times. It's as if he's in tune with everything around me.

I swallow the lump of emotions welling up in me. "How did I get so lucky to have you in my life?" I shake my head slightly. "Thank you for loving me, and thank you for showing me what love really means. I love you, Oliver, and I can't wait to become your wife."

"Loving you was easy, Sam, but keeping my feelings for you was torture." He takes my hand and kisses my knuckles.

"So, what is your opinion? Have you thought about what day you want to get married?"

I glance down at the doodles on my notepad. "I have nothing in mind. I just know I don't want to wait."

Oliver swipes his finger over his phone and opens the calendar app. "How about in four weeks, six weeks' tops?"

"Do you think we can get it done that quickly? That doesn't give us much time."

"Let your father handle it. He has a wedding coordinator lined up; we just need to be there." He wiggles his brows at me playfully.

"Okay, I'll call him and let him know. I'll see if he can fly out here and bring Kassidy to go dress shopping." Oh my gosh, I can't believe we're doing this, and if we can pull it off in four weeks... My pulse spikes with anticipation.

After having to endure a speech from my father about our decision to be married so fast, he agrees to fly out next weekend and bring Kassidy with him. He's going to call the wedding coordinator to arrange all the details of my gown fitting.

Now all I have to do is tell Kassidy that I'm getting married. She is going to go ballistic on me because I haven't told her about anything that's been going on, although it's time for her and me to have that heart to heart that we were supposed to have the night I left town. My God, it seems so long ago, but it's only been a little over a month. So much has happened. She is going to think I'm crazy, considering I've never told her about Oliver. I'll plan on that while she's here. I'll need to make sure we have plenty of wine on hand for the occasion.

CHAPTER THIRTY-NINE
CONFESSIONS

SAMANTHA

The week flew by, and before I knew it, the limo Dad hired was in front of the office to take me to the airport to pick them up.

Not only are Kassidy and Dad coming, but Bev, the wedding coordinator, is coming as well. Bev has set up an appointment at a bakery for our cake sampling. The bakery is a sister store to one back home and they have agreed to meet with us tomorrow.

I can't believe how anxious I am about seeing Kassidy. I know it's only been a little over a month, but we haven't been apart like this before, at least not since we've been roommates our first year at college.

I hadn't told her why she is being flown out here, just that my father was flying out and I thought she could hitch a ride so we could have some girl time. The conversation about Oliver and I getting married and my childhood would follow.

Oliver and I decided that I would have a nice quiet sit down with her at the condominium and he would join us later.

Butterflies flutter in my stomach when I catch a glimpse of her walking down the stairs from Dad's jet. We can almost pass as sisters, but she has more of that model figure. She is lean where I am curvier. Her wavy blonde hair dances in the evening breeze. I would love to have her hair, but I have to settle for fine straight hair that goes flat by midday. When our eyes finally met, I can see the glimmer of tears making her blue eyes even brighter.

Even in jeans and a sweatshirt, she is beautiful. I might have to rethink her being my Maid of Honor, and I chuckle to myself because she can outshine me in a gunnysack.

I've missed her so much and so much has happened. It's as if I'm in a parallel universe. One day I'm graduating from college, and the next I'm kidnapped and now getting married with a family I never knew existed. How do you explain that to someone without them thinking you are totally nuts?

As I step toward her, I wonder if she'll be happy, pissed or all the above. "Bitch if you don't get over here," she grumbles. That's the Kassidy I know and love.

A big smile spreads across my face as I run to her. She drops her bag and we take each other in a big embrace. "Well, I don't see you making any effort, bitch," I spout back as we hold tight to each other. "I've missed you."

"What the hell is going on, and what's with this father thing? The last thing I knew, you didn't have one," she whispers in my ear. "Have you been holding out on me? Not to mention, a private jet. Bitch what gives?"

THE LOCKET

Dad walks over to us. I don't think I will ever get used to seeing him again. If I didn't know he was my father, I would turn my head twice at him. He is a very handsome man, always put together, and distinguished, holding himself high, as if untouchable. I wonder if that's how he was with my mother when they met or if he just hardened over the years. I don't think I have ever seen him without a suit and tie. He's one of those men that would be happy wearing a suit twenty-four seven and it would never bother him. I remember little things about him when I was a child. I was so in love with him. He was my prince and I knew I would marry him some day. He always made time for me, called me princess, and made me feel so loved and protected. It makes my heart feel good to have him back in my life. It's just hard to think about what we went through when he left. My heart was so broken, and as I got older, I learned to resent him. I knew I must have done something wrong for him to leave me; after all, I was his princess, although if he hadn't, I probably wouldn't have met Oliver. He draws me to him in a big hug then kisses me on each cheek. As he pulls away, a petite older woman with impeccably coiffured black hair walks to his side. "Samantha, this is Bev, she will be making all the arrangements for the weekend."

She reaches her hand out to me, her large Louis Vuitton tote slung over her perfectly tailored suit-jacketed shoulder. "Samantha, it is so good to finally meet you." She takes my hand firmly in hers and holds it rather than shake it. "I look forward to making this event the most talked about and envied."

"Thank you, Bev, but quiet and demure is all I care about."

"Oh, hun, this will be the talk of the town," she says as she takes me by the shoulders almost shaking them as she speaks, "Everyone who is anyone will want and beg to be there." Her voice is full of excitement. "This is a two in one party after all." My brows knit together, trying to use mind control so she doesn't slip up about the wedding. I want to tell Kass on my own. If we were sitting at a table, I would kick Bev in the shin to get her to shut up. I glance at my father with panic in my eyes.

Dad must sense my anxiety and the panicked expression on my face and saves the day when he kisses my cheeks. "We need to be going, sweetheart, but, we'll see you tomorrow morning." He reaches out with his hand to Kass. "Ms. Day, it was nice to meet you. Samantha... tomorrow." Taking Bev by the elbow, he leads her to the limo.

We pull up in front of the condo. The driver opens our door and we step out. Kassidy's mouth is agape as she slowly gazes up at the tall structure then back at me. "And how the fuck can you afford this place?" She scans the entrance to the condominium.

I grab one of her bags as I lead her into the vestibule of the condo and greet Stephen, introducing him to Kassidy. She's trying to take in the décor of the building. The marble floors gleam as the sun hits their high polished surface. Black overstuffed sofas and chairs are placed in quiet areas that appear as if they could be someone's living room. There are plants and lamps and flower arrangements strategically placed to dampen the voices of those who might be sitting and having a conversation. Although the lobby is amazing, it doesn't feel apprehensive or uneasy. It feels comfortable, as if it's part of my own living room. Taking her hand, because she is moving too slow taking in the grandeur of the lobby, I lead her to the elevator and insert my key card as we start our ascent to the top floor of the building.

As I open our front door, Maxx and Levi bound out into the hallway investigating their new friend that is sure to show them the attention they are lacking. They weave through my legs, shyly hiding but yet curious about who is with me.

I glance down at the two fur balls that are now weaving between her legs. "Oh fucking hell, you finally got the kittens you wanted."

"Well, actually they're Oliver's although he got them for me. This is Maxx and the one with the shorter fur is Levi. Watch out for Levi, he loves to suck on your arm." She peers up at me, her brows furrowed. "I think whoever had them took them away from their mother too soon." I raise my brow and smile.

"Oliver?"

I grab her by the arm and lead her down the hallway as she pulls her suitcase behind. "Let me show you to your room, and then I'll fill you in on everything."

She glares at me, her face now very serious. "Really? everything?"

"Yes, everything. There's so much I've needed to tell you, but I just didn't know how. I should have told you a long time ago. Then I was going to tell you the day after graduation... but then Grady... well, you know."

"No, I don't know, bitch. That's the problem." She shakes her head.

I take her by the elbow leading her to her room. "I'll tell you everything in due time," I giggle.

Once she is situated in her room, I walk to the kitchen. Kassidy follows behind. "What exactly do you do at this

NEW job of yours?" I turn to glare at her, her mouth agape as she takes in her surroundings. "You can't tell me that the starting salary of an entry level marketing and business employee can get you a place like this. If that's the case, I'm moving here too."

I turn and smile at her. I pull a bottle of wine out of the cooler, knowing she is more of a Pinot drinker and me a Riesling. I take her on a tour of the condo and then we settle in the living room on the big soft ultra-suede sofa. "Before I start I have a very important question to ask you." I know she's going to go shit a brick, as she would say.

"Okay, but you're making me nervous."

I take her wine glass out of her hand and set it on the coffee table. Turning my body to hers, I take her hands in mine. She tilts her head and regards me curiously. I smile nervously at her as I say, "I'm getting married, and I want you to be my Maid of Honor." I wait for the shit to hit the fan.

"Bitch, what?"

I take a deep breath letting her absorb what I just asked then I hold my left hand out to her wiggling my ring finger. I smile and relax as I talk in her language, "Bitch, yes or no?"

"Are you fucking kidding me? You've been here a month and you're already knocked up?" There's a surprised expression on her face.

"Really?" The smile slides from my face as I give her a stern look, my eyes squinted, but deep inside I'm hurt that she would think that. "We've known each other for four years and in those years how many men have I dated," I say angrily as I pull my hand out of hers. "You think I'm just going to jump into bed with the first man I meet out here? And my God! I can't believe you think I'm pregnant!"

"Well, what am I supposed to think?" She says as she jumps from the sofa and starts to pace, throwing her hands in the air as she rants, "Some person that claims he's your father flies me out here to see you for a secret weekend getaway and now you're telling me you're getting married. Who is this guy? Do you even know anything about him? Maybe I can get Derek to check him out. It's not too late to get out of this!"

I giggle because if I were in her shoes, I probably would already have her packed and walking out the door.

"What the fuck are you laughing at? Are you punking me?"

I hold my hand up trying to silence her. "I will answer all your questions, just give me a second. I think you have already met him, he's the one that rented you mom's house."

Her brows furrow as she glares at me, "You're marrying your lawyer's assistant?"

I smile at her patting the sofa for her to sit back down and hold out her wine. I know the wine will get her to sit. "No, I'm marrying Oliver Drake."

She takes the wine out of my hand as she sits down, staring at me in disbelief. "Bitch, you're marrying your boss?" She takes several big gulps of her wine.

"Well..." Shit, what do I say? Technically, I am marrying my boss.

"Fuck, I need more wine," she says. She walks into the kitchen and a couple minutes later she returns with the bottle in her hand. She fills her glass with more wine than etiquette dictates, then settles back down into the sofa.

Studying her, I take one of her hands, leaving her drinking hand free. "Let me start from the beginning."

"This fucking story had better improve, because if it doesn't, I'm packing you up and getting the fuck out of here."

"Well, there are good and bad parts. But at the end, I think you'll feel better."

I start my story at the beginning when my father left us and how I had met Oliver. She cries uncontrollably when I tell her about Grady. She never understood why I was so afraid of him. She's just starting to manage her tears when I tell her about the baby. Then she downs what's was left in her glass.

Once I had told her about Grady, many things fell into place. She understood the panic attacks and why I had to leave town.

Then I tell her about what Oliver did for me, and I think she falls in love with him herself. Every girl wants that knight in shining armor to swoop down and save her.

As I tell her who my father is, her mouth falls open in shock. Although I tell her about the kidnapping, I decidedly leave out what happened at the warehouse. She again drains her glass.

She takes my hand and gazes at my rings. "How did he propose?"

I tell her about the lake and the bench he had made for me, well us. "I love him, Kass," I say quietly, "I think I always have. He's always been there for me."

"He's the one who took you at graduation, isn't he?"

I nod my head. "When I got the call from Grady I started to have a panic attack. I couldn't breathe, I don't know what he will do if he ever gets me alone. He's obsessed. He's told me several times that *if he can't have me no one will*. If and when…, because I know he will find out about my engagement…, it might push him over the edge. Oliver has been searching for him since graduation, but he's off the grid. No one has seen or heard from him and he's not using any bank accounts or credit cards."

"What about his father?"

"I talked to him, and he hasn't heard from him either. He had no idea what Grady did the day of graduation or when he got into our apartment with the flowers."

"So what are you thinking," she asks pouring herself another glass of wine.

I close my eyes not wanting to think about it, but knowing that I need to be prepared just in case. "I'm hoping that Oliver's men can find him before the wedding," I say in a quiet voice.

She sits up, or, at least, tries too, the wine already making her words slur. "Tell me what I need to know. When are you getting married?"

I take her empty wine bottle into the kitchen and make a pot of coffee. She follows me in, grabbing onto furniture to keep herself from falling. "First, we need to get you sober. Oliver is taking us out to dinner." I turn to her taking her hands in mine. "I want you to get to know him. Tomorrow we're tasting wedding cakes, then going with my father to shop for wedding dresses. The wedding is in a month."

Her eyes go wide. "Are you shitting me? How the fuck do you think you are going to get a wedding not to mention a dress in a months' time?"

"To be honest, I don't care. My father said he can get it done. He hired Bev, as the wedding planner, and it's up to them to get the venue and all the details in place. So... tomorrow morning we're going to a bakery to sample cakes, then we're going dress shopping. Are you up for it?"

"Fuck yeah! With Daddy Warbuck's footing the bill, I'll make sure your wedding is fan-fucking-tastic."

"Kass, before you go overboard, I really would like my wedding to be simple, elegant, and understated. If Oliver and I had our way, we would have it at the lake with just friends and family. Nothing outrageous. So, I need us to be on the same page. Please," I implore.

"Alright, I know, it's just the alcohol talking. I'll reel it in." She wraps her arms around me in a big hug. Taking our coffee into the living room, we sit and talk about what I want for the wedding.

CHAPTER FORTY
THE DRESS

SAMANTHA

I sit in the soft warm leather seat of the limo. We just left the bakery, the taste of chocolate and raspberry still lingering on my tongue. I smile as I glance at Kass. Big dark rimmed sunglasses cover her face like Jackie O. "Are you ready for some more ibuprofen yet?"

She tilts her head down pulling the frames down, and I can barely see the tops of her bloodshot eyes. She grumbles something unintelligible then pushes them back up and turns her head so she doesn't have to look at me. I reach into my purse and pull out a bottle of painkillers then pull a bottle of water out of the fridge.

"So what did you ladies do last night," Dad asks as he raises an eyebrow.

My smile fades as I glance at him tilting my head and twisting my mouth as I try to think of a way not to sound impertinent. "I told her about my childhood and the kidnapping."

He puckers his lips and in a big gesture nods his head, "I see."

"I hadn't ever told her, so last night, with the help from a bottle of wine, I spilled all my secrets. This is the remnants of it."

"Well, I can understand better now, although I think there are better ways of coping," he says as he shakes his head.

"I don't think we want to get into the other ways we've dealt with what has happened," I say.

"What…is there more you're not telling me," she asks as she whips her sunglasses off her face and stares at me with a shocked expression on her face as if trying to believe what I'm saying.

Shit, I don't want that part to come out. There is no way she could handle the warehouse.

"Uh, no, he just means going to the gym and working it out that way…don't you, Dad?" I give him a stern look. All the while Bev's head is going back and forth as if watching a tennis match between our conversation.

"Oh." Kass slowly slides her glasses back on. I hand her the water and the medicine. She tosses the pill to the back of her throat and chugs the bottle of ice-cold water making her brows pinch together. She tilts her head back onto the seat back. I would imagine trying to get a little sleep between stops.

Since we're going to shop for gowns, Oliver decides to go back to the office. The plan is that Kass, Dad, Bev, and I will spend the day at the dress shop. I want to find that one special dress that will not only look good on me but that I want to create a memory that Oliver won't forget any time soon.

Knowing that I will be changing in and out of gowns, I decided to go simple and wear a sleeveless sheath dress and a pair of sandals. Easy in, easy out.

We've gone to a couple different shops, but couldn't find *that dress.* I mean I could have settled, but well…I want the dream, although I don't know what I really like now. My brain is mush. I've seen so many dresses they all blur together.

The limo pulls in front of another bridal shop. "Okay people, if I don't find it in this shop, I'm calling it quits," I say as Kass grumbles, her sunglasses still on.

"Hun, you have to have a dress," Bev proclaims.

"I'll go to one of the chain stores then. They seem to have thousands, and I'm sure they would have my size so they wouldn't have to order one," I say, resigning.

An exclusive jeweler is on one side and an investment company on the other side of the shop. It's situated in an affluent area of downtown Seattle, not exactly the kind of place I thought I would ever step into when I thought about getting married. This is where all the rich and famous go and you can only get in by appointment, and I'm shocked that Dad was able to get us in this quick. From what I've heard, there's usually a four-week waiting list just to get in. Not to mention how long it will take to receive the dress if we have to order it, which is almost a guarantee.

Kassidy takes my hand and squeezes it with excitement as the driver opens our door for us. Obviously, she is starting to feel better. A small crowd of people stops to stare at us as if we are someone famous, some even holding their phones up taking pictures. Feeling self-conscious, I leave my sunglasses on until we are inside; the mirrored doors blocking any hint of who is inside.

We're greeted by a young woman, maybe in her mid to late twenties. She's tall with thick mahogany hair and chestnut eyes. She is very pretty. Her hair is twisted with a chopstick holding it in place and freckles dot her face. She looks as if she should be in an office rather than a bridal salon. She's wearing what appears to be a custom-made business suit. The skirt and suit jacket hug her in all the right places, and the stiletto heels showing off her long, shapely legs.

She walks straight to me and holds out her hand to me. "Hello, you must be Samantha, my name is Katherine." I take her hand as I introduce her to everyone. "I am here to find your perfect dress. All of our dresses are one of a kind, so you will not have to worry about seeing your dress on someone else." *Oh God*, my stomach falls with her comment. I can't imagine I'll be able to get a dress in four weeks. "May I inquire when your wedding is?"

Knowing that my answer will get us kicked out of here, I try swallowing down the lump in my throat. "In four weeks." I thought she was going to fall off her stilettos. Her expression is one of shock as her eyes fall to my belly as if I were pregnant.

"Oh. Well." She says and clears her throat as if stalling to think of what to say.

"I'm not pregnant," I say sarcastically.

"Oh, of course not. I mean..." She stammers around her words, and she realizes she was caught assuming the worse.

"We just don't want to wait, but if you can't help..." I turn to leave.

Bev cuts me off. "I have been reassured by Ms. Adams that there will be no issues in having a dress completed in our timeframe," Bev says curtly.

Appearing a little embarrassed, Katherine tries to back pedal. "Yes, of course. Please follow me. I would like to ask you a few questions to find what silhouette you've dreamed of."

I close my eyes trying to think of what I had always wanted for a dress, but to be honest; I never thought I would get married. I never thought I would find someone that would accept my past, accept me and my demons. Sure Oliver was always in the back of my mind, but I never thought he was obtainable. And though as a very young girl I wanted the princess ball gown, my tastes have changed.

She walks over to a desk and draws out a burgundy leather portfolio that houses an iPad. Opening it, she starts to type. She leads us to a sitting area, a cream upholstered sofa and a couple of silk damask wingback chairs strategically placed around an antique coffee table. She motions for us to sit down.

"Let's get started, shall we," Katherine suggests with a friendly smile.

I nod my head as Kassidy takes my hand again and bumps my shoulder.

"Do you like long or short?"

"I, ah..."

"Are you planning on getting married in the day or evening," Katherine asks. "If you are planning an evening wedding, they are usually more elegant and I would suggest a long dress."

"Yes, it will be an evening wedding, and I think I would prefer a long gown."

Katherine takes notes of my preferences on her iPad. "What about sleeves?" I peer at Kassidy. I never thought about that.

"You have beautiful shoulders, Sam. I think you should do a sleeveless or maybe a halter with a low back," Kassidy suggests.

"You think," I ask.

"Yes, you always looked stunning in that purple halter dress."

My mind shoots back to the last time I wore it, and I remember I did receive many compliments. "Okay, yes, I would like to see something with a low bare back. I don't like strapless dresses though, but it doesn't have to be sleeveless, I am open either way."

"Alright, what about the color? Would you like to go with the traditional white? Cream? Off-white, or would you like to go non-traditional with a bold color? Some brides go with red for good luck, or we can add a colored sash with a white dress for a touch of color."

White has never been a good color for me. It always seems to wash me out. "I think off white, but not too much yellow in the tone."

"Lace? Train? Pearls? What about a full skirt or form fitting?"

All these questions, I never thought about any of this. "I would like elegant. Lace and pearl to a minimum, a form fitted dress would be ideal. I don't want the standard train. I want something different. I never really looked at a wedding magazine so I don't know what's in style. I just want something that's unique."

"Alright, that gives me a little to go off on. Give me a few minutes to pull some dresses. I have one in mind that I think will be perfect. Help yourself to some champagne and I will be right back."

Dad pours us some champagne as we sit back a talk about what silhouette will accentuate my best features. "This is so much fun! I can't believe you're getting married, and in a month," Kassidy shrieks. Obviously, the meds are working, she's almost back to herself now.

I think about walking down the aisle and Oliver seeing me for the first time in my gown. The expression on his face is what I want to see. My stomach flips at the thought of my dad... *My dad*. For so long I never thought I would know him, and now he is going to walk me down the aisle and give me away to Oliver.

At least fifteen minutes have passed when Katherine finally returns with a rack of gowns. She rolls the rack up to the side of a room and puts them in order of which ones she wants me to try first.

I swallow the last of my champagne and follow her into the dressing room. Katherine hangs the dress up in the room and has me undress. The room is about the size of my old bedroom at my apartment. There is almost enough room for a dress with a train as long as Princess Diana's.

"This dress is the first that came to my mind as you were telling me what you like. I think it has your personality in it. It has the low back and although it has a low V-neck, the netting over it makes it appear more elegant." I didn't know what to think of it. I am skeptical. I never considered large fishnet overlay that covers the silhouette of the dress.

Katherine has my back to the mirror, she helps me with the dress, it slips over my generous curves perfectly. The netting comes to my collarbone, yet it's a low cut front.

Katherine steps back as if admiring her work. A big smile stretches across her face as she takes me in. "Are you ready?"

I nod, too nervous to speak, but apprehensive since I didn't really care for the dress on the hanger. Katherine lays out the train before having me turn around.

"Yes."

With a look of pride, she says, "Okay, turn."

I slowly turn, my eyes to the ground. I slowly raise my eyes up to glancing at her face in the mirror. Her eyes are all alight, a big smile spread across her face as I dare my eyes to peek at myself in the mirror.

My eyes go wide as my mouth falls open. Tears blur my sight as I stare at myself. I slowly turn the rest of the way and stare at the woman standing in the mirror.

"It's beautiful."

"I knew this would be stunning on you, Samantha. It's elegant and sophisticated. It's…well, it's you. At least what I have seen of you today."

I nod as I brush back the tears threatening to escape.

"Shall we see what they think?" I nod my head because at that moment no word can escape the lump in my throat. Katherine opens the door, and I slowly take a couple steps out and stand on the platform.

Kassidy inhales sharply as her hand covers her mouth, and dad, well, he had just stood to get more champagne and has to catch himself to gain his balance. "Oh, Samantha," he says with sadness in his voice. "You look beautiful, just like your mother." It's with those words that the tears begin to run down my cheeks. As a child, I had always envisioned my mother being here on this day… My moral support, helping me in all the milestones I would meet. But these are things I will never share with her.

Katherine hands me a tissue. The last thing anyone wants is mascara tears down the front of their wedding gown.

"I don't know about both of you, but I think this is the perfect dress," I say, as dad and Kassidy nod in agreement.

I return to the dressing room as Katherine calls in the seamstress to take my measurements so the dress will fit perfectly, then she helps me out of the gown. As I change back into my clothes, Bev makes the arrangements guaranteeing that the gown will be completed in the timeframe required.

When I finally walk out of the dressing room, Kassidy is impatiently waiting for me. "Oh my gosh, Sam, I can't wait to see Oliver's face when you walk down the aisle. He'll be lucky if he remains standing until your dad hands you off. The gown is amazing." She takes both of my hands in hers as I turn to look at her. Her face serious and her eyes filled with tears. "Oh Sam, I am so happy for you, you deserve it and I can tell Oliver loves you so much. Thank you for letting me be a part of this."

"Kass…I love you, you're my best friend, and, of course, I want you here for this.

After we had finished at the bridal shop, Dad, Kass, Oliver, and I go out to dinner. Kassidy asked us a lot of questions, and between the three of us, we try to answer them so she feels more at ease with the sudden marriage plans. Kassidy is what I would call outspoken and she always speaks her mind. I didn't know how that would be with Dad, but he handles her well, telling her just enough to satisfy her curiosity, and unlike Friday, she only drinks one glass of wine.

The weekend goes by too fast and before I know it, Kassidy and Dad are on their way back home. A sense of melancholy fills me.

It feels so good to have finally told her all about my past, as if all the burdens of my secrets have been lifted off my back, leaving me free. I miss not having her around. Not that we did a lot together once she and Derek hooked up, but maybe it's just the knowledge that she is there if I ever need her. That shoulder to lean on or just having her in my corner. I mean, she's still in my corner, just a corner a little further away.

CHAPTER FORTY-ONE
AND THE WINNER IS

SAMANTHA

The day is finally here to see if I am losing my office or if Lucas is going to eat crow. I know my idea is a good one. It's outside the normal box, but that's what I was looking for. No one wants to see something that has been seen a hundred times before. I chose something that will catch you by surprise, but maybe my concept is too new…too outside the box.

Oliver has made a big deal out of this competition. He has planned a big luncheon for the company, and although we haven't discussed the projects, he seems very confident that mine will be the winner. I think there is even been a pool going around on who is going to win. Of course, you have those who think that it is rigged, but I don't know what to do to stop those rumors.

I walk into the cafeteria and am surprised to see Val here. She is busy putting the finishing touches on the tables and has the room set up buffet style. Bright and shining chafers line the two, sixteen feet long tables covered in pristine white linens making up the hot food stations and two more tables equally adorned, one a fruit and veggie station the other a dessert station. It all looks amazing, and Val has gone out of her way to make this a wonderful spread.

I don't want to interrupt her, but I have to say hello. "Val, this is incredible," I say as I pull her into a big hug.

"Thanks, Samantha, it has come together so well. This is a marvelous opportunity for me. Thank you for introducing me to Oliver."

"He didn't even tell me, but Oliver is the kind of guy that always thinks of others before himself, so it doesn't surprise me," I say. "I'll let you get back to it. I just wanted to let you know how great it looks."

"Thank you, Samantha. I have a couple last minute things to take care of before they start to line up. We'll talk later." I wave bye as I turn away to find a seat.

There is a rectangular table set up at the front with a lectern standing off to the side of the table.

As the room starts to fill with employees, the noise level in the room turns to a low roar. Addison skips up to me giving me a big hug, "Congratulations, Sam."

"For what?"

"I know you're going to win; you have the best campaign."

"Thank you, Addison."

All of a sudden there is a crackling sound of a microphone. "Hi everyone," My pulse quickens at the sound of Oliver's voice. The room quietens down, "Welcome to the battle of the stars." The room roars again with applause and hoots and whistles. I search around for a chair to sit in next to Addison.

"Before we eat, I want to introduce you to our contestants, Then I will have them come to the table up here to sit." He introduces Lucas and gives a rundown of his accomplishments and acclamations. Lucas stands and in his arrogant way, he bows and strides up to the table and sits. I sit there nervous. I'm not much for taking compliments. Deep down I'm just a shy girl. The only time that really changes is if I am talking marketing. I'm confident in what I can do, and I will fight for what I think is right. That's what got Lucas and me into this competition.

"Next is Samantha Hunter. As many of you know, I have sung Sam's praises for a while now. I don't usually talk about my private life, but I want to tell you a little story." I feel my face turn red as my heart pounds in my chest. "When Sam decided to come and join our company, she didn't know who the owner was other than E.O. Drake. I didn't want to influence her to work for me because of who I am. Some of you know this story, but for those who do bear with me. Eighteen years ago, I lost my parents from a violent act. My last name at the time was Drake. I was then adopted and I took my adoptive mother's name. A year later, I met a little girl who was lost and afraid, and over the course of the last seventeen years, I have stood in the shadows watching over her and protecting her. When my adoptive mother passed, I wanted to honor the parents that I lost and changed my name back to Drake. This little girl is now all grown up and never knew of anyone with the last name Drake. That is until I told her about a month ago, so, when the rumors were going around about her knowing the owner of the company, she wasn't lying when she said she didn't know anyone with the last name of Drake. Now she does, and in the next month, we will be married." The room roars with applause. I glance over at Lucas, he hangs his head shaking it in defeat, as if he thinks I will automatically win, but I don't want to win this way. I want to win on my own merit, on my campaign. "Samantha, please come up here and sit at the table with Lucas."

As I walk up to the table, I see Lucas's face getting red. There is anger in his eyes as he abruptly stands and his chair flies backward. "This is a bunch of bullshit. You already have her pegged to win." I'm now standing at the table as Lucas is going off. "You might not have known who he was when you were hired, but obviously, you do now and there is no way this will be a fair competition."

I turn and regard him. "Lucas, all I have ever tried to do is work hard and do my job. If you can't trust the owner of this company, a security company in which thousands of people trust their lives and security too, then you don't live by Mr. Drake's mission statement. I trust everything that Mr. Drake does because I have known him for seventeen years and have seen him in action on multiple occasions. So either shut up and sit down, learn to respect your employer, and boss, learn to be a team player, or be a prima donna drama queen and get the hell out." The place explodes with applause.

Lucas storms over to Oliver. "I quit," he says in a loud voice.

"Effective immediately," Oliver says as he motions for Reynolds. Oliver reaches into his jacket pocket and pulls out an envelope and hands it to Lucas. "Reynolds will escort you out."

Oliver motions for an older gentleman at one of the front tables. I've seen him around, but don't know who he is.

He takes the mic. "My name is Mr. Pace, and I am the director of the accounting company here at Drake Enterprises. Mr. Drake had asked me a month ago to hire an independent accounting firm to make sure there was no chance in any undue influences or bias. They have the scores tallied and are ready to announce the winner." Lucas turns and glances at Mr. Pace, shaking his head knowing that he had overreacted.

Oliver knew that in order to get an undisputable winner without bias, he had to go outside the company, and that's what he had done without anyone knowing except Mr. Pace.

Although it's a moot point now that Lucas has quit, I still want to know. Mr. Pace calls the president and treasurer of the accounting firm to come up and give their findings.

"The winner, with sixty-eight percent of the vote is Samantha Hunter." The room erupts in applause, and though I am screaming and doing a happy dance inside, I stay quiet and composed on the outside.

Oliver thanks everyone and releases them to get their food. He steps over to me and pulls me into a big hug. "So when are you going to jump for joy that you beat that SOB," he whispers in my ear.

A shy smile plays at my lips and I say, "When I get back to my office and I can close my door." He chuckles and kisses the top of my head.

CHAPTER FORTY-TWO
LONG DAY COMING

SAMANTHA

I sit staring into the vanity mirror in my hotel room. My eyes fixed on the exquisite gown reflecting in the mirror that hangs from the mannequin standing in the corner of the room. With its sitrin illusion neckline, long sleeves, elegant low cut cowl back with intricate beaded scalloped lace and sweeping soft chiffon train. The column dress silhouette fits every curve and valley of my body. Katherine did a wonderful job. Silk webbing hugs the dress as stunning pearl and silver beadwork adorns the sleeves and body of the dress.

I imagine the expression on Oliver's face when he first sees me. The hitch in his breath, his beautiful indigo eyes going wide with wonder then shimmering with happiness. The vein in his neck pulsing faster and faster, and the smile spreading across his face revealing that amazing dimple as the realization hits him, we are getting married, and I will soon be his wife.

My eyes flash to the picture of Mom sitting on the vanity as she watches me get ready for the day. Tears burn my eyes as I think about her, wishing she could have been here to help me find the breathtaking dress for this of all days. To see that I made it. For her to see me walk down the aisle to the man I have loved for so long. I think that is every girls dream. I know deep down she's watching over me.

I reach for a tissue to dab my eyes so I don't wreck my makeup, Julio; my makeup artist; would get his panties in a twist if I were to start to cry before anyone had the opportunity to see his beautiful artwork. He said my face was the perfect canvas. I could hardly understand him, his English is so broken, but I have to say, he did an amazing job as did Floyd with my hair.

As I reach for the tissue, I accidently bump the picture frame tipping it over. Something pings on the vanity top. I move the bottles of lotions and perfume out of the way to find a little angel charm similar to the one that Oliver gave me all those years ago. Her body is a teardrop pearl, and I gasp as I remember that the pearl is my mother's birthstone. I pick up my phone to call Oliver. Did he set it there so I would feel close to her? No one really knows about the necklace he gave to me when I was thirteen, so I can't imagine it could have been anyone else. I love that man. He's so thoughtful. If I hadn't picked up the tissue, I wouldn't have seen it and it could have been lost.

Picturing Floyd's face and the Tsking sound with the finger wave he would make if he even saw my phone close to my face and hair, I place the phone on speaker. As I'm dressing in my lingerie, and wait for Oliver to answer.

"Hi, baby," He says, his voice low and husky, filled with need. This is the first time we haven't been together in three months. "What do you have on," he asks as he laughs.

I feel my face flush. I can't believe I still feel shy when he talks dirty to me. I giggle. I wonder if I'll always flush when he talks to me that way. "Well, that's a surprise for a little later, but I can tell you that I think you'll like it, or the lack thereof."

I hear his intake of air as he whispers, "Oh baby, you are being naughty. I think maybe I should just come up there and see you."

"You will not!" I quip.

He laughs at my reaction. "So, was there a reason you called or did you just want to tease me with the lack of what you have on?"

Shaking my head as if to remember why I called him, my eyes flash to the little angel. "Well lover, I wanted to thank you and let you know I got the little gift you left for me."

There's a silent pause on the other end of the line. "What gift, baby?"

Confused, I say, "The angel charm with the pearl body."

Again, there is another long pause. "Baby, I didn't get you an angel. Your wedding present is sitting here next to me," his voice is anxious. "Your dad is going to bring it to you when he comes to meet you. Tell me about the angel."

There's a knock at the door. "Oliver, I think the wedding planner is at the door to help me with my dress, I need to set the phone down to slip my robe on." I set the phone on the vanity as I slip into my white silk robe. Speaking louder so he can hear me, "She's a little early, hold on I need to open the door."

"Sam!" Oliver shouts through the phone as I unlock the door.

"Hi, baby sis, you're looking exceptionally fine today. I love the white."

"Sam!" Oliver's panicked voice echoes through the phone again.

The smile falls from my face. I glance over at my phone on the vanity. I wonder if I can get run back and reach it or if Oliver can hear me. I peer up into a face that I was hoping never to see again. He hasn't changed a lot in the years since seeing him, other than looking older. My eyes searching his, as a small glint flashes in them, his lip start to curl and I start to relax and take in a deep breath. His eyes begin to squint, his brows furrow and his face hardens as his eyes turn evil. I still hear Oliver hollering on the other end of the phone. "Grady, what are you doing here?" I start to edge back into the room to grab my phone, but Grady grabs me by the wrist and yanks me out of my room. I scream for help, but see no one around.

I pull my robe tighter to conceal my almost naked body. I feel his strength as he pops my wrist from the tight hold he has on me as he drags me down the hall to the stairwell. I try in earnest to pull away from him, but I only have stockings on and I slide on the carpet. "Grady! Stop! You're hurting me," I scream out. I pull against his strength as I start to hit him with my free hand. "Grady, stop this, I'm getting married today, let go of me! I have to get back and finish getting ready."

He strides down the hallway, pulling me as if I weigh nothing. He's put on a lot of muscle since the last time I saw him over ten years ago. My muscles strain to get some sort of control. His eyes are squinted, focused, and I can see his jaw clenching as he throws the door to the stairwell open tugging me through it as my feet slip on the slick concrete landing. I grab the railing, thinking if I can hold it tight enough he can't take me, but he wrenches me so hard sprigs of flowers Floyd positioned perfectly in my hair fly out. In a low growl he turns to me saying, "I told you years ago you are mine and only mine. We are family and we will always be. YOU. ARE. MINE," he accentuated the last three words.

Dragging me up the stairs, I'm confused why we're going up instead of escaping down the stairs. I slip and fall on my knees as my stockings slide on the slippery concrete. I let out a shrill shriek as the pain radiates through my knee and up my leg. Grady just yanks me harder, dragging me up the hard, unforgiving steps. As I try to gain my footing, I feel my knee go numb. Then I feel my robe stick to my leg. I glance down to see my once beautiful white silk robe daubed with blood. "Grady, stop, please. I'm bleeding. I can't feel my knee, and I need to stop. Where are we going, where are you taking me?"

He just turns and glares at me. *Oh, fuck.* I try to swallow down the big lump in my throat when I realize that he knows he isn't going to get out of here alive. I have to try and out think him. I reach up to my hair as if I am wiping it from my eyes and pull another sprig of baby's breath out of my long loose braid, dropping it on the stairs. I'm hoping the Hansel and Gretel theory will work for me. I continue until we get to the roof.

The roof is covered with little sharp jagged rocks and they quickly cut into my stockings and feet. I try to step softly, but Grady is pulling me so hard I stumble and fall to my knees. Gravel embeds into my bare legs and into my already cut knees as I cry out in pain again. With my free hand, I grab for my robe trying desperately to hide my modesty. "Grady, please! I can't walk that fast on the rock. Let's go back inside and talk."

THE LOCKET

I'm far enough from the door that I know there is no way
I can make a dash for it. I need to keep him preoccupied until
help gets here. A breeze hits my feet and they feel cold. I
peer down at them and notice my vanilla colored silk
stockings are slowly turning crimson from the blood seeping
through them. "We're soul mates, destined to be together
forever," he says in a low graveled voice, "We were each
other's firsts; we share a part of each other's souls. We're
bonded together because of this. Bound together for life. You
are mine, and if I can't have you," he glances down at me, a
mixture of sadness and anger flash over his face as he pulls a
gun out from behind his back and points it at me, "Then
nobody can."

"Grady," I gasp. I have to remember to stay calm. In a
quiet voice a say, "Talk to me Grady, what do you want? We
haven't talked in years."

Anger flashes across his face, his eyes burning into me.
"That's because your mother had me sent away."

"What did you expect her to do, Grady, you got me
pregnant, I was only twelve," I huff out.

He starts to pace, waving the gun around as he talks to
himself as if having his own personal conversation. He then
gazes at me. A softness comes across his face. "Don't you
see, Samantha, I love you. I have always loved you from the
first moment I saw you." He bends down and draws his
finger across my cheek. Then, as if a light switch has flipped,
he grabs my hair, yanking me up off the ground. I let out a
scream as the pain from my hair being ripped from of my
skull disseminates across my head and down my shoulders.
"Then that fuckin guy tries to take you away from me. Well,
there is no fucking way he's going to have you," he yells.
"You belong to me! Only me! He can't have you! I will make
sure of it!" He finally releases my hair as he begins to pace

again. "I love you, god dammit! It's supposed to be me today! ME! NOT HIM! He can't have you, I won't let him."

I hear the sound of footsteps and hollering as the door bursts open. "I love you, Samantha, you will always be mine," he says in a quiet voice, sorrow in his eyes as a single tear rolls down his cheek. He draws the gun up and, points it at me. BANG!

CHAPTER FORTY-THREE
ĐÉJÀ-VU

OLIVER

I'm sitting at the table finishing my lunch as Nicolas is talking about the security he has in place at the hotel. Grandfather, Reynolds, and Mitchell are listening intently.

I'm listening, but my mind is elsewhere. I'm thinking about Samantha and making her my wife. I fantasized what she'll look like as she walks down the aisle. Fuck, I can't believe in just a few hours Samantha will be my wife…Hell, I will be her husband! We'll finally be the family I've always dreamed. My stomach twists with anticipation and my heart begins to race. I take a deep breath trying to calm my anticipation.

"We have security on all of our floors. They are at the elevators and in the lobby watching everyone that is coming into the hotel," Nicolas says with utter confidence, but something he says strikes me funny.

"Have you received a list of hotel guests," Mitchell asks.

"Yes, we received the latest list this morning."

"That's not a lot of time to do checks on every guest that's currently registered to make sure they are who they say they are," Mitchell rebuts.

My eyes flash to Mitchell's as a thought runs through my head. "What about the stairwell?" They stare at me. "You said you had men at the elevators, but if someone is already here, already a guest or a friend of a guest…" Is it just me, or what? I feel like there is a big hole in the security. "Or for that matter, someone that uses falsified information, they wouldn't be coming through the front doors. They would already be inside. If they are staying on a different floor than we are, they can easily use the stairs, bypassing the elevators all together. What security do you have on the stairwells?" I ask

Movement catches my eye as I see Bev and the photographer walking across the room heading toward our table. My attention is drawn away from them when my phone rings. Glancing at the display I smile as Sam's face lights up my screen. "Excuse me," I say as I push away from the table pressing the button to talk to my soon to be wife.

"Hi, baby." A smile spreads across my face just knowing she's on the other end of the phone and I take a mental sigh of relief knowing she is okay. I missed sleeping with her last night. I longed for her scent and touch. I especially yearned for her to be in my arms. I glance back at the table where a black velvet box sets, which holds a handmade lace choker with pearls and pink tanzanite and a pair of long pearl and pink tanzanite cluster earrings that match the choker. According to Bev, it will match her dress perfectly. I smile thinking about the reaction she'll have when she peers inside, and although I won't be able to see it in person, I'll get to watch it on the video afterward.

THE LOCKET

It was important to both of us to keep to the old traditions of the wedding ceremony. We haven't seen each other since last night at the rehearsal and dinner. It's a wonder that I got any rest without her in my bed. I find that I sleep so much better with her cuddled up onto me, inhaling her scent. The idea of being able to touch her whenever I want and knowing that she is there next to me brings me extreme comfort.

As I step away from the table, I ask, "What do you have on?" I have to laugh, because I know that Sam is still shy, even though we have been together for the last three months. I can envision her face turning a deep shade of pink as it travels down her slender neck to her chest.

She giggles and tells me she isn't wearing much "I just put my stockings on; you know the type that are thigh high and have lace at the top? I got them especially for you, and let's not forget the matching panties." My breath hitches at the vision of her in nothing but her stockings, bra and panties.

I can't get the vision of Sam in just lace out of my head. My mind wanders as she's talking. I vaguely hear her talking about an angel that she found on her vanity in her room and thought I left it for her. It makes me wonder where it came from. She's placed her phone on speaker so she doesn't mess her hair and makeup and I have to laugh because I can just imagine what Julio and Floyd would do if they saw her with her phone pressed to the side of her face. They didn't even want me to come downstairs to eat, and I only got a touch-up and Floyd shaped and trimmed my beard. Sam mentions that Bev and Nicolas are supposed to be coming to her room soon with the photographer as she gets her dress on. I've noticed Nicolas checking his watch.

I hear a knock on Sam's door "Oliver, the wedding planner is at the door to help me on with my dress, hold on a second, I need to slip my robe on. She's a little early. Just a second, I need to open the door." I hear the rustling of clothes as she puts her robe on, then her picking up the phone again. I glance over at the table and see Bev standing by Nicolas. *FUCK!*

"Sam!" I holler into the phone. Everyone at the table glares up at me. I am at the table in a couple strides. "Sam, don't answer the door!"

Then I hear it, the voice that has haunted her for so many years, Grady. "Hi baby Sis, you're looking exceptionally fine today, I especially like you all in white, it's so virginal."

"Sam!" Apprehension and concern ignite everyone at the table. "The motherfuckers got her," I yell. "He fucking has her!"

I run for the stairs, Nicolas is on my heels as I throw open the door so hard it hit the wall with a thundering bang I start to climb the stairs two at a time trying to keep my mind from wandering, wondering what he plans to do with her. He has to know who her father is, this event has been the talk of the town, the event of all times. He has to know that he won't get out of the hotel with her. God, I don't hear anything. I hope someone is at every other exit. I say a prayer to myself, *God give me a sign, show me I'm going in the right direction.* I get to Sam's floor and I am panicked now. I open the door to the floor and see Mitchell and Reynolds running toward me. "Anything," I yell.

"No one has seen anything," Reynolds says. I turn in frustration knowing they could be anywhere. They could have taken the stairs to a different floor. Fuck, we don't even know if he's a guest here, and if he is, which room is his. I rake my fingers through my hair, closing my eyes and taking a deep breath to try to center myself. *I need a sign, God, please.* When I open my eyes, I see it. A little bunch of flowers hiding beside the railing, almost ready to fall down the well of the stairs. I bend to pick them up. I know they're from her. "Up! He had to take her up." The adrenaline kicks in again as I bound up the stairs toward the roof. About one flight up I notice something on one of the steps. I know what it is without even stopping, but my instinct is to stop and make sure. Pressing my fingers into the dark red liquid, I rub my fingers together as the tacky goo stains my fingertips. Blood. I knew it. Fuck. My stomach sinks at the thought of him hurting her. As I continue up, still not sure if they got off on another floor, I start to see more and more petals. My heart is pounding and all I can say is thank God. It's my own little bread crumb trail. She's so smart, she knew I needed to know and she set the trail.

I stop when I reach the door out to the roof. Not knowing what to expect or what my plan of attack should be.

My hand is on the door when I hear it. BANG! My heart stops beating as I gasp for air, my stomach falls as my eyes well with tears. BANG! Oh God, I'm too late, my body goes numb as I throw the door open, terrified of what I am going to see.

Sam is leaning against the ledge wall. Her white silk robe shrouded in crimson. Her eyes are closed as the remnants of tears still shimmer on her cheeks. Her face void of color. Grady is lying beside her, face down.

I run to her, needing to hold her one last time, to tell her I am sorry for breaking my promise to keep her safe. My tears are now falling down my face as I hear Reynolds on the phone with the 911 dispatcher. I slide on the gravel as I rush to her side, kneeling on the jagged rocks as they slice through my slacks piercing the skin on my knees. Pain shooting through my legs, the only thing that lets me know that I am still alive, but I don't want to be. I want to be with

My Sam. I scoop her lifeless body up in my arms, pulling her into me. I bury my head into the crook of her neck, inhaling her scent for the last time, branding her fragrance into my mind and soul, never to forget it. I rock her listless body the way I have rocked her when she was scared or had nightmares for all those years. "I'm sorry, Sam, I am so sorry I failed you."

Someone runs their hand down my back as I sob uncontrollably into her neck, but I don't give a fuck. Sam was the love of my life, my other half. She's like gazing into a mirror, reflecting everything good that I could be. She made me want to be better. She was my soul mate. She completed me.

I want to curl up and die with her.

I hear the sirens as they near the hotel. I know they're going to want to take her, but I'm not ready to let her go, not yet. "Shhh," the hand is now in my hair. "Oliver, baby."

God, I'm in shock. Delirious, I hear her voice and feel her touch. The paramedics burst through the door, the sound of the gurney wheels crunching on the rock gets closer and closer as I grip Sam's soft body harder, not wanting to let her go. "Sir, we need to see her to help her." My mind is racing, how can they help her, it's too late.

"No! I'm not ready to let her go yet," I cry out.

There's a touch on my shoulder, a sense of calm comes over me. "She's alive, Oliver, let them work on her."

I blink back my tears as I pull away. Raven is by my side. I search Sam's face as her eyes start to flutter open. "Oh God, Oh God, Sam! Sam come back to me." She moans as I pull her close to me kissing whisper soft kisses on her face.

"Sir, please."

I stand, my leg almost giving out from the intense pain from the cuts in my knees and shins, but I don't care. I lay

Sam on the gurney as they place an oxygen mask on her and evaluate her wound.

The bottom of her robe slides open revealing a gun holster on her thigh. I stare up at Raven knowing she would have some answers.

"We'll follow you to the hospital, and I'll answer all of your questions," Raven says and tears shimmer in her eyes. "She'll be fine, Oliver. Trust me." The corner of her mouth lifts into a shy smile as she places her hand on my forearm, reassuring me again.

CHAPTER FORTY-FOUR
MY SAM

OLIVER

I stand in the corner of the emergency room trying to absorb what's being said around me, but I'm in a daze.

A nurse with a kind smile and a twinkle in her soft green eyes walks over to me. "Hi, I'm Summer."

"I'm Oliver, Sam's fiancé."

"Nice to meet you, Oliver. Sam should be fine. The bullet didn't hit anything major, but we're going to take her to get a CAT scan to make sure there aren't any fragments of the bullet or bone. We're also going to examine her head. It appears as if she might have hit it, and we want to make sure there isn't any bleeding on the brain. Then we need to stitch up the wounds. The doctor will come out to the waiting room and get you when she's in her room. It shouldn't be too long. Would you like me to show you to the waiting area?"

"No, I think I can find it. Thank you, Summer, can I see her before you take her?"

"Of course. She is still unconscious, but that is normal with head trauma, but as I mentioned before, we will no more after the CAT scan." She places her hand on my forearm, smiles, and nods at me. "I'll give you a few minutes before we take her."

I walk over to the head of the bed and run my knuckles down the side of Sam's smooth cheek, and then I lean over kissing her forehead. She looks so peaceful, although she has tube and wires hooked up to her; her face is relaxed. "Sam, come back to me, baby. I can't live without you." Tears run down my face again. This feeling is so foreign to me. I don't ever remember crying before. It feels like my heart is being ripped from my chest, my insides torn to shreds. I feel so helpless.

The nurse walks back in with a couple of men. They start to place some of the machines on the gurney getting her ready to transport her to radiology.

"We need to take her now," Summer whispers.

I nod my head and lean down one more time, lightly brushing a kiss over her lips. "I love you, Sam." I step back as they pull the bed out of the room.

I reach down to the once white silk robe that lies wadded in pieces on the floor, cut from her along with her stockings. I pick up a piece of her robe, trying to inhale her scent, but all I can smell is the scent of antiseptic. I stumble back hitting the wall. As I slide down a wave of emotions flood me. I bury my face in my hands as I clench the robe and my body starts to shudder.

I don't know how long I have been on the floor when Mitchell and Reynolds help me up from the floor and take me to a chair in a quiet area of the waiting room. I run my hands over my face as I peer up at my friends.

"How is she," Reynolds asks.

"They took her to get a CAT scan. They think she hit her head when she was shot. She is still unconscious. The bullet was a through and through, but they're checking that as well," I say in almost a whisper.

Raven sits down next to me as Mitchell and Reynolds pull up chairs and sit down.

"I'm sorry I didn't say anything to you, Oliver, but I really didn't know. Well, I didn't know enough to think he would try this today."

"She must have known he would try something; she was carrying a gun holstered to her thigh. She was going to pack a fucking gun under her wedding dress. How fucked up is that," I say.

"We knew it was a matter of time, and when it didn't happen before today, she made sure she was ready," Raven says.

"Why didn't she say anything to me?"

"Oliver, you've been protecting her all her life. She needed to know that she could take care of herself and put closure to this." Raven lays her hand on my forearm as I try and absorb what just transpired. "Her intention wasn't to kill him, but he had planned to kill himself after shooting her. You know he was obsessed with her. I know you saw his attic." I glance over to Reynolds and nod my head. "He was there when Di Fonzo's men took her." My eyes flash to hers. I swallow down the lump building in my throat. If he would've taken her, we wouldn't have had the same luck in tracking him. If she hadn't been kidnapped by Di Fonzo's men, he would have taken her."

"He was waiting for her?"

Raven nod, "Yes."

I feel the blood drain from my face at her revelation. "When you both got back, you had her so protected he couldn't get to her. Today was the first chance he had. He had the room down the hall from her. No one was watching her door, just the elevator. He waited until the right time and got her. She left the trail of flowers to let you know where she was." I reach into my tux jacket and pull out a cluster of scrunched up little flowers. "Oliver, if you hadn't picked up the bunches of flowers…those few seconds saved your life. If you would have bypassed them and burst through the rooftop door and not stopped just for those brief moments on the steps, he would've shot you. You don't want to know the end of that story." My eyes go wide as I peer up into Raven's emerald eyes. She pats my hand, "Now you can be married where you really want to be married. There will be nothing standing in your way."

"What about the angel with the pearl body? That's the reason she called me in the first place."

Raven smiles up at me, "That was her mother." Tilting my head to the side, I stare at her with confusion. "She's the one that set it there knowing that she would call you. She knew you would hear what was going on with Grady and step into action."

"God, Raven, will I ever get used to your gift," I ask.

Mitchell chuckles, "No, you just learn to listen to her."

She bites her lip and quirks up a brow as she squares her shoulders. "I'm still learning, too."

Movement from the hall catches my attention. I glance over to see a woman in a lab coat walking toward us. "Mr. Drake?"

"I'm Oliver Drake." I stand as she reaches out her hand to me.

"I'm Doctor Williams, I have been attending to Ms. Hunter."

"How's she doing, doctor?"

"She should be fine. She did sustain a bump to her head and has a mild concussion, but the CAT scan doesn't show any evidence of bleeding to the brain. She should heal just fine. The bullet didn't hit anything major, just muscle and sinew. Nothing that she won't heal from. She has regained consciousness and is asking for you."

"Can I see her?"

A smile stretches across Doctor Williams face, "Of course. We have admitted her for the night and will hold her for observation just to make sure there are no complications. You can all come back if you would like. Mr. Perrotti has made arrangements for a private suite for her." I wondered where he and Nicolas have been. We're led back to Sam's room. I think about how close I came to losing her today and reflect how lucky I truly am.

As I approach the room I perceive to be hers, I hear a conversation she is having with her father. I stop outside of her door knowing that I shouldn't be eavesdropping, but on the other hand, I want to hear what Nicolas is saying. "Samantha, you should've let us know. My God, you should have seen Oliver. I knew he loved you, but what I witnessed today... well, I know he's the right man for you." My heart is beating rapidly with his revelation as I blink back the tears that threaten to fall. I gather myself as I force a smile on my face. It isn't that I'm not happy; I just have so many emotions running through me that I need to evaluate them.

I walk into the room. Sam is leaning back in her bed with Nicolas and Grandfather gathered around her bedside. I stride over to her. I can no longer fight the tears that are falling as I take her beautiful face in my hands, brushing my lips gently over hers. I rest my forehead against hers whispering, "I thought I lost you. I thought I would never have the chance to tell you just how much you mean to me and how sorry I am that I couldn't stop him. I failed you. I am so sorry I ruined our wedding. I love you so much. I was so scared."

"Shhh, I know." She brings her left hand to my face, running her fingers down it. "This was my battle. I needed to put an end to it, and you've never failed me. You had always been there when I didn't have anyone else and I thank you for that. You are my constant, my always, my forever," she whispers.

I pull away when I hear Samantha moan and wince in pain. Sam's eyes are closed tight and she's biting her lip. I leave the room to the nurse's station to see about getting her some painkillers. I hear the nurse's scrubs rustle as she follows me back into the room with a syringe and vial of medicine. Once in the room, the nurse plunges the needle of the syringe into Sam's IV port on her hand. Instantaneously her body and face start to relax, her eyes close, and the rise and fall of her chest begin to slow. I glance up at the nurse as she removes the needle from the port. "She'll sleep for a little while. She didn't want us to give her anything until she was able to see you. She's a strong lady."

I blink away the tears. "Yes, she is."

Watching Samantha rest, I notice movement beside me. Nicolas lays his hand on my shoulder. "I'm going to get some coffee; come with me Oliver." His hand grips my shoulder a little harder.

His eyes glint with unshed tears as sadness cloud his features. Though I don't want to leave Sam's side, I know whatever Nicolas has to say to me must be important to pull me away from her side. I gaze back down at Sam and nod my head in resignation.

"We'll be here. If she wakes up or starts to stir, we'll call you," Reynolds says.

I slowly stand and lean over her bed, kissing her on the forehead, "I love you, Sam." Then brush my lips softly over hers.

As I start to pull away, a whisper escapes her lips, "My Oliver."

CHAPTER FORTY-FIVE
FATHERLY ADVICE

OLIVER

We walk to the cafeteria in silence. I wonder what he might have to say to pull me away from Sam's bedside. I'm feeling a little more at ease now that I know how Nicolas feels about me.

"Oliver, I know you're probably wondering why I wanted to talk with you, but what I have to say to you can't wait."

I peer at him curiously. I wonder if he's going to try to talk me out of marrying her after what happened today, because that would be a fucking hell no. "I figured it had to be important to pull me away from her, yes."

"It is. As you very well know, the last thing I wanted for Samantha was for her to get involved with someone that had a connection with the family, but in saying that, I also want to apologize for how I treated you." I sit in my chair stunned. I don't know if I'm dreaming, but I remain quiet and sit in silence as he continues. "After what I've seen over the course of the last month and especially today, I was wrong. You...you are the right man for Samantha. You're a natural protector. You knew exactly what was being overlooked in my security for today. This was my fault, what happened today, a month ago with the kidnapping, this punk ass kid that I should have let you take care of years ago. Hell, I should have handled it myself. You were a child. I had no business relying on you. I should have protected my family. You've always been there for her, and not just protecting her, but you provided for her when I wasn't man enough to. I never realized everything you had done for her until Reno. Thank you."

He peers into my eyes; I mean really looks into my eyes, as if searching for what I might be thinking about what he just told me. I tilt my head to the side and raise my shoulders as if what I had done was no big deal, because it wasn't. "I love her. I think I always have, but I knew for sure when she was thirteen. I vowed to make her mine one day, and I knew, at that point in my life, I had one goal. My whole life has been devoted to making Sam's life what it should have been."

He reaches into his jacket pocket and pulls out his checkbook. "I want to pay you back for what you've spent on her. Her education, housing, anything you have done for her." He pulls his pen out, removing the cap with the all-knowing white six-point star on the tip as he peers up at me for my answer.

"Nicolas, I understand the guilt you feel about what has happened to Samantha, believe me; I carry the same guilt. But I took care of Sam, because I love her, not out of obligation. My employment with you was only for three years. To be honest, if it hadn't been for you, I probably wouldn't be standing here in front of you today. You showed me that I had something to live for, and if you could trust me with your daughter, then I needed to prove to you that I was worthy of her love. I don't want your money, Nicolas, I want your respect and approval."

He stands up and reaches his hand out to mine. "You have it, son. Your parents' would be proud." Goose-bumps prick my body with his confession of my parents. Yes, I know they would be.

I place my hand in his and for the first time, I'm not intimidated by this man standing in front of me. "Thank you, sir, that means a lot to me."

He slaps me on the shoulder, then drags me into a hug. "I'm family, stop being so formal. Now let's get you back up to my daughter."

CHAPTER FORTY-SIX
HERE COMES THE BRIDE

SAMANTHA

I have had to wait almost four weeks for this day, but now I know I've nothing to worry about, Grady is gone. That wasn't a fun conversation. Not only did I have to talk to Dad, but then to Oliver. I don't know which was worse. Dad yelled at me as if I were a little child. "Dad, if you would've raised me *in the family*, you would've made sure I was able to take care of myself? Using a gun and learning a martial art would've been mandatory I'm sure. This was no different. Oliver made sure I could use a gun, and I am fine." Although he didn't want to agree with me, he did concede that I had handled myself in the way of a *family member*.

Oliver, on the other hand, was a different story. He wouldn't leave my side and sex, well…that was out of the question. Not until the doctor cleared me. I know he was scared and hurt that I didn't tell him what I was thinking, but I needed to do this for me, for my closure. Grady had hurt me for so many years, and I was powerless to stop him. I felt weak, and I needed to show to myself that I could control the situation. Although it didn't go the way I had wanted, I did take care of the matter myself. I will never be a victim again.

The doctor told us that she would release me after thirty days. I'm still doing physical therapy for my shoulder, but I'm not going to let that stop me. So, we're getting married the day after I am cleared.

Once we had the date, I contacted Mrs. Golden, the owner of the little B and B at the lake, to make sure the largest suite was available that weekend. Then we started to make plans. Val is going to do the catering, and I'm confident this event will boost her clientele, too. She's bringing in extra help so she can enjoy the event as well. The luncheon that she did for the company was so well orchestrated that I knew she could manage the wedding without a problem, plus her food is amazing.

In addition to Kassidy standing by my side as Maid of Honor, Raven will join the wedding party as a bridesmaid. She and Mitchell have become an intricate part of our lives.

Mitchell and Reynolds are Oliver's groomsmen. He added Mitchell last minute, too.

It's like déjà vu all over again as I sit in my bridal room staring at myself again. I reflect on the last month. I ended up staying a couple days in the hospital due to sensitivity to one of the medications I had received. Oliver never left my side. Nor has he left my side since. He even moved my office in with his. I'm surprised he left my side last night.

Maybe because he had the adjoining room and I had to leave it unlocked.

Bev again has done an amazing job putting a wedding together in four weeks, even though we never got to see what the first one looked like. It didn't matter to me because this is where I would have preferred it. Julio and Floyd were flown in for the occasion, and as before, they did an amazing job. I glance at the round bright pink circle just below my right clavicle as I slide my fingers over the indentation. The doctor said it would fade over time, but the puckered skin would always be a reminder of the day I erased Grady from my life for good. I was okay with that. This is my life, and although scars fade, they are there to remind us of where we've been and what we've gone through. Although I would never want to relive most of my life, it made me who I am today and it brought two unlikely people together. My Oliver.

There's a knock on the door, pulling me out of my reverie. I pull my pink silk robe over me. "Who is it?" See, I learned something…I didn't just open the door.

"It's your father, honey." I smile at how close he and I have become. Like Oliver, Dad didn't leave my side while I was in the hospital. He told me stories about him and mom, and I can see just how she could have fallen in love with him. Underneath his tough exterior is a good, and loving man.

I open the door and my breath hitches as I see my dad in his tux. I wish mom could see him now. He steps inside as Bev and the photographer follow. He has a gift-wrapped box in his hands. The paper is in our colors of iridescent white with an iridescent pink bow on top. He hands it to me along with a card. "This is from Oliver."

The photographer has captured every expression on my face from the time I opened the door, making sure he captures every moment.

I open the card and read it.

My Samantha,

You know you have always been My Sam, and today, in just a short period of time, you will be my wife and I will be your loving and devoted husband. I have waited for you for so long. Like what's in this box, you are stunning and everlasting in your beauty, and as time passes, your beauty blossoms even more.

Thank you for being my life, my love, my other half, my constant.

I love you with all my being.

Your Oliver

I glance up at my father, tears brimming my eyes. "Open it."

I admire the beautifully wrapped package, my fingers shaking as I dare to open it. I peek up at my father again. He nods his head as I slip my fingers in between the papers and sliding my fingers down to rip the tape. I slowly take the paper off, dropping it onto the table. I lift the lid off the box and see a black velvet box. My heart is racing at what could possibly be inside. I glance up at Dad again as he smiles at me. I unconsciously bite my lip as I slowly lift the spring lid of the box. I gasp at the vision in front of me. Inside lies a pearl and pink tanzanite choker. The pearls are different sizes making it appear like lace. Lying beside it in the box is a pair of long pearl cluster earrings that resemble a cluster of grapes. Again the pearls are of different sizes and pink tanzanite are mixed in with the pearls. They are amazing and will be beautiful with my dress.

Dad hands me his handkerchief before the tears start to spill from my eyes. "The last thing we want is to hear Julio if he sees that I've made you cry making your make-up run."

Taking a deep breath, I giggle at the image in my head of Julio's face as I gently dab my eyes. "Dad, can you help me put it on?"

"It would be my pleasure, honey." I carefully lift my long, loose braid. Ribbon, flowers, and pearls decorate the back of it as he fastens it to my neck, and I slip the earrings in.

Bev comes around us glancing up at me, "Are you ready to put that magnificent gown on?"

I glimpse at my father… the man I dreamed I would marry someday… and know that it was my father all those years ago who started Oliver's and my journey together. I glance back at Bev and nod my head, speechless with emotion.

Bev had a privacy screen brought in for the day so I could get my gown on without my father seeing me in my lingerie. The photographer assured me that when he edits the video there will be *our* copy and a copy that can be shared with friends and family.

The dress fits perfectly. The plunge in the back stops between the low dimples on my back. The clear elastic straps that attaches the back together just under my shoulder blades can't even be seen with my hair covering it and the cowl that hangs low on my back below the plunge.

I step out from the privacy screen to Dad staring at me. Unable to speak he clears his throat. "Oh, Samantha, you are exquisite. If only your mother could be here to see you."

"But she is here, Dad." I press my hand to his heart then to mine and he gives me a shy smile, tilting his head to the side.

He takes a step to me and kisses my cheek. "Yes, of course, she is." As he steps back, he holds out a small black velvet box. My brows furrow as I pass him a curious glance. He nods at Bev and the photographer and they step behind the privacy screen, but I see the camera focused on us as he starts to speak.

"I wanted to give this to you a long time ago, back when I didn't think you would have accepted me. I know that if I had, you wouldn't have been ready for it. Hell, I don't know that I would've been ready for it. You see, in this box holds your legacy. This is who you are. Like it or not you are my daughter, and in the last few months you have shown me that now is the time." He opens the box and pulls out a gold ring. It appears as if it is hand engraved, and the result is a crisp, brilliant sparkle emanating from every cut and a contrasting natural shadow that together form the striking beauty. It shimmers and shines as the light from the window strikes it sending prisms of light flickering off of it as he moves it in his fingers.

"Oh, Dad," I gasp sharply. "It's…wow."

He chuckles. He takes my right hand and slowly starts to slip it on the ring finger. "For this ring holds your legacy. It tells who you are and where you come from."

I glance down at the ring trying to examine it more closely. It's gold with exquisite Victorian styling, a slight oval top, and wide sides that are engraved with amazing floral branches. It almost resembles a class ring from school, but instead of a stone, a coat of arms decorates the top. My coat of arms. Oh my God, there is so much history in this one little ring.

"Your grandfather and I thought it was time. You have proved yourself a Perrotti, and since this is not only your wedding but also a coming out to the world, letting everyone know that you are my daughter. You will carry on the family's birthright and legacy. Our coat of arms is blue and gold, representing generosity and the elevation of the mind, truth, and loyalty. As you can see there are several symbols," he points to each one as he explains their meaning, "First, the sides are hand carved with acacia branches which stand for eternal and affectionate remembrance. The shield represents defender. The Griffin means ferocity under provocation, velour, death-defying bravery, vigilance and most of all guardian of treasure. The helmet stands for wisdom, security, strength, protection, and invulnerable ability." He takes my hand in his, kissing the ring, then peers down at me through tear filled eyes. "Samantha, you haven't had an easy life, I know this, but if you heard anything about your heritage, you could see where you received your strength from. You are a natural Perrotti, and I am proud and honored to call you my daughter." He pulls me into a big hug, and the little air I had in my lungs is forced out with the tight squeeze he gives me. Although it does sound like me, I do feel strong most of the time. I know that I have gotten a lot stronger in the last few months, and the only reason is Oliver. He makes me stronger. He's given me the self-confidence I've needed and all I want to do right now is be with him. To be his wife.

"Shall we go and make Oliver the luckiest man in the world," he asks. I nod. "Bev, we're ready," Dad says.

"Alright, let's get you two married Aga…" She almost says *'again'* but stops herself as she and the photographer step out from around the privacy screen. "Stay here. I am going to make sure the coast is clear and Oliver is where he needs to be. Then I'll come get you." She runs her hand down my arm as she opens the door and disappears.

Emotions have me speechless today. I whisper out, "Thank you, Daddy. Thank you for the ring and my birthright."

CHAPTER FORTY-SEVEN
MY BIRTHRIGHT

OLIVER

I stand in the suite, pacing... anxiously. My palms are even sweating as my heart races. Mitchell strides his large structure over to me. He looks like a different man in his tuxedo. Shit, I'm tall but he's a beast. I would hate to be on his bad side. He slaps his hand hard on my back as I wince. "Man, you need to chill. Take a deep breath. This is your woman; she hasn't changed She's the same woman you've known all your life."

I roll my shoulders, working out the knots and tension.

"Are you telling me you weren't nervous when you and Raven got married?"

"It wasn't that I was nervous. I knew Raven was my soul mate. I wasn't second guessing if what I was doing was right. I was just anxious about getting it over with and having her as my wife. You need to remember everything from today. Enjoy it. Drink it in, because this will be the most amazing day of your life. Yes, things might not go as you have planned, but who cares, it's the union of you and Sam that's important. Seeing Raven walk down the aisle is a vision I have burned in my brain. Relax and enjoy."

There's a knock on the door. I check my watch to see if it's time yet. I glance back up at Mitchell. "Thanks, Mitchell, you're right. I'm thinking about the little things when the only thing that matters is that in an hour, Samantha will be my wife, finally."

Reynolds opens the door and Grandfather is standing there. "Do you men mind if I have a few minutes with my grandson?"

Mitchell and Reynolds close the door behind them as they leave the room. Grandfather strides over to me with an expression on his face I've never seen before.

"I thought that after all this time we need to talk."

I take a big gulp. Thinking this sounds very serious, and even though he is my grandfather, he is still the head of the family. He exudes power that intimidates and sends fear in everyone around him, including me.

"Okay, is everything alright?"

"Of course, you're marrying Samantha. What else could I wish for? My grandchildren are happy." He wraps his hand around the side of my neck in a loving gesture. Then pats my cheek. "This is a long time coming, and maybe I should have told you about your birthright, but I wanted to see what your feelings for Samantha were first." He motions for us to sit. I'm glad because I feel like my legs are turning to noodles. We sit on the sofa as he continues.

"You see, while you were watching Samantha, I was watching you. Watching you take on responsibilities that a normal man your age couldn't be bothered with, but age never stopped you. You were always there for her, taking care of her even when you thought no one was paying attention. After your job of taking care of her was over, you never stopped and it didn't go unnoticed. You are my grandson, and as so, you are entitled to your birthright. You will see that you didn't come by your character and integrity by chance. It's in your lineage, your bloodline."

He pulls a small black velvet box out of his pocket. "Oliver, you have proven over and over again to this family." He opens the box and reveals a gold ring with a crest on top, but I can't see what it is. Grandfather pulls the ring out as he continues speaking. My head is swimming, and I have to shake it to start listening and understand what he's saying. To hear everything, he's saying because I know I'll never get this opportunity again.

The sunlight hits the ring he holds between his fingers as the intricate engraving glints, radiating from every cut. My heart pounds at the acknowledgment he is showing me.

He slides it on the pinky finger of my right hand as my brows furrow. The ring fits perfectly. How would he know that? "This ring, it holds your legacy. It speaks of who you are and where you come from."

I gaze down at the ring, studying it more closely. It's gold with flawless styling and has a flat but slightly oval top and a wide band engraved with a leaf design. "This is your coat of arms." I tilt my head to the side as I study him.

"You have proved yourself as a Perrotti. You and Samantha will carry on the family's birthright and legacy." He points out each symbol and their meaning, "You see, Oliver, you are a natural defender and protector, and you were born into it. I knew it all those years ago when I asked you to watch over Samantha, but you stepped up and went further, taking on the role of guardian. You took it on your own to make sure she was financially cared for. Samantha hasn't had an easy life, but if you hadn't been in it, she wouldn't be here today. You are a Perrotti, my grandson. I am proud of you and all you have accomplished." He takes my face in his hands pulls me to him, kissing both my cheeks.

I'm speechless. Never in my life did I ever expect to feel what I am feeling at this moment. I try swallowing the lump that has formed in my throat. I am just getting used to the idea of family. Sure, I know Sam has given me everything I have wanted and longed for, but Grandfather has given me everything I never knew I was missing. "Thank you, Grandfather," I whisper out.

A knock at the door brings me back to the moment. Bev peeks her head around the door. "Are we ready in here," she asks.

"Never more ready."

She leads Reynolds, Mitchell, and I to the edge of the lake. An arbor frames the embankment, decorated with white lights entwined with ivy and pink roses. Glowing candles float across the water, their light flickering against the evening sky in a soft, luminous glow. Dark chairs filled with guests' blend into the dusk evening making this moment intimate, as if it were just Samantha and I. The aisle way is decorated with trees shrouded in white lights illuminating the aisle, decorated in a filigree design of pink and white rose petals for Sam to walk down. It's magical, I never imagined just how amazing it would be.

A small white tent sits back in the woods in the dark where Samantha is waiting with her father.

As I stand there waiting, barely breathing, the acoustic guitarist changes songs, and I know I'm only moments away from seeing Samantha, My Sam.

My heart starts to race as the strings of his guitar play the familiar song that fit Sam and I so well, because I have loved her for a thousand years and will love her for a thousand more. I see Nicolas step out of the tent extending his hand. My stomach twists and turns in anticipation and I mentally take a deep breath trying to calm my nerves as tears sting the back of my eyes. I blink them away as I see a small delicate hand slip into his, and I know the time is now. Everyone stands and turns to see my beautiful Sam step out of the tent, adjusting her hand to take the crook of Nicolas' arm. My breath hitches as my pulse spikes. I mentally imprint this moment in my mind. Sam gazes up at me, as our eyes meet, and she offers me a shy smile. It's just her and me now, captured in this moment.

A smile stretches across my face, this is it. This is our time. She's going to really be mine, my wife, my constant, my forever.

EPILOGUE
FULL CIRCLE

SAMANTHA

It's hard to believe how things have come full circle. I never thought my life would turn out the way it has. I sit in my office with my back to the door staring out over the bay at all the sailboats and yachts as they pitch and sway with the wake from other passing vessels. I close my eyes and I can almost feel the wind whispering across my ears as I remember a brisk December evening. We were on one of many yachts in a parade of Christmas ships. I should have known; it was silly of me not to realize what was going to happen.

It was December the ninth. It was a clear dry day, just as today is, although it is cold and the breeze is brisk, it's nothing compared to how it was back then.

I wasn't due for six and a half weeks but when I felt the first few contractions, I knew she was going to make an entrance on the same day that she had been taken away from me all those years ago. I hadn't said anything to Oliver at first. I wanted him to enjoy his time. It was such a magical night with all the different colored Christmas lights reflecting brightly off the water.

Oliver and I had been trying to get pregnant for quite some time, but for whatever reason, it just wasn't our time. Not being a religious person, I still believed that there is a God and he had a plan. I knew it would happen eventually because of what Raven had told me. I just had to be patient.

I remember the day we found out. *I was feeling a little off. Oliver came up to me. He stared at me for a beat before tears flooded his eyes. His eyes traveled down my body to my belly, "She's coming."*

Tilting my head to the side, confused with what he had just said, he gently placed his hand on my belly and stared up at me. My eyes widened as he smiled, showing his beautiful dimple as a tear ran down his cheek. "You're glowing, baby, and I have only seen it one other time."

He picked me up, spun me around, then kissed my belly before he took me to the bed and made love to me, so gently, and caringly, so Oliver.

We bought a couple pregnancy tests just to make sure. God, he's good. He knows me so well.

He started hovering over me from that moment, but he knew; he always knows when I need him. That hasn't changed just because we are married.

I'm peering over the bow of the yacht thinking about how our lives will change in the next twenty-four hours as I watch the second hand on my watch tick away the seconds and minutes between contractions.

I heard the deck squeak under Oliver's feet and knew he was slowly walking toward me. He wrapped his hands around my growing belly and whispered in my ear. "I told the captain to get us out of line and back to the dock."

I turned my head. I'm sure I had a surprised expression on my face. "How..."

He kissed me on the temple, "Baby, I've known you most of your life. I have watched you from afar even when you didn't know I was watching. You are standing over here watching the time tick away between contractions. How are you feeling? How quickly are they coming?"

I shook my head in amazement and answered, "I'm fine right now, a little apprehensive being early, but not in any real pain. I know that won't last though. The contractions are coming between five and six minutes apart, so I'm sure we have quite a bit of time."

"I'll call the doctor's answering service and let them know that we'll be there in an hour or so."

"Thank you, Oliver."

Six minutes until midnight our angel Anastasia was born. The sound of her soft cries brought tears to not only my eyes but Oliver's too, I finally get to meet the baby I lost so many years ago. Handing a pair of scissors to Oliver, the doctor asked, "Would you like to cut the cord?"

Oliver's face lit up in surprise. "Really?" Once he cut the cord they rushed her back to the NICU just in case there was any issues being premature.

I knew she would be fine, the thought never even crossed my mind that I might lose her. Because I had once before, and now she's back.

It was two long weeks before we could bring our Anastasia home. Once her breathing was clear, jaundice kicked in and they required her bilirubin levels to reach a normal range before letting her leave the hospital. We were able to bring her home Christmas Eve...our Christmas present.

That was five years ago, and our lives haven't been the same. The doctors told us that she would always be smaller than other children her age and a little slower too. But Anastasia, of course, had to prove them wrong. Once we brought her home, she was gaining one to two pounds a week and growing like a weed.

She started talking early. There are times I think I should have called her Gabrielle, because she was always talking. I find her talking to herself as well, as in, she's having a full on conversation. I know children have imaginary friends, and I don't want to dampen her imagination, so I leave her be.

Tonight we're throwing a big birthday party for her. We've decided that it would be good to have a big party every five years. After all, her grandfather and great grandfather spoil her every chance they get since they never had the opportunity before with their own children.

Dad and Grandfather are flying in, bringing Kassidy and Derek with them. They finally got married a couple years ago and have decided to stay in my childhood home.

We've stayed in close touch with Mitchell and Raven over the past several years also, both in our personal and business life. We have developed some new security software that Mitchell uses. We've done a little bit of work with Mitchell's company, but nothing like my rescue. They're driving up for the party too.

I talk to Raven all the time and have told her about my concerns with the conversations Anastasia has with herself, not knowing if she has a form of Autism. She asked if she could bring her grandparents over for the party to meet her. She said they would be able to tell. The more, the merrier.

Dinner is so nice. We don't socialize as much as I would like. With all of our family and friends living out of town, I miss the little get togethers. Now that Anastasia is a little older, we might see about venturing out a little more.

I've just finished clearing the last of the dishes from the dining room, and the smell of freshly brewed coffee fills the kitchen with its rich roast smell. I glance over to Anastasia, she is having a conversation with herself again. I'm starting to get concerned and I know that Oliver is, too. He glances at her then back at me as we sense the same thing. Raven's grandmother squats down to Anastasia's eye level and starts to talk to her.

The expression on Anastasia's face is one of excitement as she nods her head and talks with her hands, her body full of animation.

Raven walks over to me and distracts me. She lays her hand on my forearm and says. "She's fine, Sam, in fact, she is more than fine." I don't know what it is about Raven, but just her simple touch calms me. I can't imagine knowing what she knows or feels.

Susan, Raven's grandmother, stands and takes Anastasia's hand and leads her over to me.

"Sam, Anastasia and I would like to have a couple minutes with you when you have the chance."

Gazing down into Anastasia's beautiful indigo eyes, they twinkle with excitement, her mouth curves up into a big smile and she can hardly stand still. "Of course, let me hand out the coffee and then when we are finished we can cut your cake, Missy," I say to Anastasia as I beep her nose.

We walk back into the library and take our seats on the sofa and wing chairs. "Anastasia and I were just talking, and she knows that you're concerned with her actions lately," Susan says.

"Well..."

"I know Mommy, she said that you might be."

Anastasia is now standing in front of me. My brows furrow as I narrow my eyes in confusion. "Who, baby?" I know she's perceptive, but I've only talked to Oliver and Raven about Anastasia's unusual behavior.

"Grandmother," she exclaims as a big smile crosses her face.

I gasp as I glance over to Susan and Raven. I try not to appear shocked, but I don't think I am pulling it off very well. I try to act nonchalant. "What about her, baby?" I push a strand of hair out of her face and tuck it behind her ear.

She gazes up at me, sadness now filling her eyes as she turns and glances at Susan. Susan nods as she slowly closes then opens her eyes as if an acknowledgment of what she needs to say. "She told me what she made you do when you were a child." I gasp as my hand covers my mouth and tears flood my eyes. She's too young to know about this, hell, I can hardly deal with it and I'm an adult. "She was really, sad. She said she didn't know what else to do, so she did what she thought would be best for you." Tears flow down my cheeks and my chin trembles as I try to put a smile on my face. "She said she was very sorry for what happened to you."

"Baby, why is she telling you these things," I ask as I peer down into her angelic face, her blue eyes glittering.

"She wants to go, but she said she couldn't do it unless she knew you forgave her for what she did."

"Oh my God," I cry out, unable to control my emotions now.

"Mommy?" Anastasia places her hand on my cheek, and the same sense of calm that Raven's touch gives me is exactly what Anastasia's is doing to me now. "She loves you and just wants your forgiveness." She stands up and reaches into the pocket of her little dress, pulling out an angel. She sets it in my hand. It has my birthstone, a topaz as the body. I look down at it then back up into the face of my precious baby, so wise for her young five years.

"Baby, can you run get me some tissue out of the bathroom, please?"

"Sure, Mommy." I kiss her forehead as she skips out of the room. I want to collapse with the revelation she has just uttered to me.

"What am I supposed to do? How do I let her know that I never held what happened to me against her," I ask as I glance between Raven and Susan.

"I think it has more to do with the baby than the events of what happened. She knows you had nightmares about your baby being taken away for a long time after. She, of course, feels guilty because she's the one who made that decision for you."

I shake my head. "That was a long time ago. I have Anastasia back now. She's always had my forgiveness. I know that she was doing what she thought was the best. I know that now." A cool breeze floats over me and it lands on my cheek as if it were a butterfly then flutters away. I can't explain the sensation, but it is gone almost as fast as it was there.

Anastasia enters the room with tears in her eyes. "What's wrong, baby girl?" A look of concern I'm sure is on my face.

"Grandmother just left, and I am going to miss her." I take the tissue from her hands and dab her face.

"I know, baby, I miss her too. I'm sure she'll still come visit you in your dreams." I pull her to me wrapping her into a big hug. "You know you still have guests here, a cake to cut and presents to open!"

"Yay! I forgot about them."

"Well, we better get back out there before your daddy sends a search party out for us." I beep her nose again as I smile down into her sweet face.

"Okay, Mommy." Her little feet skip and hop toward the door, then she stops and turns to me. "You and Daddy already gave me the best present ever."

Surprised since she didn't know what we had gotten her, I give her that Mommy look and ask, "Have you been peeking in your presents,"

She shrugs her shoulders and tips her head to the side with a cute little smirk on her face. "No, Oli told me silly," she turns and continues to skip away.

I call after her, "You mean your daddy told you what your present was?" I can't believe she just called her father that. I never call him Oli, and she's never called him by his first name. I thought I would have at least another ten years before she started that.

She walks back to me as I glance at both Raven and Susan, then back down at my precious angel that is being very mysterious. "No mommy, Oli is in your tummy. I always wanted a baby brother." She throws her arms around me giving me a big squeeze. Then she is gone, skipping down the hallway hollering as she goes, "Come on Mommy, it's time for cake."

In shock over Anastasia's admission, I just stand there. One hand on my mouth, the other on my belly as my eyes fill with tears. "Baby? Samantha? Sam, what's wrong?" Oliver's hands cradle my cheeks and fear etches into his face.

My eyes slowly drift to his. We had tried so hard to get pregnant again after Anastasia, but it never happened so we resigned ourselves to only having one child. I wrap my arms around his neck. "Have I told you today just how much I love you?" I ask as I look into his bewildered face.

His long slender finger run across my face. "All the time, baby." With a furrowed brow he says, "Anastasia said we gave her the birthday present that she has always wished for? I didn't know we gave her one yet."

I peek up at him through my damp lashes. "I didn't know we did either until she told me."

Oliver steps back, cocking his head to the side as my hand automatically returns to my belly. I saw the realization hit his face as his eyes glisten and the corners of his mouth turn up, beaming at me. He draws his lower lip between his teeth biting it, glancing at my belly then back into my tear filled eyes as I nod my head in recognition.

He places his hand over mine on my belly. "I love you. Samantha. You have once again made me the happiest man in the world. Thank you for being My Sam."

The End

For those of you that have or still are sustaining sexual abuse. Please know that this was/is not your fault and there are places that can help you. If this is still happening to you, tell someone! Anyone! Make them listen!

<u>If you or someone you know is being abused, please call the Childhelp National Child Abuse Hotline at:</u>

1-800-4-A-CHILD 24/7

One out of every three girls is sexually abused before the age of eighteen.
One out of every six boys is sexually abused before the age of eighteen.
It is time to stop sweeping this problem under the rug. Tell someone, anyone, **MAKE THEM LISTEN**

There are so many things I want to say at the end of this emotional journey. Firstly, the story of Samantha and Oliver shows us that love and healing can also come out of abuse. No matter who you are, there is someone out there that is your other half; a person that will cherish and love you.

THANK YOU

To my husband:
Thank you for understanding my writing moods, and for being my biggest cheerleader and for believing in me. This one was a little more emotional than the others.

To my girls: Thank you for listening to my stories. Alex, thank you for all the medical advice.

To my PA:
Thank you, Myra, for everything you do for me. I know you have a hectic schedule and beings that we are on different continents you always make it work. Thank you for getting my name out there.

To my beta readers:
WOW! I put out the request and received an Awesome team of ladies. I couldn't have asked for a better team. Marcie Wegner, Amy Adrian Kehl, Sallyann Cole, Ebony Simone McMillan, and Liz Stephenson. Thank you all so much for all your opinions and help.

To all bloggers:
My deepest gratitude goes to the many bloggers and to all who have supported me and helped spread the word on Facebook, Twitter, on their websites and blogs. My many thanks go to Kim Bishop, Book Boyfriend Heaven, Carol Ann Wade, Sallyann Cole, Cristina Jewel Fontana, and Shaunna Armstrong, and I know I am missing a lot and I apologize, because without

you I couldn't get my book seen. Thank you for your time and diligence.

To my Street Team:

Thank you for believing in me and posting me everywhere. Myra, what can I say, you have done so much to help me get the word out about my books. Vicki, almost every day you are out there pimping me. Thank you for being diligent. One day we will get there. Kerry, Amy, as with Vicki, you are always there liking and posting my teasers. Suzanne, not only are you on my Street Team, you post me on your blog pages as well, I am glad I can call you a friend. Thank you. Sallyann, you are amazing! I don't know what I would do without you. You are always there. Thank you all for helping get my stories out, I appreciate you all so much!

To: Amy Adrian Kehl, Phyllis Bekker, Andie Robinson, Debbie Menard, Lorna Hayden, Bob Cubitt, Sammy Alexander. On that lonely sad November evening, when I didn't know if I should continue writing, thank you for all your words of encouragement, it got me through a real hard time.

To my readers:

I want to say the deepest Thank you for taking a chance on me. I hope you enjoyed meeting Samantha and Oliver.

Lastly, to the one that makes all things possible through him. Thank you, God.

♡**Did you know leaving a review helps authors get seen?**♡

Because I treasure your reviews, thank you to the readers who have taken the time no matter how long it is.

Let the author know your thoughts by leaving stars and telling her what you liked about The Locket

♡♡♡**In a Book Review!**♡♡♡

THE LOCKET

CHARACTER PROFILES

Ethan Oliver Drake
Owner and Founder of Drake Enterprises
Hair: Dark Brown
Eyes: Indio Blue
Height: 6' 2"
Age: 25
Broad shoulders, Thin waist

Samantha Hunter
Hair: Lt Brown
Eyes: Blue
Height: 5 feet 8 inch
Age: 22
BA in Marketing and Business

Tristian Hunter
AKA Nicolas Perrotti
Hair: Brown
Eyes: Blue
Height: 6'
Age: 45
Samantha's father
Father: Alonzo Perrotti

Alonzo Perrotti
Hair: Salt & Pepper
Eyes: Blue
Height: 6'
Age: 65
Samantha's and Oliver's grandfather
Godfather of the Perrotti family

Victor Di Fonzo, Jr.

THE LOCKET

Killed
Hair: Dark Brown
Eyes: Indigo Blue
Height: 6' 1"
Age: 21 when died
Oliver real father

Victor Di Fonzo, Sr.
Hair: Salt & Pepper
Eyes: Indigo Blue
Height: 6'
Age: 63
Oliver Grandfather
Killed Oliver's mother and stepfather

Savina Baldini
Hair: Black
Eyes: Brown
Height: 5' 6"
Age: 55
Oliver's Adoptive mother

Thomas Drake
Hair: Blonde
Eyes: Green
Height: 5' 10"
Oliver's step dad

Sallyann Drake
Hair: Blonde
Eyes: Brown
Height: 5' 7"
Oliver's Mother

Kassidy
Hair: Blonde
Eyes: Blue
Height: 5' 8"
Age: 22
Samantha's best friend

Grady Price
Samantha's step-brother
Hair: Dark Blonde
Eyes: Blue
Height: 6'
Age: 25

Jill Price
Hair: Brown
Eye: Blue
Height: 5' 7"
Samantha's mother

Dylan Price
Hair: Black
Eye: Blue
Height: 6'
Grady's father, Samantha's Stepfather

Val
Hair: Salt & Pepper
Eyes: Soft Brown
Height: 5' 8"
Age: 45
Owner of Restaurant at the Lake

Amber
Hair: Black
Eye: Amber
Height: 5' 10"
Age: 22
Husband: Tyler
Works at the store at the lake

Luke Masters
Hair: Sandy Blonde
Eyes: Brown
Height: 6' 1"
Age: 25

Co-worker at Drake Enterprises

Toby Mitchell
Owns a Security Business
Hair: Dark Brown.
Eyes: Green.
Height: 6 feet 4 inches.
Age: 28.
Krav Mega

Raven Lirisha Whitehorse
Receptionist Stonework's
Hair: Black.
Eyes: Green.
Height: 5 feet 1 inch.
Age: 22.
Karate Black Belt

ABOUT THE AUTHOR

Growing up in a small country town SM Stryker escaped from her home after years of abuse at as soon as she turned 18, running from a taboo life into another tragic situation as she tried to find her place in the world.

She believed that things happen for a reason and knew that one day she would understand why. She finally found her solace when she found her husband and was blessed with her four daughters.

Although she never thought she would start writing, she knew her life would make for one hell of a story or soap opera. She thought about writing years ago but finding or making the time to write was always the issue.

In April of 2014, she sat down in front of her computer and started to write. Through lots of tears, she wrote her first book, that book was Stolen Innocence. She started to write Stolen Innocence as a way to exercise the demons of her past and from there she was hooked. She has shared more of the events of her life in many of her other books. Titles include: Stolen Innocence, Never Forgotten Love, Loving Redemption, Anchored To Love, Never Expected Love, Sacrifice of love, The Locket and coming soon, Unanswered Prayers.

Now she finds that she has to write, this is her outlet her sanctuary, and in every book, she writes there is always part of her life written into it. She hopes that you enjoyed her story.

**<u>I really appreciate you reading my book! Here are my
social media coordinates:</u>**

https://www.facebook.com/Author.S.M.Stryker
http://smstryker.com
shelly@smstryker.com
https://plus.google.com/u/0/
Twitter: @smstryker
https://twitter.com/smstryker
https://www.goodreads.com/author/dashboard